# Goldy Lark

## NAOMI JUNE ROLLO

*Naomi June Rollo*

**FITHIAN PRESS**

SANTA BARBARA

1992

With the exception of Old Jack, all characters in this book are purely fictional. The only true places are St. Louis, Jefferson City, and Greene County, all in the state of Missouri.

Design and typography by Jim Cook

Published by Fithian Press
A division of Daniel & Daniel, Publishers, Inc.
Post Office Box 1525
Santa Barbara, California 93102

LIBRARY OF CONGRESS CATALOGING-IN-PUBLICATION DATA
Rollo, Naomi June, 1929–
    Goldy Lark / Naomi June Rollo.
        p. cm.
    ISBN 1-56474-018-8
    I. Title.
    PS3568.05425G65    1992
813'.54—dc20                                    91-48183
                                                        CIP

*For my moon child,*
*Nel,*
*with many thanks.*

# BOOK ONE

# 1

The world was doing its level best to shake me apart. I had to brace my bare feet on the floor and hunker low in the seat to keep my guts from slinging every which way. It didn't help, long. My breakfast, a hunk of sad bread with onions inside, rolled down one of my long squaw plaits before landing in slimy puddles on my brown toes. The fat lady beside me hurried to spread a St. Louis newspaper over the mess.

"Big girl like you do a thing like that. Shame," she said.

"I never puked in a hailstorm afore," I told her.

"Cross-state train we're on's really rocked you bye-bye. Not so much's a smell of rain or hail hereabouts for three whole long lonesome year, girl."

"It sounds some like rain against a sheet-iron roof, don't it?"

"You're too young to remember rain, child," she laughed. "Doze yourself back and dream of snow."

She seemed to be right; it didn't actually feel like a hailstorm, after all. Though the terrible rocking was there, along with the smotherness, the want to press your hands to your pigtails and scream. Not that the house don't fall in, leaving you the only one to attend Mom's funeral; it's too late to scream for that. She's

9

dead and shoveled under and at the mercy of the hungry bugs below ground. You're the one left behind to hurt.

Though you won't hurt long. Better times are just around the bend of the rails.

I shut my eyes in hopes of killing the snakes. It worked enough that I was able to again doze.

From my kitchen cot back home in Pelper County, I watched two old brown leghorn hens scratch and roll beneath the peony bush. I could taste on my teeth the dust made when they shook themselves. One, through her butt hole, laid an egg Mom fried me for supper. My stomach balked at the thought of a thing that had come from such a nasty place as that going in my mouth. It always had. I ate it because there was nothing else. Now, I could taste it, along with the sad bread and onions, coming to further mess my government relief dress.

The shaking had shifted to the front room bed where my little brown mom, Bree, lay screaming under naked white Nate Brice: "Nate, go big! Big! I'm coming, too!"

"Bree," Nate would pant at her between bed thumps, "Bree, you ever afore been fugged by a real man?"

"No, Nate! Just by boys! Little bitty boys!"

I broke out in a cold sweat at their I love yous. For the truth was, Mom and Nate Brice, deep down, hated each other like my insides did eggs. But before they could mate, he had to knock her around for bragging about other white men she's screamed under.

"Don't tell me, you hot-ass squaw. Go tell your little bastard Goldy Lark which of 'em hung like a mule made her," Nate would say.

"My Goldy Lark, she had a lawful pa," Mom would screech back. "He got his name put in the Missouri County paper, as her pa, when he died. I got that piece of paper put back, you old hairy sum bitch, any time you want to see it. I got memories of him put back, too. He was hung so big, you alongside him would've been a pissy-ass girl!"

I felt myself duck when his fist met her face.

I'd listened to them as long as I could remember, putting my hands over my ears to shut them out. The older I got the more I asked Bree why she didn't leave Nate Brice and get a man not so mean. Tears would leak from her black eyes and she'd say, "Oh, I will, Goldy Lark, when the time's right, I promise." Then we'd whisper about the big fine house we'd live in, all the pretty clothes we'd wear, what good things we'd have to eat. She always told me I'd be somebody someday, and I grew up thinking so.

Her banging of the door one morning when she started for the town's relief office to sew sheepskin coats made my world shake more. Hardly was she past the peony bush than here was Nate Brice on the corn shucks of my cot's mattress.

"Since you're giving it away, Goldy Lark, I want my share for raising you," his tobacco breath told my ear, this letting me know he knew about me and my first love.

When his big hand slid into my bloomers with a, "I'll get your little old thing," I saw only one way free. The bite I left on his lower arm caused a scar he would carry forever. He left Mom soon after, and neither of us cried.

I'd stood alone at the foot of Bree's filled grave in Potter's Field till time to get on the train and ride half the night to my new home. I thought how she'd always been more kid than me, crying when she didn't get her way. Cussing Nate Brice for not liking the funny little dance she'd do while sticking out her tongue to touch her nose. It was a "Churkey Trot," not "Turkey Trot," in his hateful way. If she cussed him and he made her bleed, I had to clean up. Blood made her puke.

I think what riled Nate Brice the most was Bree wouldn't let me call her Mom. That sounded old to her, and she'd always said she'd never be old. I thought how she'd been afraid of the dark. I couldn't run to her now to whisper daylight was on the way, as I'd done so often through the years. I couldn't do anything for her now but sob out my promise never to let life knock me down and hold me there, like it had her. I'd keep my ears and eyes open but my mouth shut so's to see and listen better and learn. I meant to be somebody soon, and I would be.

But for right now, world, help me a little bit. Don't shake so.

"Girl." The fat lady nudged me. "Sure you ain't ready to have a fit?"

"I aim to be somebody someday," I halfway heard myself say, "You watch me, see if I don't."

11

I think she shook her head. "A body'd think from the way you carry on, the world's about to end."

I was brought to by three sharp toots from Gabriel's horn. Expecting to see Jesus riding down on a white cloud to claim His own, like I'd heard a preacher say once, I turned my eyes east.

I saw instead a farmer following a team of mules up a wilted row of cane. He waved his straw katy as he passed. The little dust cloud that rose from his hat at this motion hung for a long second before settling to the ground.

"Rard, Missouri," someone called ont. "All out who's going to Rard."

That was me, I was going to Rard. Home, in my case. For little Bree, who'd carried me as a baby from my Missouri County birthplace, was now sending me, at fifteen, back alone.

"Mercy me," I heard the fat lady say as I left, "who's aiming to clean up all this puke?"

# 2

I stepped stiff-legged from the train to the station platform into the suffocating August noon sunshine, carrying at my side the dirty floursack that held my earthly belongings. The closest place to the small wood depot was a brick two-story building directly across the tracks. Cracked steps ran the entire length of the place. "Courthouse of Missouri County, Rard," the lettering over the open entrance read, and in the window east, a sign: "Marriage License Bureau." The window on the other side of the door said, "Sheriff Jessie McKay," with smaller letters beneath I couldn't make out. As this window was on the shady side of the building, several old men in faded overalls and ragged relief shirts rested under the lettering, fanning themselves with battered straw katies, gawking at me as though I had an extra head. A couple of them spat what I knew to be tobacco juice in my direction, their heads not once turning aside.

Two puny elms, one on either side of the building's front, reached past the second floor. Scraggly limbs from the one closest me managed to shadow most of the corner jail cell, one in a line of eight that, too, matched the length of the steps below. From that first cell I could see a man's hairy arm dangling downward through the bars. I could hear from a pair of unseen lips the wish, "Oh, if I had the wings of an angel," being whistled sad and low.

So this is the Courthouse of Rard, Missouri, I thought. The very spot where Nature decided, on a sleety November day nearly seventeen years ago, I'd sometime be born me. A small pretty Irish-Cherokee (Churky, to us) girl with oily black braids protected from the blizzard by a floursack scarf, was descending the stone steps. A tall red-haired Scotchman was just placing his foot upward on the second step when a sudden gust of wind lifted his cap from his head and dropped it at the girl's feet. Such had been the introduction of Harley Farker and Bree Lynch. From that chance meeting had come me, their daughter, Goldy Lark Farker.

My father had died just days after my birth, March 9, here in Missouri County, sixteen months after he and Bree met. What of, I didn't know. The few times I'd asked Mom the reason, she'd said forget it, go play, his passing was too horrible to remember. The most I knew of him, besides their meeting and that he was buried a mile from where I now stood, was that he'd been the finest man to ever breathe life. If his death had been more terrible than poor Mom's, maybe it was just as well she had never told me the finish to such a beautiful beginning.

I must have dreamed longer than I realized, for I was suddenly brought back by the hot bricks blistering the soles of my feet. Guessing the person supposed to be meeting me had been latened by the heat, I walked over to the station man's cage to ask had anybody left me word.

"Nope," he answered without looking up and wiped sweat from the side of his sunburnt neck with a smelly bandana.

"Anybody yesterday? Day afore, maybe?" I shifted from one foot to the other to lessen the pain on my soles.

He looked at me in his own good time, taking in my black braids, freckled nose, messy blue dress from the relief office back home, my filthy toes. "Injun, huh?"

"I'm part Churkey," I told him, pronouncing the Indian word the way we always said it.

"That means you're waiting for Milt Holt." His eyes opened in real interest.

"I'm to go live with some man named so. He's a sort of úncle, my mom told me. See, she died a few days back and the answer from a letter she'd writ him said to come to Rard, he'd meet me here."

"Too hot a day, reckon. Wouldn't any sooner bring his prize mule out on a scorcher like this than he'd be apt to turn Demycrat. Best you mosey on over to the courthouse, wait for him there."

"Which part?" I wanted to know.

"Jail upstairs and the courtroom, can't go there. Uncle Sam's relief office, this side to the front, that's closed today. So's the tax collector's, in back there. Man there's down with his foot broke. Sheriff's office, that's this side to the front. Best you go there."

"You tell Milt Holt I'm over there when he comes? And say what I got on so's he won't pass me by?"

"Won't have to, he'll know you right off the bat," was his surprise answer. "You look that much like your old heifer of a blood aunt he's tied to."

Which made the first mention I'd ever heard of my Bree's only sister, Aunt Ilish (pronounced E-lish) Holt.

# 3

The high-walled room I entered had a brown leather devonette, the finest I'd ever beheld, and a caned chair behind a wooden desk. Atop the desk was a calendar, a newspaper, a worn paper folder, and a black talking machine that was a "telephoney" to us. Today was Tuesday, August 4, 1937, the calendar told me, which I already knew. The *Missouri County Gazette* read how some man named Burt Troat, nineteen, had been sentenced to fifteen days in the Rard jail for stealing an Arkansaw (as we call it) razorback hog in broad daylight. His older crimes were listed on the open folder, some reading:

Threatening teacher with pocket knife; burning school toilets when he got his ears boxed; stealing seed corn; plus forgery on unnamed step-father, who could neither read nor write his own name; drunk at church; and others before the razorback's theft.

Since Sheriff Jessie McKay happened to be elsewhere, I went to the window, for a minute watching the train station swimming in the noonday heat. By reading the letters backward, I saw the sheriff kept office hours from eight to five and would pass out relief if Uncle Sam, the government man, was gone or pass letters on to the tax man till he got back.

Heavy footsteps sounded in the hall, and before I could turn, a white man entered. By the time I'd got to his desk, he had seated himself in the caned chair and was reading the paper, seeming not to have noticed me. To make sure he would, I coughed once. Twice. Three times.

"Go on up. I know you're there. Bring his plate and spoon when you come back down," he ordered, turning to the paper's second page.

I hadn't a notion what he meant, so I stood silent.

"Moved him to the shady corner cell, he hollered about the heat so," he said, his eyes on page three.

Me, I didn't care if they'd hung him in the State Pen at Jeff City.

The fourth, and last page glanced over, he finally looked halfway at me. "Can't rightly say I was expecting you on a work day. Where's his woman? She finally give up on the worthless polecat, like I told her to, even afore they got hitched?"

"Look, mister," I said.

I found myself looking into the greenest eyes I'd yet to see, gawking at what as likely the reddest patch of curly red hair in the whole United States of America. His big nose, red, too, was set in a pink face that was years younger than I'd first thought. He was so wide-shouldered he could only have entered a door sideways. A brown shirt, open at his broad red neck, bulged with arm muscles the width of my waist; over his heart hung a shiny badge. Standing, he must have been nigh six feet, because seated, his head came to just inches from being tall as my five feet four.

"Well," he said in a friendlier voice, smiling wide. "Looks like I got you mixed up with somebody else, now don't it?"

I untied my floursack and fished inside until I found Milt Holt's letter and laid it on his desk. He read it twice without looking up.

"So busy feeding my prisoner his pork and beans, I clean forgot it's Tuesday and the train's due in. First time since Jessie James, who me and my daddy—he was a sheriff, too—got named after, was chasing it, dom thing's been smack dab on time, too." He rubbed his big thumb across his big nose. "So Bree Lynch died and she's sent you back to her sister, Ilish."

"Mom never mentioned a sister to me," I said.

"Figures. Hear tell they had a bad falling-out, way back in my daddy's time. He's dead now and can't tell you what happened, and I can't neither; I was wearing diddies at the time, so I don't know what took place." He handed back my letter and watched me return it to my floursack and tie the end. "So your name's Goldy Lark?"

"Goldy Lark Farker."

"Farker, Harley Farker's kid. You must take more after Bree's side, huh?"

"We both took after our Churkey side," I said.

"For truth. Say now, what caused her to go?"

"Cancer," I lied. "Her throat."

"Cancer." I knew he knew by my look I was lying. "Too bad." Then, "You know you got a uncle here, too?"

"Is that Milt Holt?"

"Ain't him I mean, it's your Churkey gramma's younger step-brother. I think he's that, I ain't sure. Brother Dossie Lynch, preacher man. Wife's Cloma, they live in a log cabin on Lynch land." He motioned to the devonette. "Set yourself down, girl."

I shook my head. "I set too long on the train."

"Do what you want to. Anyhow, according to my grandpa, when Harvey Lynch brought Meadow Lark back from Oklahomey, nobody in her family wanted the orphan boy, so he tagged along. Boy thought white, wanted to be white so bad he took the Lynch name. Schooled himself and learnt to preach, went back later for the woman. Funny Bree never mentioned him."

"She didn't talk much on the past," I said.

"She marry again?" he asked and I nodded. "He white?"

"He thought so," I said, remembering Nate Brice.

Sheriff McKay smiled. "You know your family's the last of the mixed bloods in these parts, don't you?"

"We all have to be something," I said.

"Reckon that's so." Again, rubbing his nose, he gawked at me a long time. "Guess by now you think I'm a pretty nosey cuss, don't you?"

I felt like saying yes, but didn't dare.

"Happens I like Milt Holt a lot. Deputy of mine and my daddy's till up to a few year back. Good man, always fair. Milt, he's down these days. One foot in the grave, other one slipping, and he knows it. When I saw him Saturday he said he wouldn't be apt to come get you, he'd send his boy by his first wife. Name's Eb."

More news, me having a step-cousin.

"Milt, he says to me, 'I'm to tell you Eb hates your aunt so much he might not even say her name.' That means, if he's on the bottle or not. May's well hear from me's the next man; Eb Holt's a boozer. Anyhow, Milt didn't feel it right for you to go all the way out there expecting a glad welcome. So he asked me to tell you easy and not count on Eb to do it, what you'll be in for."

Bree's own sister didn't want me, he meant.

"Ilish says she can't stop you coming on Lynch land so long's Milt lives, he's so dead set to have you there. Said the biggest thing to welcome you back's hard work. Told me if you're smart's Bree thought she was, you'd stop off at Vestman's store, get old Villie to take you in."

"Old Villie Vestman," I said, half to myself. "Mom told me he'd used the word *mishling* to shame her, he hated her so."

"Lots of neighbors fight," Sheriff McKay said. "Long's they don't start shooting at each other, I don't always ask why."

"Is there any Farker kin, Sheriff?" I thought to ask.

"Harley told my grandpa when he first rode in that two sisters of his lived in St. Louis. The law there couldn't find 'em when he died. Maybe they had married names, I don't know. I tried myself last week'n I got word of you coming back. Still no trace."

I picked up my floursack and started for the door. "Point me the right road. I'll meet Eb Holt on the way."

"All of seven mile to Onion Creek. I'll drive you out there myself soon's I eat, if Eb's not here; show you your daddy's grave on the way. It's right close to my daddy's, Jessie Red, too, so it's not out of my way. Right now, I'm due home for Pearl's vittles. I'll bring you some back."

Seeing that I hadn't moved, he added, "You wait on the hall bench for Eb Holt. Cooler there. Toilet close and towels, you clean yourself up. Mind you, watch the warter. Drought, you know."

He picked up his hat and walked behind me out the door. "Case you're gone'n I get back, Goldy Lark Farker, I'll wish you luck ahead of time."

I couldn't deny it looked like I'd need it.

# 4

The young white man reining in a red mare at the depot I knew would be my step-cousin, Eb Holt. I also knew, and don't ask me how, that before sunset I would love him like my Bree had Harley Farker, just that fast. Maybe my being in the Rard Courthouse, where my parents had met, had a lot to do with how I suddenly felt. Whatever caused this feeling was pulling me fast to his side without me taking a step.

Thankful I'd washed my face and been able to get most of the smelly dried puke from my dress, I grabbed my floursack and raced for the open front door. I waited a few seconds on the top steps to watch him walk my way. My heart got a happy gnawing ache at the sudden thought of all the wonderful times ahead for me in his tanned, naked arms.

We met the fourth step from the bottom, stopping to gawk at each other a long while in silence. I was hoping he would first lift his straw katy before taking my shaking hand to kiss. Instead, he belched, rubbed his bare belly and said, "Let's go, Goldilocks." He may as well have been talking to a rock for all the kindness in his voice. As he spoke, he yanked my floursack from my hand so hard it nearly drew blood.

At that very second, a man's voice above us called, "Howdy down there, Big Brother Eb."

I looked up to the same cell where I'd earlier seen the hanging arm and was able now to also see parts of a bearded face. Due to the shadows, the hairy arm seemed to be floating in the air.

"Didn't you bring a chaw of baccer, Big Brother?" I couldn't tell if the voice was begging or laughing.

"You drop dead!" Eb Holt called back, heading for the depot's hitching post.

Halfway to the courthouse yard, I caught him. "That really your brother up there?" I asked.

No answer.

"My name's Goldy Lark, not Goldilocks," I tried again. "Didn't your daddy tell you?"

Still no answer.

"He called me right in the letter he wrote," I said.

To my surprise, he growled, "Pop never wrote a letter, no such thing. He can't write."

"I got it there in my floursack, honest."

Eb Holt stopped suddenly and drew back his free hand, as if it hit me. Seeing me duck extra fast, which showed I was used to such treatment, must have softened something in him. He jammed his hand in his pocket instead and, cussing under his breath, quickened his step.

"My Aunt Ilish do it?" I dared ask when he was several safe steps ahead.

"I wrote the damn thing myself, using Pop's words. Now, dry up, dammit. You outtalk your bitchy aunt."

Eb Holt stood just under six feet, taller than me by several inches. He was lean, almost bob-wire thin, with wavy brown hair, deep blue eyes that didn't match his disposition, and a newly shaved face so handsome it should have killed all my hopes on the spot. His jeans were so low at the waist his belly button showed. On his suntanned chest and back was the same kind of thick curly hair like Bree's first lover after Nate Brice left us. I noticed for the first time that instead of wearing his shoes, he'd slung them over the saddle horn, laces tied together. When we got to his red mare, he pitched my floursack atop the shoes.

There was a dirty quilt behind the saddle, where one of us would ride. Who exactly I didn't know, till he got up in the saddle first, saying, "Your pretty little ass end's no prettier'n mine, Goldilocks."

That was our talk going out of town.

Eb Holt whistled, reached inside his hip pocket for his cigarette makings. He flanked his mare and smoked, acting all the while like he rode alone.

I saw Rard Graveyard's tall gate a long time before we got to it. Rather than again rile Eb Holt by asking him to stop, I clamped my teeth tight. I could see my father's resting place some other time, if that was how it had to be. For now I'd have to be satisfied with only a roadside glimpse.

Then I was nearly pitched to the ground by a sudden stop of the mare. I waited for him to say what was expected of me before I dared ask. Finally, he said, "Well, Goldilocks, you want to see your pop's grave or not?"

"I'm too tired," I thought it best to say. "I'll come back maybe next week."

"You'll get somebody else to bring you," he growled, starting the mare.

We had traveled a short way when I twisted around for another look back. Only the big iron gate showed, standing as silent as the dead it guarded. I wondered what Eb Holt thought of my not begging him to see Harley Farker's last place of rest.

Suddenly he commenced singing, "Oh, when I was single, oh, then," which proved he hadn't been thinking of me in any way.

"You married?" I dared ask.

"Acourse," he surprised me by saying. "Like you still got your cherry."

I felt it safe to smile behind his back before asking, "She white, too?"

For a minute I thought he would fall from the saddle, he was laughing so. "Me ask my own kind to marry? Oh, run me for president of the United States and Arkansaw, any little old easy thing like that, but don't tell me to ask a white woman to get hitched."

"You're white," I said.

"Afraid not, Goldilocks, not any more. My pop's tyin' the knot with that bitch's fixed it so no decent white girl would even spit on me. Your aunt, she's so stinking a polecat wouldn't turn his tail to her. Give time, anyone round her gets the same piss-poor way."

"You're not married, then?" I asked, hoping not.

"In a way I am. In a way, I ain't."

"You said no white woman would have you, and I guess you don't want one of my kind."

"It didn't matter to Delphie Doll."

"That's a pretty name," I said, ready to duck.

He nodded. "Got it from a girl who used to kick her boyfriend out one side of bed and let me in the other, when I was in the C.C.C.s. Named her myself."

I didn't know what to say to that.

"Case you don't know, my mare's who I talk of."

Then just as I thought he wasn't maybe so grouchy after all, he turned around to say, "I remember pretty Bree Lynch, you know. Too damned bad you couldn't looked more like her'n your bitchy aunt, ain't it, Goldilocks?"

# 5

We passed several farmhouses along the road, most that were old and unpainted. Kids of all ages played in the yards while coonhounds (cooners), far too smart to overdo themselves in the heat, dozed in the nearest shade. I didn't notice any of the names on the mailboxes, so busy was I enjoying the feel of Eb Holt's back against my belly, with my eyes so often shut.

The sun was low by the time we rode in at Vestman's General Store. It looked like what people the day's miserable heat had kept from the train station had now gathered at the store to welcome me to Missouri County. When Eb Holt had lifted me down, he led his mare toward a water trough, saying under his breath, "You get the hell inside. All these folks, they've come to hear you call old Villie a bad word Bree might've missed."

I passed through a crowd of perhaps twelve, several of them kids near my age, the rest their fathers, I thought, and I stepped inside the door. It was the same sort of store scattered around Pelper County. A dry goods counter and a clothes rack were on one side, grocery counter on the other, a big black pot belly stove with more tobacco juice stains on the door than on the floor spittoon. On either side of the stove stood a big salt box. There was a wooden cracker barrel and a pickle barrel, both open. A coffee grinder stood next on a table, with several sacks of flour beneath. At the back hung everything from horse collars to cow muzzles to shoes and boots. Slightly in front was a soft drink cooler, where the customers (I knew) gathered often to talk on the drought, President Roosevelt, and the hard times.

It was here I took from my dress pocket the last nickel I owned, laid it on the counter for orange sody pop.

I opened it and turned to find the crowd had followed, halting by the stove to eye me the same way I'd look at a wagon load of dollar bills. I didn't know what else to do save drink slow so's not to choke, my eyes on my feet. When Eb Holt, a white man at his side, finally shoved a path through to me, I had counted sixty-seven of my toes, not ten.

Eb introduced the man, who was older and heavier than himself, as Urch Vestman, part-owner of the store.

"Mom spoke of you lots, Urch," I said, offering my hand. (She had, too, when of a mind to rile Brice about her other white offers of marriage.)

"It pained me to hear she'd passed on," he said, taking both my hands and the pop bottle in his.

"Nigh the last words she said was how you and Milt Holt was her two good friends." I didn't add that that had been about the time she'd had me write Milt Holt about him giving me a home.

"Milt, he'll sure be tickled to see you," he said.

Suddenly the screen door popped open and somebody whose head I couldn't see elbowed his way back. Before me puffed the shortest, fattest man I'd ever beheld, standing maybe five-foot exactly to a weight of around three hundred pounds. He was gray haired and unnaturally red of face, and his digging eyes were so blue they scarcely seemed real. I knew he was old Villie Vestman when he commenced sputtering in a foreign tongue. Everything he said either started or ended with the word "mishling."

Bree, my mom, who had never bothered to tell me I had any living kin, had told me more about this ugly old man than she had even of herself. He was rightly credited with inventing the hateful "Mishling" from his German tongue. Mom had always told me he hated her because she'd had the good looks to tempt Urch into an offer of marriage and out from under the old man's thumb. Sheriff Jessie Red McKay hadn't said this wasn't so. Whichever way it was, hate me he did. You could hear hate roll from his spitting tongue, almost smell it pour from his entire being.

Urch made one try to introduce me. Old Villie would have no part of it. He'd only come to look, like the others. He choked and sputtered in his own tongue till his breath gave out, then turned to fight his way to fresh air.

His son, now red-faced also, apologized when the old man had gone.

I had only stood silent and done what I thought best, acted dumb but unafraid. So I finished my pop, told Urch I was glad to meet him, and walked outside. It wasn't an easy thing to do with so many eyes holes through me.

A fancy house painted yellow with white trim stood behind the store. Climbing up on Delphie Doll, I caught the move of a curtain and knew the mean old man was still watching me. That naturally called for a prouder lift of my head until we rode out of sight.

"What you think of Urch?" Eb Holt asked me as we rounded a bend.

"Mom said he wanted to marry her once. He was one of lots of white men to ask."

"How's about old Villie?"

"She said he favors a pig. He does."

We passed a big white house on our right, where several kids, all girls, played in the yard. The one seeming to be oldest, nigh my age, stuck out her titties when she saw Eb and pushed at her curly yellow hair.

"Wild and woolly and full of fleas, never been tickled above the knees." Eb laughed low. "I could get a bone right easy for that one. You know what a bone is, Goldilocks?"

"No," I lied, knowing if I said I knew, he'd be apt to ask me how I knew. (That's what Nate Brice told Bree happened to his man parts whenever he saw a pretty woman he'd like to bed.)

"That's Doc Helton's place," Eb was saying. "Nigh the only other man in the county asides Jessie Red McKay and the Rard mailman and Uncle Sam (the relief man) who owns a car. Bree used to work there; Opal does now."

"Who's Opal?"

"Nobody told you your aunt's got two kids?"

"Nobody told me afore today I even had a Aunt Ilish."

"Reckon Bree wasn't so proud of her, neither, huh? Yeah, two kids by her first old man. He died in the pen."

"Both my cousins girls?"

"Just Opal."

"What's my boy cousin like?"

Eb pointed to a dried manure dumpling in the road. "That's him, right there." He took out his cigarette makings. "And your Uncle Dossie's not so pretty."

A short distance beyond Doc Helton's place, he turned left off the road and started downhill through the dark woods on a narrow rocky lane. Eb explained this ridge of rocks was called the Ozark Foothills. The Lynch property, twenty acres in all, was hemmed in by three sides of these ridges, north, east and south. Eb himself lived alone due west of my aunt, one farm removed, on creek-bottom Holt land.

"Didn't you ever live at Aunt Ilish's?" I asked.

"When I was too damn young to know any better, yeah. Pop, he up and married the bitch just about the time your folks got hitched. Matter of truth, they'd gone to get their hitching license the day Harley Farker, coming from St. Louis, met Bree. Your aunt, she'd made Bree go along to Rard so no sum bitch could hump her and your aunt wouldn't be there to hear Bree holler. I had to stay home and watch your aunt's snot-nosed kids."

Our next step was a one-room schoolhouse. Eb struck a match to let me read "New Hill," a sign above the door. His four years of schooling had been here. My mom's, if he remembered right, amounted to about the same, so did my aunt's. Dossie Lynch, as he growled out his name, had not only finished eight years here, he'd had four more terms at the high school in Rard before getting the call to preach. My great-grandfather, Joshua Lynch, who'd taught here when younger, may even have been in school a longer time.

It had been dark some time when we started the last part of the long trip, still downhill so far. I was so tired and achey I feared falling asleep and off Delphie Doll before we got home.

Finally on level ground, Eb stopped his mare. After three tries, he struck a match with his thumbnail, and by its light guided Delphie Doll across a narrow wooden footbridge.

In the yard I got down from the quilt when told and started to the house's open door, where a long length of dim light shone outside. When I was less than two feet from the doorway, my floursack came flying to smack the back of my head. Eb Holt was laughing only inches behind me as I, trying to miss a dozing coon dog, slipped and skidded through a stinking mudhole by the kitchen step.

Fighting tears, I passed through an unlit kitchen up into a front room, seeing first a lamp that burned low on an old dresser with a cracked looking-glass. It stood in one corner and in front of it was a high-back rocker. The corner nearest the creek was empty, meant to hold wood in the winter, I guessed. The last corner held a big iron bedstead painted green, over which hung an old fiddle.

In the bed, directly beneath the fiddle, lay a grayed man who favored Eb Holt enough for me to know this was his father, Milt, who was also my uncle. He smiled and held out his shaking arms to me, wordless. I had to remind myself not to cry.

Goldy Lark Farker, you won't cry anymore.

Now you're home.

# 6

The steady thump of bread being kneaded in a wooden bowl woke me at sunup. I found myself lying on the devonette, the dirty quilt I'd rode on yesterday spread between me and the gouging springs that were alive with bedbugs. Eb Holt, I guessed, had moved me sometime during the night. Across the room, in the big green bed, was a sunken outline on the spot where Milt Holt had welcomed me. There was a smaller dent in the other side, so I knew my aunt was up, too, as was likely everyone else on the place.

I arose and tiptoed across the bare floorboards to the door, thankful Aunt Ilish was too busy to look up. This gave me a chance to see her as she really was.

She so favored Mom standing there at the table, her brown fingers forming biscuits from the heavy dough. True, her all-Indian face with its snapping black eyes was perhaps a bit too broad to be pretty, her freckled nose wider at the bottom than it should be. Her thick lips, which were partly twisted into a smile, showed part of a pink tongue. Bree had always liked to stick out her long tongue and touch her nose with it while giggling in a funny little dance. Aunt Ilish didn't look like she would care to trouble herself with that kind of play.

Aunt Ilish was shorter than myself, though thinner, especially in her waist and girly legs. I could see that through the rolled-up overalls and floppy old blue relief shirt she wore. The size of her feet I judged to be a four or less, as Bree's had been. On her head was a floursack scarf, knotted at the back of her neck. It didn't take a learned schoolteacher to know that inside the covering was greasy black plaits that usually would be hanging below her waist in true Indian fashion.

Knowing now that Eb Holt hadn't liked me because I looked more like her than Bree, I suddenly wanted to run to her and twist her face into another face that didn't look like mine. Though all I could really do about it was stand and watch her work, hating her enough to kill her before she even spoke.

The last biscuit finished, she crossed to the stove, slid the pan into the oven and rubbed her floury hands on her overalled legs. Only parts of brown skin showed through the sticky white of her fingers when she reached inside her shirt front to pull forth a twist of chewing tobacco shaped like a giant hairpin. A hefty chew bit from the twist, she wallowed it in her mouth a minute, as if trying to decide whether it was the right size. When it seemed to be, she put the tobacco in the gap between her big titties. From there, she passed on to the washpan on a low table nearby, to clean her hands.

And that's when she looked up and saw me.

At first it was just a passing glance, remindful of the one I'd received yesterday from Sheriff Jessie Red McKay in Rard. I was ready to think she also mistook me for somebody else. Then she suddenly turned full face to pitch me a look as hard as rocks. It started at the part in the top center of my hair, ending with the dried mud between my toes.

"I'm Goldy Lark Farker," I said. I stepped down into the kitchen and went a step ahead, stopping to let her make the next move.

Her crackling sharp black eyes over the fast chewing jaws burned steady into mine. "I know who you are." She rubbed her hands dry on her overalls bib. "My mom, Meadow Lark, she had in her the good blood to make us all favor, no matter how bad it got mixed down the line."

"I missed seeing you last night," I said.

"Well, don't I know that, too?" Thick lips spat into the smelly mudhole inches from the kitchen door.

"Mom didn't tell me," I started to say.

"You don't have a mom anymore," she snapped. "You ain't had one in my mind's eye since you was still sucking and the bitch who claimed to be my sister run off in the middle of the night with you and a man old enough, pert near, to be her daddy. Left me to worry about who'd foot the bill for Harley Farker's grave! Left me to look out for myself without so much's a 'kiss my ruby red rear!' Other things I had to face down, too, like Harley Farker varely cold in the ground. So if you want to live here and keep your gut full, don't you ever let me hear you say her name in this house, you got that?"

I nodded, swallowed hard and said, "You got a pretty place here."

She put her hands to her hips. "That old table, it was built when the house was, during the Civil War. What we call chairs ain't chairs, they're just sticks of wood, you can plain see that." She pointed with her head to each thing mentioned. "Bucket stand here, my gramps, Joshua Lynch, a teacher up at New Hill yonder, first one there ever, built it after the big table there. Cookstove nigh's old. Rock holding up the stove's missing leg, that's even got time on old Villie Vestman. Pink dish cabinet in the corner there's the newest thing on the place. Milt won it on a drunk bet with Urch Vestman, old Villie's boy, Herbert Hoover'd be next president.

"And the green front bed, that all us Lynches, save Joshua, was birthed in, even you, that's even older'n the house. Joshua Lynch got that from some farmhouse when he was coming here, fresh off the boat from Ireland by way of Tennessee." She stuck her face close to mine. "You still call the place pretty?"

Such a sizzling pull had taken over my head at her temper fit that I found myself unable to answer.

"Just goes to show Nate Brice provided lesser for the bitch he took off with'n Milt's done for me," she mumbled to herself, and spat again.

I took a drink from the dipper in the water bucket on the stand, saying nothing.

Aunt Ilish crossed over to the only window in the kitchen, which was next to where the pink cabinet stood alongside the cookstove. "Don't know the minute you come in last night, wasn't here, like you know. Milt give you a chance to meet the King of Missouri? Poke your head in there for a look-see at how he lives."

I stepped across the kitchen and stuck my head through the window, expecting to see, for all I knew, even if I'd never heard of such a man, the King of Missouri himself. What I beheld instead was a big room almost ten feet wide by twenty long, with a flowered linoleum on the floor. In a corner was a homemade floursack mattress. The saddle from yesterday, a curry comb, and a harness hung overhead. Under the window was a shiny wash tub. A piece of old winter underwear plugged a hole in the tub's side. A long wooden feed trough with a few grains of corn stood by the tub.

Remembering what the Rard station man had said about Milt's prize mule, I knew this was his stable. But why the fancy linoleum, when the front room and kitchen had bare floors for the humans, I couldn't see. Nor could I understand why there were mule turds on the rug. For while the stable smelt of mule, the floor shone bright as winter's snow against a full sun.

"Most men stand up to go pee when they first rise of a morning," Aunt Ilish was saying. "Not Milt Holt, mind you. First off, he makes sure bread's on to cook for his precious mule and his solid gold cooner and him, then he heats warter from Onion Creek for the mule so's he won't chill his valuable guts. Next comes the corn feeding, good corn, I'll have you know, my kids could eat if he didn't think so much of that mule he'd get it ground at the Rard Mill. And then he sweeps out the stable, using this new buckbrush broom here I made with these poor old tired fingers of mine. There's the biscuit chomping after that, though when the sad bread's without salt, the mule don't want much. Milt, he eats what the dog leaves."

She spat twice in the mudhole. "That's when Milt Holt does what most other men do when they first get up. He pees."

I studied the flowered rug in silence.

"Guess you wonder why I put up with that mudhole there and all the flies it draws, for the sake of a mangy old mule, now don't you?"

I nodded I did.

"I do it acause Old Jack brings in money once a year from lassess making and helps us get the relief once ever two week. I can stand the flies in summer and the ice in winter if my belly's full."

"Where's Milt now?" I asked, not really hoping for an answer till some of her temper died.

"Cutting corn up Onion Creek a ways. Dog's watching him. Mule telling him how." She bent to check the bread. "Good thing that, reckon. Comes to brains, Old Nance's boy, he's smarter'n any Holt who ever took a breath."

"Old Nance? Who's she?"

"The red mare who brought Old Jack into the world and took Harley Farker out of it. Kicked him to death."

"I didn't know that's how he died," I said, feeling a chill.

She looked at me a long time. "Happened right out there by the woodpile, in the path to the creek. Got his foot caught in the stirrup, fell off. Spooked Old Nance. She bucked, kicked out, wouldn't stop till he was killed dead. Harley Farker, he died leaving you no more'n days old and a pile of debts at Vestman's. Milt's tried to pay off a dab at a time and let our own debts go beg. You didn't know that afore; well, you do now."

"Someday I'll even up the debt," I promised.

"Find you a pot of gold at the end of a rainbow and you do that." She hawked her chew of tobacco into her hand and slung it out the kitchen door. "Else, sober Eb Holt up long enough for him to help you somehow. It wasn't my notion you come here, Goldy

Lark. I'd sooner see you dead'n under my roof again. Guess you know the only reason you're here's Milt's to die varely soon and I'll need you that long to help out."

I nodded and set down on the step leading up the front room, no sooner getting settled than she picked up the water bucket, nearly half full. "Bring me up some warter without tadpoles in it, for breakfast dishes," she ordered, throwing last night's water into the mudhole.

Her cold hand meeting mine on the bucket handle marked the only time we would ever touch.

# 7

In spite of the three-year drought, Onion Creek turned out to be wide but lazy flowing, yet too deep to be crossed except by means of the narrow, creaky bridge. Several crawdads backed away from me to the mossy rocks when I filled the bucket. Tadpoles wiggled along the clear bottom, playing tag with the crawdads. The creek had got its name, I later learned, from the grassy-like onions that grew wild on the banks every spring. It could just as easy haves been called for the clumps of post oaks on the far side of the bridge or the thick patches of waist-high buckbrush on all sides of me. The old country saying that either could grow through a rock if it set its mind to it was just about to come true here.

Halfway back up the rocky hill was a rail fence, the gate rails laying flat by the path that ringed the yard. Inside the yard was a woodpile, three cedar trees to my left, and the house. The sheet-iron roof glared in the morning sunshine, smoke poured from the kitchen stovepipe. It was the oddest-shaped house I'd ever seen. In time I would know it had first been but two rooms, the front room and back one, built by my great-grandfather, Joshua Lynch. Harvey Lynch, my grandfather, upon the old folks dying, had added on the kitchen. Why he'd built it a step lower than the rest of the house I couldn't see, for foundation rocks seemed to be plentiful everywhere. I guessed Milt Holt had built the mule's barn against the south half of the kitchen to give Old Jack needed warmth in winter and human company all year around.

A slim, light-complected girl who looked as much like Bree as I did Aunt Ilish, not much older than me, was at the table, spooning canned peaches from a jar. She was barefoot in a blue relief dress that matched mine. Her long black hair, center parted, too, ended with a plait a-dangle over each big titty.

"Why, you look just like someone I used to know," I said, feeling my heart give a jealous pull.

Why couldn't I have looked like pretty little fair-skinned Bree and this girl take after her own mom? I wasn't sure I really could ever like her, because of that.

"Don't think I don't hear that all the time," she said.

I put the water bucket on the washstand when she patted the nearest stick of wood.

"Welcome to the fold, you poor little stray lamb, as Brother Dossie would say. Glad you're here, cousin. Fish farts! You look more like my sum bitching mom'n I do."

"You must be Opal," I said.

"And pert nigh eighteen and single, dammit, but still hoping." She laughed. "Set down. Don't look so ready to run. Nobody'll swipe your cherry without your say so."

I dropped onto the stick of wood and looked around.

"Talk about Aunt Bree, if you want to. I won't cut out your tongue."

I shook my head and looked at her closer, the jealous feeling coming again.

"Mom's out fanning the backbrush for hen nests. We don't have a chicken coop, maybe you've seen. My lazy brother wouldn't cut much winter wood last fall to brag of, and Eb Holt, he wasn't talking to us more'n usual, and Milt wasn't up to work, so we used what wood was handiest. Chicken coop hadn't been in the family near's long's Great-Grandpa Joshua's rail fence. So Eb, he built us the coop when he got out of the C.C.C.s."

She giggled. "Didn't matter a coon's tail, nohow. Chickens still freeze their asses off, same's others does ever winter in the coop. We've always stood there and waited for 'em to drop, left 'em lay till we got hungry enough to walk that far. Their coop was out by the woodpile, handy if the weather started to thaw, then look out, old dead hens. Biggest worry was to beat Old Mame there. She's the dog. Want some peach juice?"

"Not now," I said.

She drained the juice from the jar and licked her Bree lips. "Say, it true you're fifteen and your middle name's Lark?"

"Yes," I said to both questions.

"Ain't that funny, me never knowing afore Milt got your mom's letter, I had a cousin to share my Churkey middle name?"

"Me, too, up to now."

"Opal Lark, Goldy Lark. Belly buster, if you ask me." She tipped the fruit jar, stuck her tongue inside to lick the last drop of juice. "By the way, what do you think of my pretty step-brother?"

"Delphie Doll wasn't mad at me for being born," I said.

She snorted. "Oh, he don't mean to be sour, I think. One good lay and old Eb, he'd die with a possum's grin all over his pretty little face."

"You recollect my folks, Opal?" I didn't like the way she spoke of Eb Holt, who now belonged to me.

She shook her head. "My brother does, though. Aunt Bree's white husband, anyhow, just varely. When Old Nance kicked out his guts by the woodpile, he says he tried to help Harley Farker stuff 'em back."

"I saw the graveyard yesterday," I said, chilling again.

"My old man's there, too, in the proud Lynch family spot. Got arrested for stealing seed corn from Vestman's store six planting seasons in a row and died in jail while I still sucked. From a knife fight. Mom, she was so proud of him being all white, she ought to pickled him in vinegar and kept him on the dresser to look at. She claims my brother's just like him. Other words, sucking hind tit and hind tit done run dry."

"What's Brother Dossie like?"

"Oh, he's prettier'n a toad frog, guess," she said with a giggle, then added, "Well, asides being the biggest turd from here to Arkansaw, you mean? 'Save us from sin! Build us a great church in this wilderness, drop your money offers right in here! Be saved.' Above all, one of the womenfolk. Last night we went up to the churchwomen's prayer meet at his cabin, east up Onion Creek a ways and you know what? When he gets Mom and all the others so stirred up they talk in tongues, he hightails it outside and tries to fugg this girl no older'n me right by the creek, so help me." She laughed. "Hope the chiggers bite hits old balls raw."

I smiled to please her, not really believing, and asked what her brother was like.

"Eb Holt, he didn't tell you he's in jail in Rard for stealing Eb's razorback hog?"

"Oh, that one with the long arms and his name in the paper. He called Eb his brother, but I didn't know."

Opal Troat stood up. "Burt's been in jail so much I hear tell they're ready to name the town Troat. Best'n he ever pulled was sign Milt's name for a Model A he tried to buy. Reckon he forgot Milt don't know how to write." She touched my shoulder. "I'm off to work now at Doc Helton's. Be sure not to piss in Onion Creek, or you'll go to Arkansaw'n you die."

She was barely out of sight down the path when Aunt Ilish, now wearing men's shoes, clumped through the front door. Wallowing a tobacco chew in her mouth, she carried a dirtified egg in each hand. These she placed carefully in a bowl inside the pink cabinet, going on her way like I wasn't there. From the cabinet she drew a cracked cup and filled it with coffee from the granite pot bubbling on the stove. Scooping up three biscuits from the hearth breadpan, she came to the chair Opal had just left and sat. She removed her unfinished chew, put it as carefully inside the peach jar as she had put the eggs in the cabinet.

When I got to know her better, I found out she'd done this not so much to protect the table as the tobacco. For where her chewing tobacco was concerned, Aunt Ilish was the most particular person alive.

I watched while she broke the sad lumpy bread into her coffee, sprinkled sugar from a bowl on the table over the bread and added water. Her arm almost touched mine as it snaked past to pick up Opal's spoon. Still forgetting me, she commenced to eat.

The cup empty, she then remembered my being, "Biscuits and coffee to make you soakey." Her voice actually dared me to go ahead and eat, despite just having asked me to help myself.

"I'm not hungry," I lied, hoping she couldn't hear my growling insides.

"Good. All the more for me."

"I mean, I can't go soakey. Sugar sharps my teeth."

"Make yourself up some fried bread, in that case. Whole lot of flour in the sack, whole lot of warter in the creek."

"Fried bread—"

"Can't give you milk. Ain't got a cow."

"I don't like milk," I lied, trying not to lick my lips when remembering the few times I'd been lucky enough to drink it.

She rubbed her stained mouth on her shirt sleeve and took up her unfinished chew. "Don't let yourself start craving any eggs, they're not for the likes of you. All laid here's for my baby Burt. No need my telling you he's in the Rard jail, now, is it?"

I said I'd glimpsed him yesterday.

"Up in the woods atween the schoolhouse and Doc Helton's, Burt sees this razorback rooting in the moss, nabs it, ties it up with bindertwine and starts leading it to Vestman's store to ask who owned it. Right this side of the store, Jessie Red McKay comes driving along, big's you please in his brand new car, and takes my boy to jail." She spit in the mudhole. "Pig turned out to be Eb Holt's, who'd turned it in as lost day afore when he went to get our relief. Acted like his name was on that old hog, Eb Holt did. Since it wasn't, how was my boy to know? And don't you ever let nobody else try to tell you different, Goldy Lark."

"Nobody tried to," I said.

She waggled her chew to the other side. "Burt didn't rape the New Hill teacher, I'll tell you that right off the bat, too. Me, I say it takes two to diddle and that girl knowed how to run. She married him the next month, anyhow. But just acause his dad, Henry Troat, died in the pen—he got sent there for stealing—they watch my Burt, always expecting him to do the same. I tell you right now, and you'd best hear me, he'd no sooner steal'n Brother Dossie would cuss."

"Could I go visit him after a while?" I asked.

"No, you can't, and his name's not him. He's Brother Dossie to everybody he meets, and he meets everybody. You got that straight?" At my nod, she added, "You know how to cook and make bread and housekeep?"

"Yes," I said.

"We'll be in from corn cutting to eat when the sun's due south," she said and stood up. "You see to it the house's shiny as Milt keeps the barn." She trained her sharp black eyes on my face. "Milt, he likes warter sop with his sad bread. Can you fix sop?"

"I make good gravy," I said.

"You call it sop," she ordered me.

Horses hooves sounded on the lower creek path. I followed Aunt Ilish to the door in time to see Eb Holt rein in on Delphie Doll. Lashed to his saddle's side was a cornknife, its blade flashing in the morning sunlight. His straw katy was pushed back from his face, showing his good looks to the whole wide world.

"Ready to hie, Ilish Troat?" he growled, his eyes fixed on the creek.

"Minute, Eb." She first had to check the size of her tobacco twist before shoving it down into the neck of her dress.

I watched, a peculiar ache in my throat, as she followed him down the path. For the man I meant to marry hadn't even noticed me.

# 8

Judging by the sun, my aunt having no clock, it was past seven when they went to work. Not a very long time between now and noon to do all the chores I knew were expected of me and still have dinner on the table when the sun's shadow said high noon.

I started by eating the three leftover sad breakfast biscuits, which did little to stop my hunger pains. A cup of coffee, nearly half sugar, followed. I then searched through the pink cabinet in hopes of finding more eats, being extra careful not to touch the precious eggs. On the top shelf was another biscuit, rock-hard, probably left from last week. I spread it heavy with relief lard in a syrup pail under the cabinet, and wolfed it down.

I was now fairly fixed to commence chores.

In my new home in Missouri County, like in my old, a big dishpan filled with greasy water and dirty dishes sat on the middle of the stove. A ribbed rag of old winter long johns lay atop the dishes. There didn't seem to be a cake of lye soap in the pan or anywhere else close. About the only thing left to do was try and dry the grease from the dishes I'd wash by means of a bigger piece of underwear I found inside a big box in the back room. Maybe, by listening for Eb Holt's mare to come in at noon, I could have the eats dished up before my aunt got in to notice the dishes weren't any too clean. At supper, I could work it the same way. What she'd do to me come breakfast time tomorrow, I could pretty well guess.

The breadpan I decided to leave be till after baking sad bread at noon. I couldn't see the use to go over it twice and it still not be clean.

Having slid the greasy dishrag over the stove top, I remembered to check the coffee pot, always so important in my old home. The outside showed it had been used many times over without washing. Inside, over half the pot held grounds boiled several times over, thanks to the hard times. But before deciding to clean the pot, I searched the kitchen for a coffee poke, finally finding one in the pink cabinet. I told myself then and there to always know how much coffee was on hand. People like us would do without eats till the relief was ready at Uncle Sam's, be it a day or a week or longer, it seemed. But I'd learned early they could get close to dying if the place was out of coffee.

I found the ash pit on the far side of the woodpile and dumped the smoking grounds nearby. After filling the pot with a few inches of ashes, I threw another rag inside. I went down to the creek, the coffee pot swinging at my side. Kneeling on the bridge, I dampened the rag to scour the pot's outside until it shone like new. It took a much longer time to clean the inside. That done, I rinsed the pot, filled it with fresh, tadpole-free water for dinner coffee and took it back uphill. I laid the kitchen fire next so's to be ready to cook in a hurry.

In the front room I made the big green bed, careful to ruff the dried leaves stuffed inside the floursack mattress. I noticed tear stains on one pillow while shaking it.

I thanked Milt Holt for that part of my welcome home.

My tied floursack, which I would use as my pillow, still lay on the devonette where Eb Holt had probably put it last night. Since this and the dirty quilt were the only things there, I left them be. Using a homemade buckbrush broom I'd found in the kitchen, I swept the cobwebs from the newspapered walls of the front room only, the kitchen and back room walls being covered with card-board. The newspapers were the *Missouri County Gazette,* a barely readable portion dating back to 1910. I dusted the dresser with a clean rag from the back room rag box. Its cracked looking-glass I wanted to clean and would have, as well as dust the old fiddle on the wall, except the coffee pot scouring had used up so much time. There was a King Heater in the middle of the room. Directly north was a window with two of its missing panes stuffed with rags. In front of the window stood a high-back rocker, so warped it only moved sideways.

In the stuffy back room were three doors, one leading north, one south towards the creek, the last into the front room. A sagging cot to my left kept the south door from opening all the way and a double bed was jammed solid against the one north. The rag box was pushed against the beds, that's how small the room was. Little fresh air was able to enter, so the place smelled of human use, dust, and very old age.

It was here, I told myself, Mom had slept when young. Maybe in the double bed with Aunt Ilish. I guessed I would sleep in the big unmade bed tonight with Opal. The cot's undisturbed covers told me this was my cousin Burt's bed, waiting his return from jail. Under the cot was several quilts stacked for use in winter. When I ran the broom beneath the double bed, it brought forth a blue relief dress exactly like me and Opal's. Wadded inside was a pair of homemade bloomers that nigh matched those I wore. The sack's red-and-blue initials, M.F.A., meaning Missouri Farmers Association, was printed on the straddle. Neither the dress or bloomers my property, I slid them back under the bed with the broom handle. I swept the dirt of many days into the front room, shutting with wide-cracked door behind me. The dirt I then swept into the kitchen, on out to the mudhole.

When the sun told me I was ahead of myself, I wandered back into the front room, opened the top drawer of the dresser. A bottle of green pills bearing Milt's name lay atop a worn Bible. I opened the Bible to find these words: "Joshua Jeremiah Lynch, husband of Annie Nora Guthrie, who begat Timothy, Pansy, Harvey, and Mary, Harvey being the only one to live to prime."

On the same page in the same hand, though penciled at another time, was: "Better that Harvey had died as a babe, too, than darken the home of his parents by taking to wife a heathen Cherokee squaw." The writing was old time and swirly. I guessed it to belong to Joshua Lynch, first New Hill schoolteacher.

In a separate paragraph, in a different hand, I read: "I, Harvey Lunch, was lawful to Meadow Lark, no last name, at what was the Ft. Sill Reservation in the Oklahoma. Possessed of no earthly worth, I promised to raise her younger step-brother, a half-Indian, as my own. I was made to build a log house at the mouth of Onion Creek to house my new family till Papa learned of Meadow Lark's earlier conversion to Christianity. Then, she became the daughter they had never had. My own two daughters, birthed in the green Lynch family bed, Ilish Opal Lynch and Bree Annie Lynch, were brought into the world by my mama, Annie Guthrie Lynch."

The reverse page, in yet another hand, went: "Rev. Dossie Lynch, wedded to Cloma of Ft. Sill, not quite right in the head. Loss of baby girl Nonnie unbearable to us both. Blessed are the meek, for they shall inherit the earth. Amen.

"Ilish Lynch, wedded to Henry Troat, father of Burt and Opal. Henry died in the pen at Jeff City. My oldest niece then wed Milton Holt, him that I myself saved in the holy waters of Onion Creek. Young Eban Milton Holt, issue of Brother Milt by his marriage to the late Jane Bell, joined our family against his will. Sister Ilish, as I could and would call her after her salvation in Onion Creek, backslid twice, hardly was her hair dry, with two neighbor men. Neither shall I name.

"Younger niece, Bree Lynch, married to Harley Farker of St. Louis, Mo., who died on Lynch property right after the birth of baby girl, Goldy Lark. God grant that Harley Farker rest in peace. He was liked by all who knew him. Amen. Bree Lynch Farker ran off with Nate Brice, neighbor, and baby girl. As of this day, February 4, 1927, nobody save God above knows what has happened to my youngest niece and her babe. Let us pray.

"May God have mercy on the souls of my Meadow Lark's two wayward daughters. Signed, Brother D. Lynch of the Gospel of Jesus Christ, our Lord and Master. Amen."

A few lines on the pages for deaths, undated, in the same hand read: "Annie Guthrie Lynch and husband Joshua both died of scarlet fever. Harvey, Meadow Lark's husband, passed on during a big drunk. My gentle Cherokee sister in spirit went to her Maker soon afterwards of homesickness and heartbreak. Her last request in life was that I take her to her Oklahoma birthplace for burial. On sad journey, my borrowed team and wagon, I left heavy of heart and returned happy with my bride, who became a sister in my church due to baptism the next Lord's Day. The blessings of God, our Father in Heaven, will always prevail, today and forevermore. Amen."

For an unknown reason, I felt as guilty as if I'd been caught stepping on the graves of the mentioned dead. I shut the book, glancing about to see if someone was watching, and closed the drawer. How I wished, now that I knew there was nothing I could do about my mom's past, I could change the words just for me. But the ending of her life, if I'd been writing it in the Lynch family Bible and had to tell the truth to those who would follow after me, I would have to say:

"Whore Bree Annie Lynch Farker Brice, mother of Goldy Lark Farker, died August 1, 1937, in Pelper County, Missouri, of the beating several days earlier by C.C.C. boys, who'd claimed she'd tried to sneak away after being paid first. Out of her head most of the time, she'd cussed Nate Brice for leaving us hungry and without a way to get our relief eats home. 'Hey, mister, you give me a ride to town and back and I'll sell you a ride in my bed.' The man with the thick curly hair on his chest and back, just like Eb Holt's, had been the first I knew of. Anything in pants had soon followed him.

"Bree remembered that first man the last few minutes of her life, when her breathing was little more, she said, than a hard black knot in her bruised throat. 'He give me the two-bits I'd asked for, acause he thought, Goldy Lark, you looked so starved and skinny. I was so glad for his kind words for you I fell so deep in love with him, I asked him to stay. He laughed at me and spit in my face and never got back by.'

"And the last words of Bree went: "Goldy Lark, this Milt Holt you writ to asking for a home, ask him to help you get even with old Villie Vestman for what he once promised he'd give to me. Mishling, poor mishling Bree.' "

Poor mishling me, too, I thought, dropping to the step at the kitchen door. Life hadn't always been too kind to me, either. I'd always missed not having a father. How wonderful it would have been to be touched without being hit or slapped by the man who had your mom. Your very own father, imagine that! Though I'd tried for most of my life to think of Harley Farker, Bree and me together as a family, my imagination just wouldn't work. Part of that might have been due to Bree's not having his picture. Now, I didn't have one of her, but her memory made up for that. I had felt her warmth, heard her happy laughter and kissed away her tears, which made all the difference.

My mind now back on her grave and Pelper County, I thought of Roy Cox again. He was the son of Miss Emmer Cox and Freeman Cox, a traveling drummer salesman. I'd despised Roy Cox from my primer days. Dark-haired himself, he'd always called me "Squaw," tried to beat me at dare base or scrub or anything else. He tried to outshine me in class. At our weekly spelling or geography matches, I'd skin him good. At arithmetic matches, he was made to look sick. In poetry class, he'd try to find out which poem I'd be memorizing so's to outdo me there.

Since we shared a March 9 birthday, Miss Emmer always invited me home for dinner that day with her and Roy. Her living just across the road, she'd leave a bigger girl in charge of the school. In her fine home I'd be seated at a fancy table and eat whatever she'd fixed before school that morning. The first time, she'd made a big cake with pink icing just for me and her and Roy, and gave me two cups of cold milk to go with it. I could have died happy right then and there. The next year, and the next, it was the same. I always got to take a big piece of cake home to Bree, being careful to hide it from Nate Brice because I didn't want him to have any.

How I always lived for March 9 to finally come!

Miss Emmer was always fair. She knew Roy was almost two years older than me but not any smarter because he had trouble reading. New glasses didn't help much, I saw, when he still couldn't always get words right. He was just plain old dumbheaded, to me.

His last year in grade school before he would board in town to attend high school there, I'd had a bellyful of Roy Cox. He'd stood up one day in history class to say Indians couldn't be very smart, else the white man wouldn't have got their land. As Miss Emmer hurried to say my people had been too kind and trusting, I felt every eye in the place on me. She made Roy sorry himself, which didn't stop the pulling sizzle in my head. I knew I had to get him the worst way. The whipping he got from Miss Emmer in front of the whole school, with a witch hazel stick he'd had to cut himself, just wouldn't be enough for me.

I got my chance next poetry class. Miss Emmer had let the whole school pick their favorite poem, so when Roy Cox asked me about mine, I smiled and said, "Bo Peep." I'd asked to be called last on purpose, and when Miss Emmer allowed it because I'd never asked a favor before. Roy went close to last, making several mistakes on the eight-line poem. I got up to recite "The Cloud," by someone named Shelley. I didn't know what some of the words meant, but the ones, "Like a child from the womb, like a ghost from the tomb," sounded so beautiful I wanted to cry. The poem was eighty-four lines long, but I learned it in a week and made only two mistakes reciting it. I got an E, Roy got a D, for dumb, from his own mother.

"Who's smarter now?" I asked him when school was out.

"Squaw," he hissed back.

He came home from town one weekend in my eighth grade year and I saw him in the general store, where he asked if he could come to the house sometimes to study. His "You've always been so smart in school, Goldy Lark," made me feel even smarter just because he'd finally admitted it.

He cut across Nate Brice's pasture next day for his first lesson. We got along for about a minute before he forgot and called me "Squaw." I hit his shoulder with his history book and stomped out to the woodpile to split supper's kindling wood. He was fast behind me, grabbing my arms and pinning them to my back so's I couldn't slap him, and kissing me smack on my mouth. I forgot how much I hated him when he ran his tongue over my teeth.

After that, Roy Cox came over whenever he was home. He told me he loved me and asked if I'd wait to get married till he was through high school and had a teaching job himself. I whispered I would wait, I loved him that much, too. Each time we got together, it got the harder not to make love. But he wanted everything to be right on our wedding night. So's not to have to have a shotgun marriage, he showed me how to pleasure him with my hand. I let him do the same to me. The first time I become a woman that way, I shivered for hours afterwards, so happy for knowing something in this world could be that good. Roy said someone had once told him it was ten times better when done the right way in a bed.

Then Nate Brice left us and Freeman Cox, of all Pelper County men, started hiding his car in the roadside woods the times he visited Bree. I begged her to stop seeing Freeman because of me and Roy and got her promise his next visit would be the last. So it was Roy who caught his dad and my mom in bed together when he came earlier than usual that weekend. Thinking it was me, I guess, in the dark bedroom, he was at the bed before realizing his mistake. He was crying so hard when he ran from the house I didn't think he saw me at all, which was maybe the best thing for us both.

So our love ended without a word, and he left my life forever. I cried myself sick over him, and Bree cried with me. Knowing the relief would only stretch so far, I couldn't really blame Bree all the way, only for picking the wrong man again. It hurt to be hungry, nobody knew that better than me. It hurt twice that much to also be hungry in your heart.

# 9

A pale Milt Holt staggered up the path more than an hour before dinner, dragging behind him in the dust a bridle, which he dropped upon seeing me. I ran to meet him at the woodpile, my arms stretched wide. He caught me to his skinny chest and bent to give me a whiskered kiss. I led him inside for a dipper of water and a pill when he asked for one. He drank deep and settled on the room-dividing step, lowering his upper self into the front room. After several minutes he was breathing easier, his color was coming back.

"Better now?" I asked.

He shook his grayed head, patted my hand. "Get these weak trembles often lately, caused by my bad lungs. Worser one yesterday, why I sent Eb to fetch you. How you like that boy of mine?"

"More'n he likes me," I honestly said.

"Sometimes Eb don't like Eb," he said shakily.

The big cooner I'd seen last night leaped up through the front door and padded on giant paws to Milt's side, where she lay with her nose resting in his hair. He reached overhead to pull her floppy ears. The dog met that with a kiss to his cheek. She sniffed the air to pick up my smell, making no move to leave her master's side.

"Pretty old, ain't she?" I asked.

"Same's my mule, eleven. Old Mame, she's not too fair fixed for teeth, hard of hearing, too, but she's still spry enough to catch a rabbit off and on. Time was I'd take her out coon hunting, half the Ozarks tagging ahind to watch us tree one or two."

"Where'd you get her?"

"Urch Vestman. Funniest bet ever made in my life." He laughed loud at the memory. "Started up the hill one day, couple nanny goats tied to Old Jack's saddle. Opal was six or so then. Started bawling what would I bring her back, a baby sister? See, your aunt was in the family way then—she lost it later on—and Opal had heard us talking, I guess. Said yeah, just to shut her up. Get up to Vestman's store, here's all my neighbors gathered round swapping lies about their dogs and I didn't have one to fib about. Urch hands me a bottle. Couple swigs later here's me in front of the crowd, bragging about how fast my nannies can strip a buckbrush bush. Pointed to Old Mame and bet Urch, against his dog, my goats could strip a bush afore his hound can run a mile. Bet all the others, a dollar apiece on my goats. They took me up on it, to a man. Urch, he started the dog running, him riding Old Jack to time her."

I brought him another drink, to hear the story's end.

"Now, I was dying more with every second to have that dog. Was the booze doing it, nothing else. Knew danged well I'd get nagged all night long if I come in with Old Mame, even if there was a wad of money to go with her. Anyway, while Urch was mounting my mule, someone led my nannies to the nearest buckbrush. We all got so busy watching Old Jack run to outrun the cooner, clean forgot the goats. Time Urch got back, them damn nannies had clumb on top of Doc Helton's Model T, chawed off the roof, fell through it and eat up half the seat inside. We all thought it was a belly buster, save Doc."

"What happened?"

"Doc was cold sober, like usual. Had the bet money, to boot. Sees what my goats done, he just jams the money in his pocket, says, 'Thanky, Milt, aimed to get rid of that flivver last three year anyhow.' He wound up with a newer car. Urch Vestman, he took the goats. I got Old Mame."

"She the baby you brought home to Opal?" I guessed.

"Rode in and here she was. And you think I didn't catch it? Opal got over it in time. Ilish, she never did."

At his mention of Aunt Ilish, the dog sneaked out the front door backward, tail between her legs.

"I swear she heard you, Milt."

"She did," he said.

"Aunt Ilish much like her mom?" I asked, remembering Brother Dossie's Bible mention of Meadow Lark Lynch.

"Nobody's like Ilish," he said back.

I walked to the kitchen door and glanced at the mud hole, which was now drying somewhat in the hot sunshine. The sight of a pair of long pointed ears walking slow toward the house greeted me when I looked up. They sat atop the face of the homeliest mule I'd ever seen, or would see if I lived to be a thousand. The face was hooked onto a broad-shouldered reddish body that rippled in the sunlight with every step the grand animal took. Though I was no mule judge, this one, I knew without being told again, was what nobody on his right mind could call ordinary. Or even close to it. Old Jack was the grand-daddy of all mules, if really not the King of Missouri. His height alone, nearly a foot over the everyday mule, told me so.

He was built more on the order of a giant plow horse than a low-born mule. The closer he got, the clearer it was the only mule parts of him were face, ears and tail. His feet were horse feet, thick and muscled from fetlock to thigh. His rump was inches wider than Eb Holt's Delphie Doll's. The proud backbone was smooth rather than V-shaped like the roof of a house, as are all other mules. He'd gotten his deep reddish-brown color from Old Nance, his mother, who'd been Harley Farker's mare.

When he reached the mudhole and showed no sign of stopping, I stepped aside to let him enter if he liked. And that's exactly what he did, stopping low at the door. His footsteps were slow, careful, almost as if he knew I'd swept a while before. His shiny tail was almost sticking out the door when he reached his long face through to the front room to nuzzle Milt's forehead.

Milt raised upright to return the greeting with a kiss near the mule's watery, gnat-filled eyes. "Goldy Lark," he said, hugging the smooth back, "my baby boy, Old Jack."

"He's big's the train I come in on," I said.

"Nigh sixteen hand high, he is. Stouter'n all other mules the day of his birthing. Prettier, too. Folks in these parts all say me and Old Jack favor one another. Republican, like me. Only two of us hereabouts. Everybody in Missouri County, they know that." He winked at me. "Wouldn't let him vote for a president last year, though. Cussed law again it. Wouldn't let me neither. Can't read or write."

Old Jack kissed him again.

"Go rest up a spell while I warm your warter, boy, fetch you some corn nubbins."

Milt pushed him away easy. "Goldy Lark, she'll have your biscuits ready by time you get set."

The big mule backed out the kitchen door. A minute later, I heard him rolling himself on his bed mattress.

"How many mules you know of who'd come hot creek warter and not drink acause they know I'd sooner they drink up here?" Milt asked me with a smile.

"Man at the Rard depot yesterday said he's a prize mule," I said. "He forgot to tell me he's part person, too."

"Demycrats just tell the truth partways," he laughed.

"Who was that depot man, Milt? He knew Aunt Ilish."

"What man don't?" His eyes were sad when he answered.

"What become of Old Nance, Milt?" I asked, to change our talk.

He scratched his chin. "Funny you ask that, Goldy Lark. Since you did, no harm you knowing. Stray mare got to her down by

45

the creek when Old Jack was a baby, cornered her, pert near kicked her to mincemeat. She died just like my friend Harley Farker did. One of them things."

"I'm glad you liked each other so."

"I'd die for him any day of the week, Goldy Lark, and him for me, that's no lie. I sure wish he'd left kin for you to get to, since you ain't much welcome here."

"Yeah. So do I." I sat down beside him. "Milt, I was just wondering on Mom's last words right afore you come in. She said I should ask you to help me get even with old Villie Vestman for what he done to her. What asides naming her a mishling did he ever do to hurt her so?"

"She didn't tell me." He yawned. "Look, you hungry?"

I nodded.

He rose, reached for the drinking bucket and emptied it out the door, a good part of it landing in the mudhole. "Fetch my mule a few buckets of creek warter, I'll bring in eats from the barn. How's that?"

The first bucket I brought, Milt kept on the fire till it felt the right warmth to his fingers. Then he poured it through the kitchen window into the mule's tub. I watched as Old Jack drank deep, his giant sides swelling with each swallow. Most of the other three buckets I toted up he managed to drink. Just enough leaked from the tub to again fill the mudhole. The fifth bucket I brought for dinner for us humans.

While Milt went to the barn for Old Jack's corn nubbins, I started the first batch of sad bread. I hoped Aunt Ilish didn't expect me to make it rise, which couldn't happen when made with only flour and water. Salt would have helped the taste. But nothing on hand could have caused the bread to be anything but soggy lumps inside.

Milt returned with a handful of withered potatoes, which he called "sputaters," two relief grapefruits, and a brown poke of relief raisins marked "Not To Be Sold." I hurried to wash the potatoes in the creek, then slice and peel them all into a rusty iron skillet sizzling with relief lard I found in a syrup bucket.

Not saying much, Milt helped himself to the coffee, stoked the fire, wiped sweat, watched me make the second batch of bread.

The dog and the mule would get the first batch, us humans the second. While the first pan cooled, I started water gravy, or sop, in another rusty skillet, got the grapefruits skinned and the raisins boiling in a battered pot.

Old Mame, who was missing many teeth, managed to down her soggy biscuits whole. But they stuck in Old Jack's teeth, causing him a hard coughing fit. Milt's worried concern, till the mule was breathing right again, was so pitiful I wanted to cry.

I had the table set when I heard Delphie Doll's hooves on the rocks somewhere upcreek. A quick glance at the doorway showed the sun's shade centered even, so I hurried to get the grapefruits and raisins on the greasy plates.

Eb Holt made it picture plain nobody but him sat at the table. He ate with his eyes on his place, looking through the rest of us when he looked at us at all. Once, seeing he was nigh out of potatoes, I offered him the bowl. He made his jaws keep chewing on nothing till, my face burning, I put down the bowl. Then, he picked it up and helped himself.

Finished and ready to return to the cornfield, Eb came round the table where I was next to Milt. He slapped his father's back in play.

"Best damn eats I ever downed, Pop."

"Don't tell me, son." Milt hugged my shoulder. "You tell the one who done it."

Eb Holt crossed over to the window, where the mule's raised ears awaited a friendly word. He said, "How's come you never told me you could fry sputaters and fix sop and sad bread, Old Jack?" and went on his way, leaving my heart to flop in pieces on the floor.

# 10

I had done the dishes, took Milt a pill, and was wondering if he would talk of my parents a while, when he spoke from the front room floor. "Goldy Lark, you do me a favor?"

"I can try," I said, stepping up to where Old Mame snored at his side. "What you want, Milt?" I was surprised to see how sick he looked in his eyes, which were now glossy and fevered. I hadn't seen them that way before.

"If something gets in my mouth, I cough, puke up my grub. You take my hat yunder, fan off the flies while I sleep?"

I sat on the long hewn log that served as the front porch, behind Milt and his dog, listening to Old Jack snoring along with the others, my wooden arm shooing flies for what seemed like hours. When the shadows told me it was nigh four, both feet were asleep and my back about grown to the door frame.

As I started to stand, I stumbled against Milt's arm. He stopped snoring, propped himself up on one elbow and looked at me funny.

"Don't you ever be like Ilish, Goldy Lark. Don't you ever be," he begged.

"I aim for folks to look up to me," I said.

"I had that dream once." His thin shaky fingers touched his whiskered chin. "I was all set to take my wife Jane and Eb to Jeff City and fiddle on the radio station there. I'd saved enough money fiddling at square dances and being Old Jessie Red's deputy to do it, too. Then, Jane, she just set down in the rocker that day and died. Took all I'd earned to buy her a good coffin, bury her fine." Big tears was standing in his sick eyes. "After I married Ilish, my dream just died. I couldn't even hope then. Don't you ever let anybody stop you."

And he fell back, never having been full awake.

I went down for water when he woke, now feeling better, and I came on Eb Holt taking a wash near the bridge. He saw me just as I saw him, but didn't bother to turn. The late sunlight was directly on him, and I could see his whole lower body; my straddle started thumping again with that funny little ache I'd had last year for Roy Cox. Trying not to notice that he had a bone, I dipped in my bucket and turned my head to the house.

"Where's my aunt?" I asked, starting off the bridge.

"Gone to meet Opal when she gets off at four from Doc Helton's, to keep her from walking home by her little old sweet self," he growled. "Afraid I'll jump out ahind a tree and fugg Opal, reckon."

"Supper's on," I called over my shoulder.

I quickened my step when he didn't answer. At the rail fence, wondering if he was watching me, I turned halfway, only to stub my toe on a rock. I fell down in the path, water spilling on all sides.

Eb Holt was on the bridge, facing away, drying himself with his shirt on my second trip to the creek, humming a song. I was nigh back up the hill before it changed into words.

> I got a gal in Kansas City,
> She's got a gum boil on her titty.
> That don't bother me.

Supper was quieter than even dinner. Opal had seemed friendly when she came in ahead of my aunt, but when Aunt Ilish came in she settled, sullen, on the stick chair in the farthest corner. She didn't look up before Eb Holt and Milt were in from the hewn log. Through dinner she gave Eb Holt one eye. Save for that, the rest of us may not have been acquainted.

When Eb finished, he stood up and took out his cigarette makings. "See you at lasses time, Pop."

"Corn crop all laid by, son?"

Eb rolled his smoke and said, "Tolerable yield this year, with the drought and all."

"Thank Onion Creek and these poor old tired hands of mine for toting corn warter to the field all summer long," said Aunt Ilish.

"You need me afore, send word down, Pop." Eb hadn't noticed my aunt speaking. He scratched a match with his thumbnail, puffed on his cigarette, and blew the smoke in Opal's face.

"Dollar put back, son, to pay you with." Milt commenced to fumble in his shirt pocket while he spoke.

"Pop, I won't take no money from you."

"Know it's not much . . . " Milt stopped to cough, letting the wadded bill in his hand finish his words.

"I swear to mule turds, Pop, you beat all."

"Come on, boy," Milt said when he'd finished his cough. "Buy you something you want."

"Dollar wouldn't stretch near far enough to get what I hurt for." Eb winked at Opal, and I think I'd have pasted her one if she'd winked back.

49

"Well, it'll sure buy me a heap of chaws," Aunt Ilish said, grabbing the money from Milt's hand.

It went down her shirt front with her Harper's Homespun tobacco twist.

# 11

Opal told me while we done supper dishes my least worry here was want of soap. "Only known cake on the place Mom keeps hid for when she wants to smell prettier'n the rest of us. Oh, Burt, he'd let him have it, I guess, if he asked. Trouble there's he ain't had a wash since the day he got birthed, I know of, save for his wedding day."

I looked at my aunt safe out of hearing atop the woodpile, talking to Milt. "She sure likes herself and your brother Burt a lot."

" 'Buy me a heap of chaws'," Opal mocked. "Buy me some storebought silky bloomers, dammit! Turn over the dollar I earn a week to the old sow, never do get back a penny. Someday I'll show her, bet your ass on that. Dollar buy you a lot of silkies, too, Goldy Lark. Two, three, four pair."

"I always did want some silky bloomers," I said.

"While we're waiting, how's about a warsh in the creek?"

"I'm so dirty, Opal, a warsh without soap wouldn't help me much."

She laughed and held open her dress pocket. Inside was a partway used cake of soap that smelled like spring lilacs. "Burt's not the only thief in the Troat family."

"You find your mom's soap?"

"Me finding hers, that's about as apt as her finding a man who says no," she laughed.

"Where'd you get your soap, Opal?"

"Swiped it from Doc Helton's, where else?" She slung the dishtowel towards the cabinet, paying no mind when it landed instead on the floor. "Ready?"

I picked up the dishtowel when it was clear and she didn't aim to and went into the front room to take my other dress and dirty bloomers from my floursack.

"Bring your dirties," Opal said, going into the back room. "Better to do 'em now than Saturday, when we won't have any soap. If Mom won't bring hers out, I sure's hell won't show her mine."

"All the dirties I own, I got on," I said.

She clapped her hands in mock fun. "Well, fish farts! Finally I found somebody in this old world poorer'n me."

Opal kept up such a constant run of talk while we washed ourselves and our clothes that it was a job just to hear all she said.

"And the cracks in the back room door, they're big enough to pitch any mule asides Old Jack through. That's where me and Eb and Burt would watch Mom and Milt's daytime fugging when we was younger. Stand there and whisper and fight over who'd get the biggest crack. Pull hair, shove, spit, bite. One time, Eb, just to be ornery, wouldn't let Burt see boo. Made him stand ahind him. Burt, he got so carried away, always, he'd bite his fingers raw when the folks started to come. This time, though, he just took out his pecker and pissed all over Eb's foot. Eb give him his own crack from then on."

"Didn't your folks ever catch you?" I asked.

"Now how could they see us with their eyes shut, Goldy Lark?" she asked back.

Laughing so hard it hurt, which wasn't like me at all, I raced her to the creek, shedding our clothes as we flew. I beat her to the bridge and was in the water before she caught up, so busy was she trying to shed her bloomers while running fast. She stood on the bank a minute to let me eye her big titties before wading in, carrying her pink soap in her hand.

"You ever let a boy feel you?" she asked, gawking at my body.

"No," I lied.

She flipped water in my face. "That's why you ain't got titties my size," she said, laughing.

I took her pretty soap and washed myself everywhere but the bottoms of my feet, not looking apurpose at her better body. I rubbed my dress between my knuckles to get it clean, then did the same with my bloomers. After rinsing, or "wrenching," as we called it, I laid them on the bridge boards and jumped up to dry myself with a big piece of old long johns Opal had said we could share. She followed me out, for once saying nothing. I walked behind her up to the yard, where I slung my clothes over the rail fence to dry overnight after she put hers there. Then I followed her into the kitchen, where Milt sat at the table alone.

I put my arm round his shaking shoulders and hugged him tight.

Old Jack gave a sudden snort, and I was nigh scared out of my skin by the sound of a hundred bells clanging against one another in the still evening air. The dishes in the pink cabinet rattled and danced, it was that loud. Opal, hands over her ears, smiled at two more louder clangs. Her mouth worked to say something the ringing in my ears wouldn't right away let me hear.

"Mom's telephoney," I finally understood.

"Her telephoney?"

"Brother Dossie and her rigged up a line of tin cans strung on bob wire back afore Burt was born so's they could call each other quick. The way they ring means something special. One ring means we're fine, how's about you? Two says we want company or we got eats left over for him and Aunt Cloma. A lot of quick rings means big trouble. What Mom give now's the company ring. He'll be along to meet you, right off. Listen."

I listened and, sure enough, from somewhere up Onion Creek a man's voice was giving out a song.

Opal, stepping up to the front room, gouged my ribs hard. "Lucky you, to get to see Brother Dossie Lynch. I have to go to bed; I been bad."

# 12

At first he was just a deep voice floating slow up the path, singing, "When the roll is called up yunder, I'll be there." Then he was a dark shape the size of a picture book bear, walking very slow, singing low. In the little daylight left, I could see he was clothed only in overalls. Fat and hairy arms were folded across his Santy Claus stomach. His giant feet were shoeless. His face was nothing but a blackened shadow, and it took a minute to realize he wore a beard that grew from his sideburns an inch or so past his chin.

Almost to the mudhole, he suddenly knelt in the dirt and raised his bare heavy arms skyward.

"Repent, Sister Ilish," he thundered in a voice that almost shook the house, "I say to you, repent of your sins and be cleansed whiter than snow by the Blood of the Lamb. Throw out your sinful thoughts, filthy chews. Give to the Lord what you wallow in your dirty mouth. Then, watch. Watch my great church on its foundation of solid rock rise past yunder tree tops till the spires stretch within sight of the Pearly Gate. Amen."

"Amen, Brother Dossie," Aunt Ilish called, coming in ahead of him to light the lamp.

Milt, on my stick chair, motioned me to his chair, the one nearest the kitchen door. "Howdy, Brother Dossie. Come on in."

"Evening, Brother Milt. Reckon I'll do just that."

He stepped sideways into the kitchen, as I was sure Sheriff McKay would have to do. They were nearly the same size, but any other likeness ended there.

"Something the cat dragged home and the kittens couldn't eat," a saying of Bree's, was my first thought at seeing him in the light. Ugly may not have been the right word for him, but because I didn't know a better one, it fitted fine. He was so hairy and had such heavy eyebrows it was hard to figure anything on his face save his nose. It was freckled in the Cherokee-Irish way, but much longer and broader than Aunt Ilish's or Bree's. His sharp, deep-sunken eyes were two black marbles, with just enough water in back to slide from side to side. If he had ears, his long greasy hair hid them.

Seated next to Aunt Ilish, he stared at me. I was wondering if he would ever ask me the first question all preachers ask when he smacked his fat hands together and boomed, "You sure ain't been saved, Goldy Lark Farker, I can see bad, bad sin in your evil eyes."

Half afraid to speak, I nodded.

"Neither was poor dead Bree, may The Almighty have pity on her soul."

"Brother Dossie, there's coffee," my aunt hurried to say.

"Nobody knows how bad I could use it, Sister. I've been kneeling out under my sycamore the whole day long, praying Goldy Lark here might already haves seen the Light." He turned

back to me. "Well, you look like I thought you would. Gentle
Meadow Lark's kin, no doubt about it. I look to you like you'd
always thought I would?"

I nodded yes, I don't know why. Maybe I thought that would
be kinder than saying that till yesterday I didn't know he was even
alive.

"You scared of me, girl, or don't you have a tongue?"

"I believe in God and Jesus. I just never got to church much."

"You live that far away from The Almighty's House?"

I looked from him to Aunt Ilish and decided I may as well tell
the truth today as tomorrow. "Nate Brice wouldn't always let me
go. He said Heaven was just a place some preacher man dreamed
up."

"Didn't Bree ever make you go, to save your soul?"

I nodded no.

"You want to go up there and see for yourself who's right, me
or Nate Brice?" he snorted. "You want to see Harley Farker to
know him, don't you, girl?"

"I guess so."

"Well, you sure better start to pray the Spirit touched you afore
it's too late." He reached inside his back pocket and took out a
letter. "This come for me Monday from Pelper County. Here take
it. Read. You can read, can't you?"

I was gawking open-mouthed at the letter written in Bree's
hand, addressed to Rev. D. Lynch. It was news to me. I'd only
known of the one sent to Milt Holt, the reply being a long time,
with twenty dollars for a train ticket to Rard. Mom must have
been afraid she'd never get an answer from Milt and wrote the
second one to beg that Uncle Dossie take me in. Either the doctor
or Miss Elmer Cox, who both visited her every day, must have put
it in the mail.

"Sister Ilish, all day long yesterday, I could feel it, the power of
the Man Above." Watching me take out the letter, he licked his
lips. "It was working inside me, tormenting me so bad I could
varely stand the burden. Sister, I just now understand what's been
tearing at me so."

"What, Brother Dossie?"

His eyes were shiny wet when they met mine. "There's good

fortune finally coming my way. I can feel it tearing, twisting at my poor old tired heart."

"What's the letter say?" Milt asked me.

"Dear Brother Dossie, I won't live long," I read aloud, a lump rising in my throat. "I never hated you. See to it Goldy Lark gets my share of Lynch land so I can rest easy in my grave. Help her get all the promised money I earned there that's due. She don't know of it yet, but you can guess what I talk of. Your sick niece, who will be in her grave when you read this."

"See? What did I tell you?" asked my uncle.

"Well, if that means her two-bits a week wages from Doc Helton the year or so she was up there's supposed to be paid back to you, Goldy Lark," snapped Aunt Ilish, "you got a long hurty time ahead. Most of what she made went to fill her own gut."

"Don't worry none," I said. "She was out of her head a lot."

"Bree have any money put back you know of?" Milt asked me.

"She had to borry from you to get me here," I reminded. "And Pelper County buried her in Potter's Field free."

My aunt and uncle traded quick glances. He reached over to touch her hand before they trained their sharp eyes on me.

I gawked back. I had nothing to hide. Mom had been out of her head to write about all that money just waiting there for me to collect. That was all there was to it.

When Aunt Ilish, wallowing a brand new chew, got up to pour coffee, Brother Dossie, turning to Milt with a question on the corn, also lost interest in me.

During Brother Dossie's visit, Old Jack had been asleep in his room, his heavy snores drowned out only when Brother Dossie spoke. Suddenly he snorted, his hooves hitting the wall hard. Old Mame, at Milt's feet, give a friendly bark, her tail thumping the floor.

"Sister Cloma's coming. Clean forgot she was along, Lord, forgive me."

A thin dark Indian woman entered the room. She wore a gray bonnet and a faded brown dress that almost dragged the floor. She wore no shoes, and the slime of the mudhole squished between her toes. In her arms was what I thought to be a floursack-wrapped baby. She noticed the others one by one, her eyes at last coming to rest on me. Tears then spilled down her wrinkled cheeks.

Brother Dossie took the bundle, which I could see was a stick of wood when the cover fell away, and laid it on the table. "No call to cry, Sister Cloma. Your little baby's right here."

The woman sat beside him, still gawking at me. "Poor, poor little Nonny," she said.

"Dossie's wife Cloma," Milt told me. "Went all the way out of her mind when their baby girl died."

This was the woman I'd read of in the Lynch family Bible.

Aunt Cloma stopped crying to reach across the table, touch my hands with hands every bit as dead as her wood baby. "Poor little Nonny." She picked up her Nonny and soon seemed to forget us all.

"Well." Milt stood up, stretched. "Reckon you aim to pray over Goldy Lark's money she says ain't there, for a spell. So I'll roll in. Don't need Goldy Lark, do you Ilish? She looks powerful beat to me."

"You sleep on the devonette," Aunt Ilish told me.

"What's wrong she sleeps with Opal?"

"Nothing, Milt, save it's a little cooler in the front room and lesser bedbugs. On top of that, I want her close to me, so she'll be safe from Opal's sinful talk. That too much to ask?"

"Ain't, if she gets that money Bree spoke of, along with her fair share of Lynch land," Milt said. He pointed to the dresser. "You fetch me a pill, Goldy Lark? No, now, make it two. One don't work enough when my heart's troubled so."

He wasn't the only one with a worried mind.

# 13

My aunt cooked relief oatmeal for Thursday breakfast, and we ate it with sugared water on top. Milt stayed at the table for three extra cups of coffee, explaining that with the corn cut, he hadn't much to do the rest of the year. "Goldy Lark, day or so I'll help you carry the corn ears to the barn. We can bring in the fodder just afore the first frost."

The telephoney caused us all to jump. Aunt Ilish, starting to unplait her waist-length hair, hurried around Old Jack's barn to return the one ring.

"Brother Dossie give me a nickel last night for a poke of salt to share, case you ride the mule up to the store, Milt," she said when back. "He called me now to remind me. We both been out afore the new moon." No answer from Milt.

"Coal oil's gone, Milt, and I'm pert near out of chaws."

Milt's reply was to fan his face with his hat.

"And you ought to fix it with Urch to get his wagon and team for the relief next Thursday. And Goldy Lark, she's got to be signed on, recollect?"

"Cooler. Guess it wouldn't hurt Old Jack to go this early," Milt finally decided. He looked at me. "Ever ride a mule?"

"Nate Brice's old girl jenny mule," I said.

"A girl mule's no harder to ride'n a boy," said Aunt Ilish.

"Take Opal up to Doc Helton's on your way," Milt told me. "On Old Jack, you'll be safe's here with me."

"Not if some glassy-eyed man grabs the reins and starts to unbutton his overalls fly, she won't," butted in Aunt Ilish.

"Oh, I'll beat her to him, no worry there," Opal said.

Aunt Ilish slapped her hard. "I mean on the way back home, Opal."

"That happens, Goldy Lark, I hope he ain't so ugly's Brother Dossie." Opal ducked as she spoke.

"It's only the sinners who see ugly in Brother Dossie's looks, Opal. Like you and Eb Holt. The believers think he looks holy, maybe even something like Jesus."

Opal gave such a snort that Old Jack snorted, too, causing even Milt to smile behind Aunt Ilish's back. I thought my belly would pop, I wanted to laugh so much.

I rode behind Opal on my bed quilt, my arm tight around her. For Old Jack didn't walk, he trotted fast and his being so high gave me an awful feeling I'd fall. The gallon coal oil can marked "M. Holt" clanked against the saddle, and my legs went *whush, whush* as they rubbed the mule's middle. Above me up the creek I could hear Brother Dossie singing. He was too far away for me to catch the words.

"Asides wanting your money," Opal suddenly laughed, "Mom's really got a good side. She truly is worried you'll get laid."

"She sure sounded so," I said.

"Just afraid there'll be a little fugging she's not in on, that's all. That's why she meets me'n I get done at Doc's. We ever run across a glassy-eyed man undoing his pants, why, I'd have to fight her to get him first."

"Opal, I swear you're the funniest person I ever seen."

"Being funny runs in this family," she cackled. "Funnier and uglier'n anyone ought to be. Leastways, with Brother Dossie claiming us as kin, we won't never want to fugg him. I ever had to, I'd put a poke on his head. I don't know what you'd do."

It was anything but easy to hang on for the uphill ride, what with laughing so hard and the quilt's slipping sometimes nearly to the mule's tail. Many times Opal's warning to duck a low limb from a post oak tree sounded too late. I got smacked so hard in the face I nearly fell to the ground. At one time, Opal scratched a bedbug bite on her arm as I lifted my bloomers to scratch a red bedbug welt at the elastic casing above my right knee. Both of us seeing at the same second what we were doing, we had to laugh until the tears came.

"I didn't see your mom scratch at breakfast," I said. "The bedbugs afraid they'll die if they bite her?"

"She's got goose grease to use," Opal screeched.

"Where's that come from?"

"Same place's the canned peaches. Bode Jenkin's farm down-creek a ways. Bode's a gooser. He raises geese, that means. Mom's white lover."

It wasn't funny anymore. "Milt know?"

"Like he knows his own name." She didn't laugh either. "Look, cousin, I tell you something you don't know, it makes no difference if you believe me or not. You forget it was me told you?"

I leaned around for her to see me cross my heart.

"That letter Brother Dossie let you read last night, it didn't come Monday, no such thing. It come nigh a week after Milt got his from Aunt Bree. I forgot to look in the mail one day after work and the next day on my way to Doc's, I saw the letter to Brother Dossie. It was gone on my way back home that night."

"I don't know why he would lie," I said.

"He don't want you to know he had pert near the time Milt did to get you here, along with the money, without having to borrow money for your ticket, like Milt had to, and he didn't. He don't want you here, and neither does Mom."

"Did Milt truly want me, Opal?"

"Me and him was the only ones. Poor cuss, he had to beg her a week, about, to let you come back. Had to go on his knees to get you train fare from Eb. Brother Dossie could've made it so easy for Milt, and he didn't lift a fat finger to do it."

"Then him and my aunt decided I might have money," I said.

"They'll use ways you ain't heard of to get you to tell where it's at."

"They got a long wait, Opal. Little dab we got from Mom sewing sheepskin coats for the relief office, we eat up."

"Write it in blood, they still wouldn't believe you." She scratched another bedbug bite. "All I ask's you don't tell on me. And watch Mom. She's bound to treat you better, acause she figures you're telling a lie to get yourself caught in."

When Opal was happy, she was all ways so, even talking, and that also worked the other way. Except to tell me at New Hill about Joshua Lynch first teaching there, she did nothing else but point to four leaning mail boxes across the dirt road, saying, "Eb Holt's, Nate Brice's, Bode Jenkins, Milt Holt's, used to be Henry Troat's. Piss on the whole shooting match!"

Probably halfway up through the dark woods toward Doc Helton's, she closed her mouth for the first time since leaving New Hill.

She alighted at Doc Helton's and, wordless, handed me the reins. She seemed like a girl I almost didn't know. She slapped Old Jack's flank when I was halfway in the saddle, keeping me so busy climbing over I couldn't look back.

I was glad it was Urch Vestman and not his mean old father tending the store. He hugged my shoulder, put two twists of Harper's Homespun into a dress pocket without my asking, then filled the coal oil can from a keg in the back of the store. A green gumdrop was used to plug up the can's spout so's the fuel couldn't drip down the mule's side and cause very bad burns. The nickel poke of salt Brother Dossie wanted was so heavy Urch had to use both hands to pick it up.

I held out Aunt Ilish's dollar.

"That all for you?" Urch's eyes was the same pretty blue as Eb Holt's, but he'd learned how to smile with his.

"Milt needs your wagon and team, week from today, to go get the relief in Rard," I said.

"Burt Troat'll be out of jail by then; it's his turn for the relief. Eb took Old Jack and Delphie Doll last week when he picked it up. Guess Milt's got to go along this time to get you on the government rolls, him being head of the house. Powerful long way for a man in Milt's shape. You'd think they'd mail out the papers for him to X."

"Urch." My throat had just gone dry at the sudden thoughts of the question I had to ask. "Can I ask you about Mom, you and Mom?"

"Guess you want to know was we in love."

"I already figured that out partway. Three white men proposed, she told me. She married two, my father and Nate Brice. What I want to know most, what happened atween you and her?"

His eyes teared. "There was a fight, that's all."

I didn't say anything, for fear he'd cut loose and cry.

He wiped his eyes on his sleeve. "Goldy Lark, I'll dang nigh bet my life Ilish won't let you talk of little Bree down home, will she?"

I shook my head no.

"Well, any time you want to think about her out loud, I'm up here." He went to the counter and bent down. "You're fifteen and pretty, and pretty girls always like good little things, don't they. Shut your eyes. There."

Whatever he pushed into my empty dress pocket was soft. "Ain't for nobody but us to know, now," he whispered.

"Thanky. Nobody won't," I said, wishing it had been a Baby Ruth candy bar. I hadn't had one yet this year.

"Come on," he said. "I'll put you up on the mule."

As I mounted Old Jack at the water trough, a big truck loaded with C.C.C. boys pulled to a stop at the gas pump. About ten had alighted before I could start the mule, all acting like they'd never seen a girl. Most were pointing to my bloomers that reached down to my knees. I tried to cover myself with my dress, which couldn't happen with me holding the weighty sack of salt in one hand, the bridle reins in my other.

"Sure tell they ain't been raised right," I told Urch, who was fastening the coal oil can over the saddle horn.

"They's good boys," he said, not knowing what had happened to Mom. "Some come to church at New Hill. Friendly, likely homesick. Always speak when I meet one. Remember not so long ago Eb Holt wore clothes like that in a far-off town of Oregon. He told me how much lesser he missed home if somebody took the time to say howdy."

I flanked Old Jack and stuck out my tongue at the howling boys in green as he trotted away.

At Helton's, seeing Opal at the clothesline, I stopped, meaning to show her Urch's present, and slid from the mule. What I pulled from my pocket, too late to hide since she'd seen it, was a pretty pair of pink silkies.

Mule sense told me I couldn't take a present like this down home.

"Opal." I held out the silkies. "A pretty for you."

Her black eyes flashed in happy surprise. "You swiped these from Urch to give me?"

My nodding head lied for my tongue.

"Mom, she'll skin me, sure's little green apples."

"You're smarter'n me. Hide 'em like you and her hide your pretty soap."

I left her holding the soft, soft silkies against her teary cheek. For her sake, I truly hoped my aunt would never know they were on the place, and I knew Urch would never tell the truth if it caused me trouble, either. All I'd done was give her a pair of silkies that was from a man, which meant I couldn't keep them. Since Opal really thought I'd swiped them, she couldn't be to blame.

I started to believe her at the bridge, where Aunt Ilish, fish line in the water, awaited me.

"Reckon you can have a egg some mornings, Goldy Lark, you won't blab it to nobody else," she greeted.

Thinking fast, I told her, "I can't eat eggs."

"What you mean, you can't eat eggs? What kind of crazy talk's that?"

"I just can't choke 'em down, knowing they come from a hen's butt. I puke."

"Can't eat soakey, can't eat eggs. Real puny in the gut, ain't you?"

But my head's on straight, I thought. Catch me letting you think you'll get any of my money, if by any chance in a million there is some, for a few sickening eggs.

"Here." She handed me her line. "Give me my Harper's Homespun. I'll take the mule up to Milt, and the salt to Brother Dossie. Stay here till you get us a fish for dinner." She turned away, only to turn back fast. "Though, guess you'll be apt's not to puke it up, too."

Still smiling because I'd outsmarted her in two ways, nigh fifteen minutes later, I landed a hefty cat.

# 14

I rubbed coal oil over me before going to bed nights, but the bedbugs seemed not to notice. Friday night, after I'd caught a dozen tasting me, I gave up and took my quilt outside. I threw it under one of the cedar trees, and lay thinking of Eb Holt and how good it would feel kissing him, until I finally slept.

Saturday, wash day, me and Opal got up before daylight. With four big flat rocks behind the house, she built a square under the shadiest cedar tree. I laid a fire in the rock square, over which we put a heavy screen Opal got from the barn. In a leaky wash tub—one usually kept on the hewn log, Opal told me—we let the wash water heat while we ate. I then brought up Old Jack's drinking water to heat, as Milt was still abed. My aunt was quieter than usual, I noticed, and Opal hadn't said "Fish farts!" all that morning.

Milt, too, seemed to be deep in thought when he finally made it to the table. His animals fed and the mules watered, he took the rifle from the front room wall and stumbled down the path.

"Aims to do away with his critters, then put a bullet in his own head to keep from dying like a man," Aunt Ilish said, watching Milt from the yard.

"Oh, hope, you bitch," Opal said. "He's going to Eb's."

My aunt kicked at her rear, but missed. "Why God let you grow up'n He must've knowed the day'd come you say such sinful words to the one who suffered to give you life—well, that's way past me."

"Ask Brother Dossie why. He knows it all."

"And you, Goldy Lark," I was told, "next time you decide to sleep outside, you'd better ask me first."

"The bedbugs—" I started to say.

"Puny gut, puny hide, too puny bad," she snapped, spitting in the mudhole, and went inside.

I carried out the drinking bucket table we'd use for a tub stand when Opal bade, and placed it under the cedar tree. After I got the outside fire going, we placed the washtub on the screen. Opal swept a pile of dirty clothes from under hers and Aunt Ilish's beds, holding her nose and gagging at my aunt's wash. I took my dirty relief dress and bloomers from their hiding place between the devonette and the front room wall, then followed Opal into the yard.

Helping sort out the floursack bedsheets, our underwear, and Milt's B.V.D.s, I noticed only Opal and me had any bloomers in the wash. "You forgot to get Aunt Ilish's bloomers?" I asked Opal.

"Mom forgets to wear 'em, apurpose. Catch some glassy-eyed man undoing his overalls and her not ready all the way," she snorted.

We had to quit laughing when we looked up and saw my aunt, hands on her hips and the usual look on her face, watching us.

Opal commenced by scrubbing the dirty floursack bedsheets— three all told, now that Burt was due home soon. Her thin back hunched over the tub of soapless water, she scrubbed so hard sweat poured down her body in a steady stream. When I offered to spell her, she said, forget it, the stinking rotten wash was nigh done anyway.

"Pert near done?" The piles on the ground were waist high.

"Wait and see," she said.

I said no more and laid down in the grass to wait my turn at the tub.

Soon Aunt Ilish, her hair fresh-combed and plaited, garbed in a storebought dress and white high heels, pranced outside. "Going to look for mail," she called at the path. "See you two have eats ready when the sun's due south. Make sure that warsh gets spanking clean."

"Go nail your tit to a tree," Opal said.

"Why's everybody so het up?" I asked when Aunt Ilish was out of sight.

Opal dropped down beside me. "Mean you didn't hear the fight last night?"

"Not from out here. Guess I slept sound."

"Started when Mom wanted her lay from Milt and he ached so bad he begged her to wait till morning. She commenced saying he ought to die, damn him, he wasn't any good to her nowadays in any way. Milt, he starts bawling like a little boy lost in the woods. More of it he done, the more she went on. I stood at the door listening, trying to get nerve to reach ahind the dresser for Milt's rifle, shove it up her crack. Damn if I won't next time, the fugging old sum bitch."

"Where's she going now?"

"The Jenkins place to line her up some for tomorrow, that's where. Bode, he don't allow none of his kids or his wife, Virgie, to go for drinking warter acause Mom leaves him a sign there when she wants to fugg, in a big gooseberry bush on the creek banks there. You ask me what sign it is, I'd guess she leaves some pee on a rag. Bode sniffs it and it's oh, I'm going to have to holler, I'm going to come."

She grinned, and for a minute I almost tried to like her. "Hope she left something in the house I want you to see. Beat you to it!"

From inside a dresser drawer she pulled out a narrow box, longer than my hand. She opened the lid to show me a round brown rubber thing with a black rim. I thought she'd choke to death when I asked her what it was for.

"Goldy Lark, ain't you never heard tell of a tap?" she asked when she'd finished sputtering.  .

I hadn't.

"It keeps you from having babies if you shove it up in you afore you fugg. Works for Mom. Catch her with a snot-nose kid."

"What's that other thing for?"

Opal gave a loud giggle. "That's her glue gun. The glue she puts on the tap to hold it in tight, else she'd cough it up through her teeth, the way Bode goes at her," she snorted.

"I didn't know there was such a thing in the world," I said truthfully.

"There's something else you ain't seen, in the barn," she promised. "Race you!"

The barn was unfinished save for one stall and a high manger stretching the length of the room. In the manger's center, our government food was separated from the mule's corn nubbins by a two-by-four. A homemade bed with filthy quilts on it stood in a corner of the finished stall, which was on the side nearest the creek.

"Burt sleeps out here sometimes in the summer with his wife. Providing he's not in jail and her dad lets her live with him, I mean. That way, he can guard the relief eats from the rest of us," Opal explained.

"Who's his wife?" I asked.

"Bode and Virgie Jenkins' girl, their oldest kid. Burt, he got her knocked up when he was sixteen and her twenty, four year back. They was married at New Hill her second term, when Burt was in seventh grade. Look, Goldy Lark, you like butter?"

I licked my lips in answer and she jumped into the manger, where she dropped from my sight a few seconds. When she called, I reached to take a syrup pail, its lid closed tight. It held melted butter, none that we'd ever put on the table, so I asked, "This Burt's, too, like the eggs?"

"Ain't now," she laughed, pointing to the bed.

We spent a long time on the dirty bed, licking the delicious butter from our fingers and talking.

"Why does Burt and Miss Maudie sleep out here in hot weather? So's he can mistreat her, I think, and not have Bode or Milt threaten to call the law. Even Mom couldn't like what he does to her. You know by that it's pretty damn bad."

"What's he do, Opal?"

"Nothing, to hear him tell the law. But if you'd been married four year and been knocked up a dozen times and didn't have kids yet, you know what I'd think?"

"What?" I asked.

"He gets rid of babies that way afore they're born," she whispered.

I didn't know whether to believe her or not; I'd never heard there was a way like that to get rid of babies you didn't want. "What makes Miss Maudie stay with him, then?" I asked, hoping she'd laugh and say she was funning me.

"She don't believe in devorce," Opal said.

Later that night, I lay awake smiling to myself about Burt's butter we'd swiped and Aunt Ilish's tap she didn't know we knew about and the dirty clothes Opal had said not to wash. She'd overturned both tubs in the dirt, filled them with the clothes and sheets, motioning me to help carry them down to the creek. Weighted with heavy rocks, the water moving past on all sides, we left the clothes to wash themselves while we dangled our toes over the side of the bridge.

"Why sweat over the bastards at all, without soap?" Opal asked after we'd wrung the wash partly dry and slung it over the rail fence to let the sun finish the job. "Nobody'll never know the fugging difference."

Nobody ever did.

# 15

Church time Sundays we were the second comers to New Hill, Brother Dossie Lynch being first. He'd opened the windows, placed a bouquet of wildflowers in a fruit jar on the teacher's desk, which would serve today as a pulpit. His white shirt was topped off with a brown necktie stuffed into his overalls bib. I'd seen another tie like it at Vestman's store the day I'd come in with Eb Holt. He smelled of goose grease, and I knew if it wasn't in his blue-black hair, it was on his shiny brown shoes. Though he did look better this time, nothing could have helped his homeliness.

"Welcome, Sister Ilish, Brother Milt." He bowed low. "Welcome to the House of the Lord." Opal and we weren't entitled to so much as a nod, till he remembered my imagined money, anyway. "Any new word, Sister, from Pelper County?"

"Soon, Brother. I can feel it right here." Aunt Ilish was pointing to her heart just as though she had one.

"Amen," said my uncle and led us inside.

"Ugly old fart," Opal hissed.

Milt and my aunt sat on the black (boys) recital bench on the right. For the time being, my cousin and me shared a red (girls) bench in the very last left side row, near the stove. She'd told me beforehand we should keep toward the back of the school. When the room was overflowing, the young people had to stand. It was smarter to always settle in some open window. Once the preaching commenced, the boys from the C.C.C. camp by Rard, who seldom came in, would pinch your bottom. Turn around, they'd slip you a stick of chewing gum and ask to see you later. Knowing Aunt Ilish, Opal had never asked if she could go any place with them. The closest she'd come to wrongdoing with the camp boys had been to let them think her first name was Lark. She never planned, she'd told me, to go beyond seeing them at church.

Aunt Cloma, in a newer dress than the one she's worn when I first met her, came in next, carrying her bundle. Instead of me, the flowers caught her eye this time, and she slipped up to the rostrum to smell them and cried a little. She then sat down almost directly under the pulpit. Patting one shiny shod foot, she commenced singing baby Nonny to sleep.

I caught the creaking of wagons and buggies along the road. The first, a wagon loaded with people of all sizes, drove past the window. An older man close to Milt's age stopped the team of horses, jumped from the wagon seat, and tethered the horses next to the post oak tree where Old Jack and the buggy were tied.

Opal pushed me over to the window. "Gooser Bode Jenkins and half of Missouri County, all of 'em his," she whispered.

My aunt's butter-bean-bald lover, whom I'd seen at the store last Tuesday, was at the head of his family, plainly proud of his big brood. His sad-eyed wife, Virgie, in a relief dress like mine and Opal's, her hair hardly combed, walked close behind. Virgie was taller and heavier than the usual woman. So was Miss Maudie,

Burt Troat's wife, who was next in line, dressed in pink and holding a fat, black-eyed baby, her brother. She spoke kindly to Opal, then thumped the ear of the taller boy behind, who looked about seventeen. His sin had been to wink at me, find my belly button with his finger and go "cuck" with his tongue. He was named Green for Virgie's home county, Greene, I later learned. Seven more children moved up the line after him. Most were girls, all wearing relief clothes. Counting Miss Maudie and the baby, they totaled ten. "One's not here," Opal said in a loud whisper I pretended not to hear.

When their parents went to join Milt and my aunt, the Jenkins kids scattered by threes to the windows across from us to stand looking bashfully at their bare feet. Green Jenkins put one long leg out the back window, showing he might not stay very long inside.

The bench group was peculiar. Milt sat on the far end, Bode next to him, my aunt next to Bode, Bode's wife by Aunt Ilish, my uncle by Virgie Jenkins. They all talked across each other's heads in such a friendly way strangers might have mistook them for the best of friends. Odder yet was when Miss Maudie held out the baby to her mother, Aunt Ilish reached first, smiling. She held him closer than Aunt Cloma did Nonny. I could no more picture Aunt Ilish really liking a helpless, useless baby than I could see Old Jack doing without his breakfast biscuits.

Miss Maudie, Opal said, was church solo singer. She picked up a stack of hymn books from the top shelf of what we called "the liberry," began passing them out at the door and benches. My cousin introduced me when we were handed a book to share.

"I hoped you'd be able to come to New Hill this year, when I got word Milt was taking you in," Miss Maudie smiled. Her face held nearly the same quiet sadness as her mother's.

"I got out of school last March," I told her. "The week I turned fifteen."

"You come visit New Hill anyhow, Goldy Lark. Term starts tomorrow." She crossed the room to offer Green Jenkins a songbook, only to have it slapped to the floor, with a wink at me.

If Green Jenkins had been at the store with Bode Jenkins last Tuesday, I hadn't noticed him. It wasn't possible I had forgotten him, not with him now taking notice of me the way I hoped Eb Holt would.

Other people had been coming in meanwhile, scattering to both sides. Opal told me some of their names, which for me held little interest without their history. A family with three children, all redhaired, redheaded, and freckled, I marked in my mind as the Theron Copeland's. "Live smack across Onion Creek from Bode and his bunch. Theron and Bode's been into it for a hundred year over some gooseberry bushes they both claim—one of 'em's where Mom always leaves her love sign for Bode. Ain't spoke since Columbus discovered Arkansaw. Good feud's always a belly buster in these parts. Better yet, Green Jenkins and Theron's oldest girl there, Lucy Lee. Bet you my silkies they play house for the fiftieth time on the way home from school tomorrow."

"Opal, I swear."

"You can't cuss in church. Brother Dossie don't allow it." She nudged me hard. "Watch this."

I looked up to see a very pretty dark haired girl near my size and age, not much taller, enter. Garbed in relief gear and barefoot, she had a wild daisy pinned to each plait. She went directly to the occupied right recital bench, bent to kiss the Jenkins baby, then went on to the pulpit to sniff the altar flowers. I noticed that Brother Dossie, talking to Mrs. Copeland with his back to us, had also marked her entrance. Turning, the words: "Afore the sun has set in yonder west, be saved!" thundered throughout the room.

The girl knelt beside Aunt Cloma, taking extra care to tuck her dresstail under her feet. Brother Dossie laid his hand on her head in silent prayer. One of his long fingers was reaching down to touch a flower.

"Another Jenkins," Opal whispered. "Hollyhock. Likely stopped to pick her flowers, got out of the mile-long line."

"That really her name?"

"Suits her, too. Cries when she sees a flower in a picture book. She's the one Brother Dossie always begs to be saved. Watch how they shine to each other. She must think he's flowerdy, and I'd hate to say here what he thinks she is."

The girl's prayer ended, and she arose and came back to join us.

"I'm trying to get myself in the notion of bringing salvation to my soul, Opal."

"Meet my cousin, Goldy Lark," Opal said.

"You been saved?" Hollyhock asked me.

"No," I said.

"Brother Dossie's still looking at you." Opal's whisper was almost a laugh. "Praying for you with his eyes wide open, you think?"

"Just trying to drive out my sin," Hollyhock said.

Almost every seat save the left recital bench was filled by now. People were fanning themselves, babies were fussing, and little children were squirming. Then Urch Vestman entered. Dressed in a white shirt and black pants belted at the waist, he nodded to everyone and headed for the right recital bench to ease in between Milt and Bode Jenkins.

"Where's old Villie?" I asked Opal.

"He don't come."

"Where's Eb Holt?"

"Someplace cussing out us mishlings, same's old Villie. Quit thinking of pretty Eb Holt and use your finger to scratch that itch atween your two big toes."

More people entered. Most of them stood, yet the left recital bench stayed empty. And then, above the noise, I heard a car chugging down the road.

"Doc and Evelyn Helton. He pays the church to hold their bench," Opal said. "Get a gander at her."

Skinny Evelyn Helton, in a yellow dress, white spikes, and a hat that could have outdone a flower garden, came in first. She had bobbed hair the color of goldenrods and a powdered face white as snow. She was also the only woman in church wearing lipstick. Her six daughters, all shod with pretty dresses and combed hair, followed her to the bench. Doc, who'd taken off his thick glasses at the store on Tuesday to see what I looked like, brought up the rear, talking to himself.

Those who weren't standing rose as Brother Dossie went to the desk and lifted his arms. His opening prayer was short, doing mostly with salvation and his great church to be built in the wilderness. When it ended, my aunt, Virgie Jenkins, and Evelyn

Helton stepped up to the rostrum on Brother Dossie's right. Aunt Ilish, in the center, announced that the first hymn was page number seventy-eight. I watched the three women in the choir. How very different they were. Virgie Jenkins, with her bent back, saggy titties, and stomach swollen from so many children, looked the holiest—also the homeliest. Standing so straight she may have had a hoe handle poked down her back, Evelyn Helton was the best singer and should have been the prettiest with her store-bought face, bobbed hair, fancy new hat and clothes. Beside my aunt, she, too, was a big aught.

Aunt Ilish stood straight and natural, her sharp black eyes glimpsing a land I couldn't see, a thick plait hanging over each titty. She was holding the book for the others. She didn't need face decorations, a good voice, or several children to let the congregation know she took a rumble seat to none. She did it just as naturally as she chewed tobacco at home.

Partway through the second song, the Jenkins baby set up such a howl that Bode turned red and passed him to Miss Maudie, who was standing near the wall. Miss Maudie bounced him, but without luck. Virgie Jenkins left her place to step down from the rostrum, unbuttoning her dress front on the way. The baby was chewing her nipple and she was back in line long before the song ended.

Miss Maudie's solo was "The Old Time Religion," and her voice was like a bell. The choir joined her at the chorus. After this, the women returned to their places and Brother Dossie opened his Bible. He said a short prayer on giving while Bode Jenkins and Doc Helton each passed a pie plate.

A prayer to end the long drought was next. "Dear Lord," prayed Brother Dossie, "we thank you for the everflowing warters of Onion Creek. We thank you for the deep hole by the bridge down home, where so many lost souls have found salvation these many year. So thankful are we, in this time of drought and famine, for Onion Creek's fresh warter to be hauled home today by our neighbors for their families and thirsty stock, their truck gardens and fields that would have burned but for Your bountiful gift. Amen.

"Now, I beg you, Lord, let rain fall from the skies on these good people here today. Let the dark clouds gather and the lightning and the thunder tear asunder the blackened sky. Let the blessed rain pour upon our scorched land far as the Christian eye can see. Let the fields be soaked knee high with Your blessing. Make new rivulets on the Ozark ridge above us to run to the home of every parched animal nearby. And let the poor farmer and his family, who have always held fast to their faith, fall in the mud at Your feet and say, 'Thank you, Lord. We knew all along we were being tested, not forsook.' Amen."

The congregation then stood to sing "Showers of Blessings We Need. Mercy drops round us are falling, but for the showers we plead."

While this happened, two C.C.C. boys were behind me and Opal, trying to see inside.

And then the sermon, based on salvation, commenced.

For perhaps a full hour Brother Dossie preached, his tight fist pounding the teacher's desk when he wanted to get a point across. It was almost comical to watch Aunt Cloma jump when this happened. And then he was preaching louder. "Come unto me, all ye that are weary, saith the Lord," and tears were flowing into his beard.

"Weary? Who's weary? You, Brother Milt, from your daily toil and your lung sickness? And you're ready to go home, ain't you? How's about you, Brother Bode? A lifetime spent at tilling your fields, bringing forth your sheaves, raising up your young—ain't you tired out, too? And you, Brother Doc, caring for the sick and the helpless, the lame and the blind, telling 'em rise, take up your bed and walk, like our Blessed Saviour done when He trod this evil earth—ain't you sick of it all, sicker more knowing the only way out is death? What lies beyond is two paths: the left one leading to damnation, the right to life everlasting, the pathway home.

"But tell me, brothers and sisters, how do you get home if you don't know the way? You *don't* get home if you don't know the way. Like a baby turned loose in the woods to root for himself, there's no hope. You, without salvation, you're as helpless as this little baby here afore me—what's his name, Brother Bode? You're all as lost as little—did you say, Elmer, Brother Bode?—little

Elmer Jenkins would be turned out to take care of little Elmer Jenkins. Death claims you and you burn forever and evermore in the everlasting flames of hell fire. Amen?"

"Amen, Brother Dossie," echoed the congregation.

Brother Dossie stopped to wipe sweat and tears from his face with his shirt sleeve and to loosen his tie. "Brothers and sisters, I stand here afore you today telling you, trying to show you, lead you by the hand, on the only road Home." His voice had dropped to a coarse whisper. "Kneel here at this altar at my feet and I'll kneel at your side, begging our Lord and Master to help you see the way. It's the only beginning to the only Christian end.

A woman in front screamed, "Glory Hallelujah!' and I saw Virgie Jenkins come running down the outside aisle across the room. Her Green slung his other leg out the window when she was just inches away and disappeared. Virgie fought her way through the crowd to Hollyhock. She grabbed her arm, trying to pull her forward.

"Don't, Mom," the girl begged. "I ain't ready yet."

"Die after morning and you're lost for good, Hollyhock."

"Maybe next Saturday, not today. The feeling just ain't all there."

I'd been so busy watching that I hadn't noticed Aunt Ilish racing down the outside aisle toward us. She reached Opal first, and pulled on her as Virgie Jenkins was on Hollyhock. Upon Opal's balk at budging, her mother tried pushing her.

"Get away, Mom," Opal said, low as could be.

"What if the buggy tips over going home, Opal, and you die without salvation?"

"Good!"

She went back up the aisle, stopping in front of the Helton family to say something to Evelyn. Doc's wife jumped up and commenced to speak in tongues, her arms waving wild, eyes rolling backward. Next, my aunt and Evelyn were both talking in tongues on the rostrum, moving round each other in circles. Several other women, enough to fill the stage, soon joined them.

Brother Dossie Lynch ran down to help Virgie Jenkins persuade Hollyhock to join. Each holding an elbow, they dragged her to the rostrum, where she knelt, screaming, "I'm trying harder now!"

"Praises be!" shouted Brother Dossie.

Virgie Jenkins joined the women on the rostrum to talk in tongues. As she circled in and out of the crowd, I noticed one of her titties kept flapping through her dress opening without her seeming to know.

When Brother Dossie turned to look dead center at me, I didn't know what to do. I found a way out, in the same manner Green Jenkins had taken, upon seeing Milt, his hand over his gagging mouth, fighting to get out the door. Opal, a stick of C.C.C. chewing gum in her hand, hit the dirt seconds after me.

We found Milt trying to crawl into the buggy's shade, coughing and puking up blood. The camp boys helped us get him in the buggy and I drove him far's Onion Creek home. I raced up to the house for his pill, praying he'd be able to keep it down.

I was halfway back before I remembered I'd last seen Opal behind the school, laughing with the camp boys like nothing whatsoever was wrong. One had his arm round her waist. The other was trying to feel her titty. The way she laughed and said, "Go ahead, but it'll cost you!" would ring in my ears a very real long time.

# 16

Milt was in bed sleeping when my aunt returned later, shoes in hand. I expected her to ask how Milt was, where Opal was, and bawl me out for making her walk home. Instead she surprised me by dropping down to the cold eats and asking a blessing.

"Going to be a baptizing in Onion Creek next Sunday," she said, eyes shinier with every word. "Doc Helton's two oldest girls, asides Hollyhock Jenkins, finally joined us, praises be."

She ate slow and, when she finished, reached with some sadness, I thought, for her chew. "Powerful glad my Burt'll be out of jail to see it. I miss him awful." She gave a loud sniff. "Something awful."

A minute afterwards she was counting the eggs, telling me to let her dishes be till supper and not to leave Milt.

Returning to the table, she suddenly asked, "What you think of Doc Helton's wife, Goldy Lark? I want your truthful thought."

"Well, she's pretty and can sing, I guess."

"That makes up for her keeping a roomful of spare clothes she don't want a needy neighbor to have?"

"I sure wouldn't think so."

Aunt Ilish spit in the mudhole, wiped her mouth with her hand, and began to sing:

> Some people, they jump up and down all night
>   at a d-a-n-c-e.
> Then, they go to church to show
> Their brand-new h-a-t.
> Upon their face they smear great gobs of p-a-i-n-t.
> Yet, they've got the breath to say,
> I'm s-a-v-e-d!

"I noticed Evelyn Helton's hat," I said.

"It's like Old Jack. You couldn't miss it." She re-spat and went on:

> He stands and pours the whiskey in his neighbor's c-u-p.
> Then, he's got the breath to say,
> I'm s-a-v-e-d!

I watched while she bent her head on folded arms, her mouth working hard a time or two.

"Amen. Well." She blew her nose on the dishrag. "Crying for Evelyn Helton's and Urch Vestman's sins won't likely get me to Glory Land."

She went into the front room to put her shoes in the dresser, not once glancing at Milt. "Going for a walk. Be back when the Lord wills it."

Hawking her chew in the mudhole, she left the house.

I dozed in the rocker, coming awake at the sound of someone by the front door.

Opal's dirty feet stepped upon the hewn log and into the room. Her eyes were shiny wet, her hair hanging loose, her legs covered with brush scratches. The clean dress she'd worn to church might as well have been slept in for a week, it was that wrinkled. Why, I still don't know, but I asked where she's been.

"Praying for rain. Where's Mom, piss on her?"

"Gone to walk."

"She know I didn't come home with you and Milt?"

"Guess not."

"She ever asks, tell her I was here with you two," she said, heading for the back room.

A while later, Milt went out of his head and started wanting Jane Bell, Eb's mother, to fetch his fiddle. No amount of talk would quiet him. Opal wouldn't budge when I asked for help. Since Milt looked too weak to get out of bed and stray outside, I ran for the bridge, calling my aunt's name in hopes she might be where I'd had to leave the buggy.

Old Mame, stretched out in the path, stopped me from running headlong into a farmer I'd seen in church, standing by a rain barrel he'd just filled in Onion Creek. His wife, in a relief dress, stood in knee-top water scrubbing a pair of jeans with a cake of homemade soap. Under the bridge, several little kids laughed and splashed in a crawdad catch.

The man lifted his straw katy to me. "Brother Dossie said it's alright we get warter here anytime."

"You help yourself," I told him.

"We lived downcreek, like Bode and Theron Copeland does, and Eb Holt, we wouldn't need to bother you none."

"Milt's abed and you don't bother me."

I looked across the bridge to his wagon by our buggy, holding maybe eight rain barrels all told, his mules tied to a post oak. Could be ten wagons had been down for water since church, judging by so many tracks in the dust. I'd been so busy with my own thoughts and Milt, I hadn't heard even one.

The wife slapped the clean jeans up to a bridge plank, bent to pick up a boy's relief shirt soaking in the water, and rubbed on it the homemade soap. She never noticed me at all. Neither did the man when I left.

Remembering Milt again, I headed up to the buggy crossing, a shallow place in the creek we'd used on our way to church. But Aunt Ilish didn't answer when I called there. There wasn't time to see if Brother Dossie was home. I headed back to the house, walking in the buckbrush rather than the creek path, so's not to bother the family at the bridge.

It was the farmer's call of, "We're all looking the other way, Effie," that caused me to glance downhill. I was even with the woman when she peeled off her dress and dipped it down in the water. She then took the lye soap and washed with it under her arms and in her straddle before reaching down for the dress. Soaped good, she rubbed it hard between her thumbs a minute. Pitching the soap on the bridge, she swished the dress in the water, wrung it out and pulled it down over her head.

"You can all look now, Lester. I'm done."

Opal had told me she'd finally met somebody poorer than she was, meaning me with only one other change of clothes to my name. Now, I'd finally met somebody who looked like she was poorer than me.

# 17

Opal dragged herself to breakfast next morning when I'd done dishes. "Going to walk with me a ways today?" Her eyes, over her soakey, wouldn't meet mine.

I counted my toes in silence.

"Mom out egg hunting?"

"Checking relief. Said your brother's due home in a day or so."

She was drinking coffee when the notion came to face me. "You're sure acting powerful damn funny. I didn't do anything yesterday save go riding, if that's what it is. No harm to that."

"I just don't like you with the camp boys, Opal. They're all trouble. I hear they do bad things."

"Worser things than my mom sleeping with a neighbor man? Or my dad dying in jail a thief? Or my own blood brother the biggest bastard in the Ozarks, with our good churchy Brother Dossie Lynch damn nigh holding second place? You think now, Goldy Lark, there's any hope for me?"

I picked up the water bucket and headed outside. While my toes touched the mudhole, Opal passed me, jumping across it clean.

She was at the bridge waiting, her skirt heisted to show me the new pink silkies I'd have done better to keep.

"Well, cousin, what if I ain't got my cherry? You knowed I was lying to you all along, you had to. Thanks for my nice new silkies. Both the boys I laid with yesterday liked your present so much they give me this to pay you back."

The shiny coin she pitched toward me was a fifty-cent piece, as I saw when it glanced off my hand, rolled on its side into the water, scaring a fish back under the bridge.

"I won't touch it, Opal."

I filled the bucket as she waded in to bend over, find the money and—the exact picture of Aunt Ilish—slip it down the front of her dress.

"You act like there's something wrong about getting laid, Goldy Lark. Shows how young you are. Try a fugg for yourself sometime, it's pretty damn good. Why, me and Ivy Helton, we been with the camp boys on and off since last spring. I don't know what it's done for her asides make her feel good when she comes. All I know's I need a nickel for sodey pop, I got a nickel for sodey pop."

"You'll wind up with a baby."

"Fish farts! Didn't you hear me the day I showed you Mom's tap? You can't have a kid when you wear a tap, Ivy Helton told me so. She heard Doc tell Mom so when he give it to her, paid for my Uncle Sam's office in Rard. Guess the government don't want poor people who's on relief having more kids'n they can feed. So he gives taps free."

She jumped up on the bridge by me. "I aim to get me one of my own next week or so. I'll let you use it sometime if you don't tattle on me."

"I got no call to blab," I said.

Opal tried to thank me with a hug, but I moved away, sure she would feel dirty to touch. Not letting it bother her, she wrung out her dresstail on the bridge boards and gave a big cackle. "You know what I used to think gets you knocked up?"

I said no.

"Bode Jenkins, he's got a big one, nigh to his knees, and Virgie has a snot-nose kid once a year. Mom never had any, so I thought Milt's was too little. I figured a big one's something to run from fast."

Not knowing what to say, I kept still.

"I felt the first one I fugged to see if he was safe. It was about like this." She held up her little finger and laughed. "Next one, he slung me down too quick. He could've made Old Jack jealous with his. I couldn't move all that day. Turned out I didn't get caught anyhow. So I figured now I can't have a snot-nose kid, ever. Some girls can't, Ivy said." She nudged me. "How'd you like your first lay, Goldy Lark? Holler a lot?"

"I ain't had it yet," I said.

Her eyes bugged wide. "You trying to tell me a man's never been on top of you?"

"A man ain't never been on top of me," I said.

"Well, no wonder you got such little bitty titties." She started from the bridge laughing. I could hear her cackling to herself way up the hill. The same sizzle that had come in my head when Roy Cox said Indians weren't very smart crackled again to tell me someday I'd have to get her good, too.

That same day I got my first letter from Miss Emmer Cox.

"I think about you a lot," she wrote, "and wonder why I haven't heard from you. You did promise to write, you know. So please let me know if you're happy in your new home."

The P.S. said, "Roy will be going to Lotoe College this fall for a term. I'll miss him as much as I have missed you. Please write."

Rather than show her letter to Aunt Ilish and be accused of hiding any money she would think had been in it, I tore it in a hundred little pieces and threw it in Onion Creek. Pelper County was far behind me now. The only thing I cared to remember there was my little Bree's grave.

# BOOK TWO

# 1

Tuesday, I'd been living in Missouri County a week. Aunt Ilish reminded me of this during suppertime. She let me know as I heated the mule's water that I'd done a better job than she'd expected keeping Milt fed, watered, and a cool rag on his forehead between pills. If he felt good enough tomorrow, her Burt would see to it he got a good creek bath when Burt got home, if Burt had to carry him downhill himself on his weak back. If Burt agreed, Milt might also get an egg for his very own. Milt looked able to stand the long ride to Rard, now didn't he?

Before I could open my mouth, she said the two of us would be going up to Brother Dossie's cabin tonight for prayer meet, to pray for rain (and the money she thought I had coming, too, I guessed). Opal could stay home with Milt.

"Can I ride along to Rard, see my father's grave?" I asked.

She pitched me a hateful look. "What you aim to do, Goldy Lark, go live in the graveyard? You was at the graveyard just a week back, wasn't you?"

I told her Eb Holt had been so mad at me I didn't want to rile him more, so I hadn't seen Harley Farker's grave.

"Too puny bad. You'll be too busy working here."

"I'm all caught up on work," I said.

She bit off a chew. "I'll make more work for you, you can bet your last penny on that."

"What if Milt gets sicker and needs me?" I tried.

"Burt's bigger'n him," I was told, and that was that.

Shortly before sundown we started up Onion Creek. At the buggy crossing, Aunt Ilish stopped to take a final chew. In the cornfield she halted to watch the fodder shocks drying for winter. My great-grandfather, Joshua Lynch, had dynamited tree stumps to clear this land, she said. Every seventh year since, from his time down to mine, the land was rested, as the Bible said to do. A careful record was kept in the Lynch family Bible, at the back of the book. Next year, we wouldn't plant anything at all.

"Couldn't you clear off a new field?" I asked.

"A mule make a dumpling and not raise his tail?" she asked back.

A few steps in a row, she told me she sure could use a new dress. "Folks look down too much on people who's got mostly relief gear to wear."

Don't I know? I thought.

At the field's edge, she suddenly commenced raging about how Evelyn let dresses she wore only once a year be piled to the ceiling in a spare room of her house rather than giving them to a needy neighbor, which was contrary to the Good Book's rules. What pained her most was her and Evelyn Helton were the same size all over save for their titties.

"Her with a titty harness! She's got lesser there'n I've got in the Rard bank. One old one she wouldn't miss, and it'd sure make a dandy place for my baccer."

We passed more trees and then we rounded a sharp bend in the path and came into Brother Dossie's front yard before I knew it. His log cabin faced south, about as far from Onion Creek as our house was. On the rock step leading to the only door sat poor Aunt Cloma, rocking her baby. Strong gurgling water drowned out her lullaby's words. We were close enough to whiff the smelly unwashed dress and see the stiffness of her stained gray skirt that had been used for a handkerchief many times over. The stale sweatiness of her tangled gray hair almost caused me to gag. I didn't think she'd ever had a bath.

Straight ahead was a high bluff of solid rock, twice as tall as the sycamore tree overhanging the cabin. From a marble-size hole in a rock gushed a steady stream of clear water. It foamed to form a clear and wide whirlpool not thirty feet from the cabin door. Beyond the whirlpool, the water, through time, had cut Onion Creek to the width it was the bridge. After Old Jack, this was the second grand sight Missouri County had.

I stood rooted for a long while, within me a feeling of littleness at such a wonder. Here before me was a hole not much bigger than my hand that helped keep life in hundreds of folks, for all anybody knew. Alongside it, I felt like a gnat lined up with Old Jack. Who could tell I was even there at all?

The sight had stirred my aunt the same way. "There's a rule women can't warsh their dirty rags in the creek or it'll go plumb dry. Meadow Lark, she told me so."

"Where do I warsh 'em?" I asked.

"Soak 'em in a old pan, like I do, hang 'em on the rail fence to dry. Mind, you remember that now."

I promised I would.

"People would've dried up and died long back in this drought if it hadn't been for Onion Creek. Folks come from far's Rard with their barrels to haul warter home for over three long year now. Acourse, the creek's a little low from that. But it won't run dry, never. This here's blessed land, truly blessed. Kind of like a picture, ain't it?"

"Aunt Ilish," I asked, "why didn't Joshua Lynch build up here astead of further downcreek?"

"To be closer to New Hill, reckon, to teach."

"Where's Brother Dossie's great church to stand?"

She pointed to the high bluff. "Up there. On a foundation of solid rock, just like he says. He's got a good notion to dig the whirlpool deeper and wider for the baptizing. There'll be pure solid gold steps set in the rock so's the congregation, being God's soldiers, can march down to watch. You looked long enough, let's go in. The women, they'll be here varely soon."

I turned to the cabin. "No men coming?"

"Menfolk don't talk in tongues much nowadays. There'll be just us and the Jenkins women and Evelyn Helton with Ivy and Louise."

"They walk all this way?"

"Just the Jenkins. Evelyn, she drives Doc's fancy car far's the schoolhouse. Catch her not grabbing a chance to show off."

We almost had to climb over Aunt Cloma in the doorway to enter the cabin; she didn't seem to notice she was in the way.

My first thought of the one-room house was that it was hot as a cyclone cellar before a storm. There was only one window to match the door. More daylight than fresh air got in through several cracks where the clay mud chinking had washed away. The only furnishings were a bed, a washstand, and a table with chairs like we had down home. A rock fireplace stood in the east side of the room. Coals still smoked from the supper meal, and a giant black kettle, its rim smeared with rice, hung on a big hook. Alongside the wall towards Onion Creek were several stacks of books higher than my head. People in several counties, I learned later, had given the books because of Brother Dossie's great love of reading.

The bed, on the north, was made of two-by-fours held off the dirt floor by flat rocks; the mattress of floursack material was likely stuffed with leaves, like ours. In the corner of the bed, grizzled Brother Dossie outsnored even Old Jack.

"I'll leave him a minute," said my aunt, seating herself by the table. "Poor Brother Dossie's so burdened these days he gets little enough rest, as it is."

Looking for a place to drop down, I accidentally kicked a covered tub that was mostly hid by the books. The mattress leaves rustled in time with the loud clang the tub made, and I turned to see Brother Dossie upright on the floor. In his hands was a shotgun with the hammer cocked.

It was leveled straight at me.

# 2

Throughout the new few months, I was to think of many things that happened that night. Aunt Ilish's telling why I disturbed Brother Dossie would be but one: in that tub I'd kicked was the money Brother Dossie had gathered from his "flock of ever-straying sheep, to return them to the path of righteousness" for more than twenty years. He naturally slept with a loaded shotgun at his side to protect the means to his "church in the wilderness rising higher than yunder trees." A share of these offerings, enough for him to live on without government relief, had been marked by the givers for Brother Dossie's own use. So far he had touched not a penny. He got his food by begging, or "visiting," as he called it. Working for Vestman's sometimes paid for his clothes. A store owner in Rard gave him and Aunt Cloma new shoes after the first frost of the season and medicine, if needed, because he'd once saved his oldest daughter from pneumonia by praying it out of her body.

Aunt Ilish and Brother Dossie, unsmiling when they uncovered the money tub, said I was granted this sight only by being Meadow Lark's kin. If I ever told any outsiders about it, I'd answer to God third.

There was more than three hundred dollars in the tub, Brother Dossie said, most of it in small coins.

Lipsticked Evelyn Helton got in soon with her two oldest daughters, Ivy and Louise. Virgie Jenkins with Miss Maudie and Hollyhock were not far behind. After Brother Dossie lit the lamp, we formed a circle in the middle of the floor, me between Hollyhock Jenkins and Doc Helton's wife. Brother Dossie began with a prayer for rain, blessed rain, that shook the log rafters. When it ended, we joined hands and the others prayed for God to deliver to the church enough needed money (guess from where?) to allow the realization of Brother Dossie's early-lifetime dream.

When I say the others prayed without me, I mean just that. For Aunt Ilish, sitting spraddle-legged across the room from me, had, true to Opal's words, forgotten to wear her bloomers. Wondering without meaning to, if Bode Jenkins would meet us on the way home, I forgot to hear the rest of Brother Dossie's words.

Soon, somebody other than myself wasn't believing either, for Brother Dossie suddenly became very riled. His dark marble-like eyes gawking under heavy eyebrows to find the sinner, came to rest on Hollyhock Jenkins. She jumped to her feet and flew through the door.

This left the circle broken, but most failed to notice, and soon

Evelyn Helton was on her feet, swooping around the room, talking in tongues. Ivy and Louise sat back and watched her, maybe scared. Miss Maudie was next to feel the Power, then Virgie Jenkins. Brother Dossie was kneeling, asking for the answer, show us the answer, when Aunt Ilish came to my side.

"Watch Doc's girls. That oldest one steals," I thought she whispered before joining the others.

Probably half an hour had passed—at least it seemed that long to my backside—when Brother Dossie stood up and wiped his eyes and his long nose. Seeing him head for the door, I jumped and caught his arm. "I'll find Hollyhock for you."

"Hollyhock's likely run home, with Satan racing after," he said. "It's Sister Cloma I'm worried for. She gets out of cabin-sight after dark, she can't always find her way home."

"I'll go look."

He shook his head. "Too dark outside, and bad things happen to little girls not in the Light of Faith."

For the next fifteen minutes, I and the Helton girls looked from one another to the four rejoicing women. We squirmed, coughed, changed positions. Miss Maudie was the first to finish speaking. When she stopped and sank to the floor dripping wet, I stepped outside with the intent of helping Brother Dossie search for Aunt Cloma.

I found her and Nonny hunkered on a low rock, swaying slow, listening to the creek give birth not twenty feet from where the lamplight's shadow casts its glow. Low, hurried voices behind the stone stopped me from trying to take her inside.

"I can't, Brother Dossie! I tell you I just can't let you do this to me no more. And don't you stretch across me so. It's a bad, bad sin!"

"It won't be after Sunday noon, Hollyhock, when you'll be made white as snow."

"You won't do it to me no more after Sunday, you swear on a stack of Bibles?"

"You just meet me by the bridge early mornings till then and I'll promise, Hollyhock, I'll promise."

I turned to run for the cabin, bumping into Miss Maudie at the door. She caught my arm to stop me, asking if I'd seen Hollyhock or my aunt or Brother Dossie. Before I could answer, Brother Dossie stepped into the lamplight, gently guiding poor Aunt Cloma by the arm. Hollyhock Jenkins, crying, followed a step back.

# 3

Two jars of gooseberries had been in the pink cabinet since Sunday. "Bode Jenkins, he always pays Mom that way," Opal said when I asked where they were from. "You don't like goose-berries, next week there'll be plums maybe or peaches again. Hell, sometimes we even get goose meat or rabbit. Anything that stands still, Virgie Jenkins cans."

At noon Wednesday I got the job of washing and drying several fruit jars Aunt Ilish said I'd find under the barn bed.

"Do it on the bridge. Then put 'em back under the bed, careful, in a poke," Aunt Ilish ordered. She took a bite of Harper's Homespun. "Bode can tote 'em home next time he's here."

I later guessed Burt Troat must have cut through the woods instead of taking the New Hill road or he'd have had to pass by me at the bridge. But when Aunt Ilish left to meet Opal, she stepped across the last of the jars without saying boo.

"Get taters abile for supper," she called on her way up the hill. "And you heat up some lard to dip our bread in."

Nothing did she say about Burt's being home for maybe the past hour.

My first glimpse of Burt showed a much bigger and younger man than Brother Dossie, without the fat. Shirtless in overalls and barefoot, he was throwing the eggs his mother had so carefully saved against the side of Old Jack's shelter. Burt Troat, when it came to height, was a good way under six feet. He just gave the notion of extra bigness by having the widest of shoulders. His hairy arms were so long they dangled way past his knees. I watched, with a bad chill, as he wiped his giant hairy hands on his overalls leg without bending one inch.

I managed to get to the woodpile and was hoping to make it to Milt before Burt saw me, only to have him turn when we got side by side. The face he showed me was Aunt Ilish's from the tobacco stained lips to the half snarl. His black glassy eyes were part mad dog, part drunken man.

Since I had the choice of running and showing my fright or trying to bluff my way past, I chose the latter. Holding forth my hand, I smiled, hoping he couldn't hear the pounding of my heart.

"You're Aunt Bree's Goldy Lark," he said holding out a dirty hand. "Reckon I seen you get off the train in Rard, Tuesday last week."

"I've heard a lot about you, Burt. From your mom." My fingers itched for clean water where he'd touched.

He laughed, slapped his thigh, and ran his fingers from his nose to his bearded chin. "All of it good, bet you a pretty."

"You didn't steal the razorback apurpose, I know that," I said. He laughed louder. "Reckon you're part right, Goldy Lark. I didn't steal it, but I sure's hell tried to. Went down to Eb Holt's pigpen in broad daylight and coaxed the bastard out. Bet you a fart that sum bitching step-brother of mine was inside, watching me all the time."

"Aunt Ilish told me you found the hog in the woods." I was at the mudhole now. In a few seconds, I'd be safe with Milt.

"Hell, I told Mom right out I stole it to get Eb's dander up. What's this god damn world coming to, you tell me, when your own mommie goes round telling lies on you all the time?"

Milt was asleep, but it didn't really matter. If Burt Troat decided to harm me, at any time, any fight would have to come from me alone. And so I began supper, using the eats he'd brought in, while he sat at the table whittling with his pocket knife on a long stick of wood. One end was pointed. The other, I saw with a sudden sickening, was rounder, with brown stains on the end. He guessed that I'd heard from Opal of its terrible use, for from time to time, he'd rear his head back and laugh, scratch his hairy armpit with the stick. He'd gawk at me till my eyes dropped, and hee-haw again.

While I was spooning up relief lard, Burt walked to the door and pissed in the mudhole. "You see this, Goldy Lark?" He had turned to face me, leaving his overally fly open. "You know it makes babies, don't you?"

I was so surprised I was unable to turn away.

Burt laughed as he buttoned his pants. He walked back to the table and picked up his whittle stick. "This little pretty here, it ain't so good-looking neither but it's got a good purpose, too. It gets rid of the babies my other pretty makes. Too damn many Lynch bastards been birthed in that green bed anyhow. Acourse, you don't go round blabbing that, hear me? Somebody might find you laying in a ditch with your throat cut and some little pretty you wore on your neck missing, if you do. That's what happened to Almy Copeland."

"Almy Copeland?" I dared ask.

"Theron's oldest girl. Had a pretty locket round her neck she'd let other kids look at close, but not me. Mailman found her in a ditch by New Hill, bleeding like a stuck pig, bloomers up to her neck, and that little pretty of her missing. 'Burt Troat done it' was her last words."

I was too smart to ask if he had.

"The first Sheriff Jessie Red McKay and Milt, him being a deputy then, comes to take me to jail, meets Mom on her way to Doc Helton's. I'd been deathly sick all week, I ain't got out of bed, or the house neither. Milt, he swears to it, too. The law wouldn't take Almy's word against Milt's and mine. That's how I got off. Copelands, they buried poor Almy at Rard, and the whole bunch bawled till their eyes got red's little Almy's hair had been."

He fed Old Jack a biscuit. "Heard tell poor Almy Copeland had been fugged hard afore her asshole was cut with bob wire, too. Now who'd be that damn ornery? Sure wasn't me, I was only thirteen at the time."

With what sense I could gather, I quickly decided to have the same look-out for my cousin Burt Troat I'd always before had for coiling copperhead snakes and, lately, my Aunt Ilish.

Soon Opal came up the creek path ahead of my aunt. Seeing Burt, she pretended to smile through gritted teeth.

"First smell of you," she told Burt, "I'm always happy you're close kin, acause the one thing on earth I'll never have to do is marry you."

"Now, you wouldn't look at me twice, kin or not. You got to find yourself a white man or go plumb without one. Why, that's the Lynch law."

"Piss on the Lynch law," Opal snorted.

"That's what I say. So I just up and took the first one who looked at me cross-eyed!"

"Took's right!" Opal shot back. "Poor Almy Copeland."

"Was itchy old Miss Maudie I meant," Burt laughed.

"She's that good, why don't you hightail it down to Bode's and get you some?"

"I don't run after a damn woman; they come to me," Burt said.

The first thing Aunt Ilish saw a minute later was the rotten eggs running into the mudhole. Before Burt knew what she was about, she had him by the ear and was screeching for him to get the barn shovel. "Not my fault, Burt, them eggs got rotted up."

"Ain't mine neither." Burt wouldn't budge.

"You don't move this minute, Burt Troat, I'll pop you one."

"Hop to it, if you want to throw your hand out."

Aunt Ilish, still not bested, sat down beside him. "Son, you aim to mind me or not?"

Burt laughed and reached down her dressneck for her tobacco and helped himself to a giant chew. "To tell you the truth, Mom, no, I ain't. My back's not up to a shovel tonight. Tell Goldy Lark to."

While Opal finished fixing supper, I shoveled up the rotten mess, gagging with every breath I took. It turned out to be just as well I wasn't hungry. When at last I had finished, I saw Burt had downed all the eats by himself, including the batch of sad bread meant for the animals. Opal was making more for Old Jack, Old Mame, and us when my aunt asked Burt if he was going down to his father-in-law's tonight and bring Miss Maudie home.

"Her not visiting me once all the time I was in jail!" Burt's big fist banged the table. "Hell, I'd sooner play with myself's go crawl to her!"

"She won't have any part of you from now on out, son, less'n you get yourself baptized afore the year's end. She told me so herself. Miss Maudie, she's religious as me nowadays. She means it this time," and Aunt Ilish's mouthful of giant spit landed in the middle of the mudhole.

"Well, I mean it this time, too." Burt's healthy spit landed on top of his mother's. "Mom, damn it, I ain't having any whiny bitch telling me what to do. If she wants me, she'll come here."

My aunt and Burt stayed at the table late, she listening quietly as he told her all about his latest stay in jail.

# 4

From the beginning, I never knew exactly what to expect from Burt Troat. One minute he'd be an over-sized little boy begging my aunt for a chew, and the next he'd be twisting her arm till she cried out in pain and allowed him to help himself. Opal's teases were taken in what seemed good nature, but when she wasn't looking he'd study her in a way that said he'd like nothing better than to cut her throat. There was also in him the same odd tender streak Opal held for Milt. I first saw it the night the relief had been brought home.

"The butter and grapefruits and prunes, raisins and sugar belongs to me," he'd said after supper. "Butter beans and rice, and the noodles, that kind of mule turds, is for you—and me, too. Anybody I catch swiping mine, they'll have a hole where their teeth used to be."

He had hardly finished speaking when he peeled a grapefruit and pitched it across the room to Milt.

"Go to hell," he told Aunt Ilish when she ordered him to pick up the rinds from the floor.

After our first meeting, Burt all but forgot me, and of that I was very glad. Everything about him had warned me whatever evil he was waiting to cause, I would rather have it happen to somebody else. The closest I got to him for a long while was at the table. He had the stick of wood nearest mine, where he'd hunch over his plate eating with both hands, his whiskered chin nearly resting in his plate. Aunt Ilish called him on his manners his second night home. He threw a biscuit at her head without missing a bite. It rolled out the door, to be claimed fast by Old Mame, who'd been sniffing round waiting for her share of bread to bake. Since I was almost doing the same—for the rest of us had to wait till Burt had his fill—I was tempted to fight the dog for the bread.

I was to sleep every night with a troubled mind, waiting and listening for something terrible to happen. My biggest worry was Burt's getting up in the night and passing by my bed on his way outdoors. I didn't want to be found some morning like little Almy Copeland. So I took to sleeping with a pair of rusty scissors I'd found in a crack of the devonette held point outward in my hand.

Since the prayer meeting my aunt hadn't once mentioned my coming money, and, so far as I thought, Burt knew nothing at all of my imagined fortune. It was on that Saturday morning early when I got sent to the store for Harper's Homespun, coal oil, and flour, that I saw Burt at the table, deep in thought, his hairy arms circling a picture of a shiny black car. I knew then my fairy tale fortune was expected to be split still another way.

Since both storekeepers were busy with farmers, I didn't have a chance to talk with Urch till he helped me back on Old Jack. "You ever hear tell my mom had any money put back here in Missouri County?" I asked low. "You said I could ask about her."

He heaved the fifty-pound sack of flour ahead of my belly on the saddle and hooked the coal oil bucket's handle over the saddle horn before saying, "No."

"Uncle Dossie got a letter from her days afore she died. It asked him to help me get all the money she'd earned here. I can't figure out what it meant. We was so poor back home I had to lay her in Potter's Field. My uncle says he don't know what the letter means, and Aunt Ilish seems not to. Even if they pray about it and go on a lot, they act like I'm a liar. Milt also said it was news to him. I thought maybe you'd know."

"Oh, boy, Goldy Lark." Urch suddenly bent double, his hand over his mouth to stop gagging. Snowy white, he turned his face away from me. "I'm sick, I got to go in."

"Feel better," I called after him.

If he heard, he showed no sign.

Sometime in the dark night, I heard a woman in the direction of Onion Creek screaming for her very life. Thinking, "Burt's killing Opal, cutting out her heart to eat it," I skidded fast across the mudhole. Through the buckbrush, I could see a lit lantern on the bridge. My heart was trying to jump out of my chest at my wild

thought of how to save Opal from Burt. Milt's rifle? The axe?
A big rock?

"Goldy Lark, what you doing up?"

I could just make out Opal's form on the woodpile.

"What's all the hollering for down there?"

"Nothing to lose your cherry over," she told me. "Looks like
Brother Dossie's finally sniffed Aunt Cloma up close. That's just
her fighting another warsh."

# 5

Sunday morning I told Aunt Ilish I'd rather stay with Milt than go
to church. To my surprise she allowed it, providing I come down
to the creek when I heard the congregation gather for the baptism.
These were always held by the bridge at the deepest part of Onion
Creek, she told me, due to the drought. "But just you wait till the
Almighty sends rain, and then watch. You watch the great church
with its solid gold spires rise above the tree tops, see the whirlpool
upcreek cut wider and deeper to let the weary sinners wade in for
salvation and everlasting life," she added.

Milt was asleep when I first heard "Bringing in the Sheaves,"
led by Brother Dossie, coming down from New Hill. I stood by
the buckbrush on the bank nearest the house and watched the
slow march to the bridge.

Brother Dossie led the way. Evelyn Helton, Virgie Jenkins, Miss
Maudie with Burt behind her, and Aunt Ilish followed. Hollyhock
Jenkins and the two Helton girls to be saved were behind them.
Green Jenkins walked alone. Urch Vestman and Doc Helton
walked side by side with Bode Jenkins, who carried the baby
Elmer. Lucy Lee Copeland and her family were next, and I
wondered if they hated Burt Troat as much as I would have had I
thought he'd killed my daughter the awful way some thought he'd
killed Almy Copeland. Behind them was Opal, with three of the
camp boys instead of two. A crowd of perhaps forty, some of
them farmers with water barrels in their wagons, were the last in
sight save for Aunt Cloma, whose newly washed hair flew loose
on all sides.

She seated herself on the bridge to nurse little Nonny. My uncle, along with the three to be saved, knelt near Aunt Cloma's feet. The true believers of the church which didn't include either of my cousins did likewise in the grass.

When the prayer ended, Brother Dossie sat down to remove his shoes. He stood to test the water with his big toe before lowering himself in. He worked his way about five long steps upstream, slipping often on the mossy rocks below. He halted in rump-high water. As if by a sign, his followers stood and the choir commenced to sing of fathering at a beautiful, beautiful river. Hollyhock Jenkins, in a faded relief dress mended many times, slipped into the water. The lower tips of her flower-decorated plaits hung in Onion Creek as she made her way forward.

There was something in the quick way Brother Dossie turned to lead her that caused me to wonder why only me and Opal could see the truth about those two. If not in his way, then why not hers? She looked more like a bride going to be mated with a husband than she did a young girl about to make her peace with God. They met about halfway between the bridge and the deep hole, where he took one hand and put his other about her waist. As their eyes met, Hollyhocks reminded me of Old Mame's when she heard Milt say her name.

Hollyhock was crying by the time they reached the deep hole. Brother Dossie clasped her hands in front of her and held both with one of his, while his other hand, behind her neck, lowered her easy into the clear water. For the second or so she was under, I could see the water lapping at her hair, trying to pull it on down the creek without her, it looked like. Sunlight danced on her slim brown legs. There was a strawberry birthmark on her lower right thigh.

When he brought her up, she had a look of misery you'd expect to see at a fresh grave. She stood in the water, shivering and crying, her eyes glued on her hands, while my uncle saved Ivy and Louise Helton.

Later, when Doc's daughters had received dry clothes and been sent into the brush to change, Brother Dossie led Hollyhock partway across the bridge. Once out of my Brother Dossie's reach, Hollyhock ran straight for Virgie Jenkins and held her tight.

"I didn't mean to do it, Mom! I swear, I didn't mean to," she screamed.

Virgie Jenkins, nursing the baby now and still singing of the beautiful, beautiful river, reached out to gather Hollyhock to her side.

I saw Green push through the crowd to shove a bundle of dry clothes to his sister's arms. For a minute, Hollyhock didn't seem to notice. Then she suddenly let go of her mother with a loud scream.

"Can't any of you hear me when I tell you all I'd rather be dead?" she screamed on her way into the bushes.

Nobody but me seemed to have heard her. Brother Dossie stepped over Aunt Cloma to talk to Doc and Evelyn Helton, while Urch Vestman went to say something to Virgie Jenkins and Bode. The Copelands started downcreek without saying anything to anybody else. Burt Troat pulled Miss Maudie toward the barn, his big hairy arm hard around her waist. The farm families needing to load water commenced to roll their barrels across the bridge when Aunt Cloma left to follow Brother Dossie. Some of the women toted washtubs of dirty clothes to do while they had a good chance. I couldn't see Opal or the camp boys anywhere.

Aunt Ilish turned her head, either to look for Bode or to look for Opal, giving me time to duck up through the buckbrush and fix a dish of gooseberries for Milt.

# 6

The day Burt took Milt to Rard to get me on relief, Milt came home sick and stayed sick all night, keeping me up with him. By the next afternoon I was so tired I was numb. Aunt Ilish sat in her rocker and didn't say "boo" to me till I put the mule's supper water on to heat.

"Whole lot of warter just for you to drink up, ain't it?" she said, blocking my way outside.

"It's for the mule," I said, my head starting to sizzle.

"Why, I sure thought you was heating it up for you." She moved to one side. "If the mule can't drink it, reckon you'll have to, huh?"

Then my head sizzled a lot.

"Ain't you caught on the mule's not here today, Goldy Lark? Eb Holt, he come and got him afore daylight. He's cutting New Hill's wood today and needs you about now to help. You go up there right now and don't you dare come back till Eb's all done for the night."

"Won't Milt need me?" I asked.

"Bode's coming up to see him." Her voice was softer now. "He'll help in your place."

"Ain't you going to meet Opal?"

"Eb, he's busy with the woodsawing, he won't go smelling after her," she said. "She'll be safe."

Vestman's woodsaw was in the schoolyard when I got there, and Delphie Doll was tied to a blackjack tree, but Eb and Old Jack weren't there. He was likely on No Man's Land felling trees, which left me a little time to visit at New Hill. When I knocked on the door, Miss Maudie said, "Come in, Goldy Lark, I'm glad you're here."

I took a red seat close to Lucy Lee Copeland, trying not to think so many eyes were again on me all at once. Of the fourteen kids I counted, exactly half were named Jenkins. I wasn't surprised Hollyhock hadn't come back to school after she'd found faith, like Opal had told me last night.

The other kids were the four younger Helton sisters and Lucy Lee Copeland's two brothers, both a lot younger than she. Due to Burt Troat's being thought of as Almy Copeland's killer, I hadn't expected Lucy Lee to like me, and she didn't. I never got a chance to be friendly with her. She'd see me looking at her and with a sling of her long silky red hair, stick her nose in a book.

"She knows I'm stuck on you, that's why she acts so," Green Jenkins whispered to me as I passed by him to see if Eb had come back yet with the mule. I tried not to look at him after that, knowing that when I did, he'd make it his business to wink.

But I did laugh inside till my belly hurt during his trip out to dust the erasers; he was singing, "The farmer in the dell, he died and went to hell," at the top of his voice. Miss Maudie shamed him, with tears in her eyes. She did the same to all the others who failed to mind, which about took in the rest of the school.

Once she laid her head on her desk, and I thought she was

crying till she raised up and said, "Well, since you all want to act like heathens in front of our company, you can recite The Lord's Prayer to prove you're not. Green, you start." I figured Miss Emmer Cox back in Pelper County would likely have done the very same thing.

I looked outside just as the last bell rang, my heart leaping as Eb Holt's straw katy rounded a corner of New Hill. In jeans and a torn shirt, he was astraddle Old Jack, smoking and whistling, looking straight ahead. I got outside to see him loose the two big logs the mule had been pulling behind him in the dirt, waving to Miss Maudie as she passed by me. Eb Holt didn't even know I was there when I spoke his name.

"Well, if you don't want me to help you till dark, I'll go home," I finally said, starting away.

"Goldilocks, get your ass back here," I heard five steps later.

"What do you want me to do, Eb?"

He pointed to a pile of logs he'd brought in earlier. "Can't start sawing till I get some more logs. You take Delphie Doll down to drink while I'm gone," he said.

As I led the red mare back up from Onion Creek, I met Opal going home. "Where's Eb?" she asked.

I said he was on No Man's Land getting logs with Old Jack. "We're going to work late tonight," I added. "Aunt Ilish let me come to help."

"That means Bode's down home," she laughed. "Well, don't tell Eb I was here. I can see him any time I want to, just like that." She snapped her fingers as she started away, leaving me to hate her even a little more.

We had about two hours of daylight left by the time Eb got done dragging in logs and getting the woodsaw's motor to work. When it was finally sputtering right, we started sawing the wood.

"You work the short ends," I was told. "Don't let 'em pile up underfoot. I got enough to do cussing this bastard machine without getting my hands sawed off."

I did as told, pitching the short ends that would be split into school kindling out of his way. By sundown, we'd done most of the logs. He planned to cord it tomorrow so's to see how much more would be needed before taking the woodsaw home.

"High time you went home, Goldilocks." Eb, rolling a smoke, was talking to New Hill, not me. "Come morning, I'll know how much more to cut. If you can help me, you got a dollar. Don't you tell your aunt about it, now. Bitch'd keep it."

"If she lets me, I'll be back. Any word for Milt?" I asked.

"Yeah. Tell him I said when I'm done here, I aim to go out and find me a pair of itchy bloomers. With a girl in 'em."

"You want me to tell him a dirty thing like that?"

"One thing you'd best get straight about Eb Holt, Goldilocks, he don't never say something he don't mean. And now you'd best get that pretty little ass-end of yours out of here afore I forget you're a Lynch and lay you."

I led Old Jack down the hill, shaking with the same warm happiness I'd once felt for Roy Cox.

Hearing Aunt Ilish out on the hewn log singing a happy, "When The Work's All Done This Fall," I hoped it meant I'd get to work with Eb Holt again tomorrow, and it did. So, for the better part of a day, I got to be touching close to the man I loved.

That was two days after Burt Troat took Milt to Rard, first by buggy and mule, then by Vestman's team and wagon so Milt could lie down and rest. His long trip just to sign me on government relief was to be the last time he would ever rise from his bed.

# 7

It was odd the way friends and neighbors came to the house after that, almost like they were reminding Milt, in a kind way, he was soon to die. For me there was feeding, medicine, washing his clothes and dishes separately from the family's, keeping his forehead cool, and cleaning him all over fast if I heard company coming. This meant my staying on the green bed, listening as they talked, for some time he couldn't find the strength to use his voice. Whenever this happened, whoever was visiting would keep talking like nothing was wrong, but at the same time keeping his eyes fastened on the floor while I talked in Milt's stead. I learned fast the best thing then was to brag on his mule, his cooner, or Eb, the only things in life he really loved.

The Missouri County Sheriff started visiting Saturdays, always to sit in the rocker and talk over old times with Milt. Then when Milt's pills made him doze, Jessie Red McKay would always talk to me.

"Well, Goldy Lark Farker, how you faring out here?" he'd want to know. Or did I think it was going to rain, just like I might know it first.

On his third visit, after he'd mentioned seeing Aunt Ilish waiting at New Hill for our mail, he asked, "Well, Goldy Lark Farker, they treating you good out here?

Knowing by "they," he meant Aunt Ilish, I looked him straight in his eyes and said, "I'm bigger'n her, I do alright."

He laughed and said, "Reckon that's so." Then, his reddish face straight, "Eb Holt, he show you your daddy's grave the day you come in?"

Not wanting to maybe cause Eb trouble, I nodded yes.

"See the first lawman Jessie Red McKay's grave, too, close by the Lynch family corner?"

"I saw your daddy's grave, too," I lied.

He got out of the rocker, patted my head as he passed by, smiling to himself, maybe over something I'd said. (I hoped it wasn't the big fibs I'd just told about seeing the graves of his father and mine.)

Doc Helton was down weekly, Urch Vestman every other day. Maybe twice weekly, old Villie tagged along. The piggy old man would wait in the rocker while Urch visited, his sharp blue eyes shooting here and there as if he expected bedbugs to crawl out of the corners. His special look for me was one of pure hate. During my lifetime, I'd had lots of whites look at me in several different ways, but there was something about me that really riled the old man.

One noon they came just after dinner. It had been the first meal in a long time Milt had wanted to finish. I was thankful he'd been able to keep it down for a change, but then he suddenly started to cough. Before Urch could move, I had turned Milt and fixed his head over the spitpan. There was a cold rag waiting in my hand when the spell had passed. While Urch kept up his steady talk of how business was, I got some fresh water spooned down Milt.

This was followed by a cup of cool mashed peaches I'd kept in a shady spot in the creek all morning long. I brought Milt a clean shirt and helped him into it, fed him a pill, and dropped on the bed to hold his hand. He dropped off while Urch still talked.

Old Villie got to his feet and puffed past, spitting something in what must have been German at the door.

Wondering what he'd said, I walked outside with Urch, aiming to ask him about it, if the old man had gone. He hadn't; he'd stopped by the woodpile and, hearing us, turned to face me. To my surprise, he stuck out his fat tongue and put a fat finger to his nose, giggling as he did the little dance exactly as I'd seen Bree do it so many times in the past.

I didn't need to ask what he'd meant. But I did have to know when old Villie Vestman had seen Bree cutting up that way.

"I guess he watched Bree once when she done it for me," Urch said low, his face redder than the old man's.

"Well, you tell him he done it wrong. Your tongue's supposed to touch your nose. Your finger ain't."

"Mishling!" old Villie shot back at me.

Urch grabbed him by the shoulders and marched him down to Onion Creek. I could hear them jawing at each other all the way up the hill.

# 8

Halfway through September, some of the neighbors' cane crops had been cut, hauled to our place, and stacked in separate piles awaiting Old Jack and Eb Holt. It was during this time, 'lasses making season, that Milt's mule proved his true worth. Until this year, when bad lungs and hard times had so snowed Milt under, Old Jack had always earned enough to keep the family going part of the year. Milt told me this sadly while waiting for Eb to come for the mule. This was the first caning season ever Old Jack would work without Milt.

I was working, too, thanks to Burt's bad back, which was suddenly worse. "I'm trying to save a dollar here and there to get him to Jeff City on, see if he's caught cancer or something worser," Aunt Ilish told Milt when he mentioned he didn't want me to be the only girl working with so many men. "She can wear your old overalls so's nobody'll see her bloomers. Her plaits, they can be pushed up inside your old hat, Milt. Nobody'll know she's a girl lessen'n she shows 'em so. That one's going to earn her keep if I have to stand over her with a hoe. You dry up, Milt," she snapped all in one breath.

Eb whistled, sometimes sang, about the gal in Kansas City all the while he led the way on the harnessed mule up to Urch Vestman's to pull down the 'lasses mill. I followed on Delphie Doll, a helper like myself. Her job was to help Old Jack pull the mill down to our place. Mine, besides firing, from best I could understand from Eb, would also be to stir the cane juice as it was being slowly cooked into 'lasses.

The mill looked smaller than I'd imagined. It was a square piece of wood and iron standing maybe five feet high, set on four low iron wheels. Directly atop was a bent pole nearly twelve feet long. Old Jack would be hitched to an end. As he walked slowly around in a circle all day long, Urch had explained, someone, generally the owner of the crop, would feed the cane pieces into some gears that turned when the mule walked. The owner's helper, usually a boy my age, would squat opposite the gears with a bucket to catch the green juice that oozed out of a tiny tin hole. My job wouldn't start till there was enough juice in the giant square ten-by-four-foot pan so it would sit on the creek bank in a pit, built up slightly by rocks on all sides; I would pitch pieces of wood into the pit's fire when it threatened to get low, and stir it often to make sure the pan stayed hot enough to cook.

A long ladle, which was lashed to the mill along with the pan, would be used to stir the juice. Beside each owner's pile of cane was a stack of wood for his own cooking use. I'd counted seven stacks on the way up; more would be coming in when Urch spread word the mule was working.

Both the mare and Old Jack pulled the mill until we got past Doc Helton's, where the level road started running downhill. At this point, Eb unhitched the mule and harnessed him to the back end to serve as a brake. He did this by means of two log chains harnessed from the hames at the mule's shoulders to the back axle of the mill. All the mare had to do was guide the machine down to Onion Creek. Old Jack, with Eb riding him, would see to it Delphie Doll and the mill both got there in one piece.

It had been real early when we'd passed New Hill going up. On the way home, classes had started, and I could see several kids through the open window. Miss Maudie Troat waved as I walked by.

Coming down from Doc's had been fairly easy. The road was traveled often by cars and had been cleared of jagged rocks, and although it ran downhill, it was flat compared to what we'd pass over from the school on down. Old Jack had made the trip without really trying, as I could see from where I tagged along at his side.

Past the school was the dangerous part. Big sharp rocks lay in the road. They had been loosened in the last year, likely, and nobody had bothered about them because the buggy and the relief wagon could pass over without worry. Now they had to be cleared by me before the mill got to them. The first lesson I learned was to keep at least thirty feet ahead of the mill so as not even slightly to chance the pole running through me. What rocks I couldn't heave aside, I started rolling downhill, hoping they'd all land out of the road. There was one jagged snag that my quick judgment said would cause no trouble, and so I left it, hurrying on.

A minute later, I heard Eb's warning call and looked up as the rock flew past, missing me by inches. Frozen with fright, I could only watch him point, swearing mad. I was extra careful after that.

But not careful enough, it seemed, for another rock I'd somehow missed seemed to have jammed the axle, nearly tipping the mill. I climbed fast when Eb called and got to his side to see it hadn't been a rock at all. The first chain link hooked to the axle had snapped. I had to climb up on the mule and steady him while Eb slipped the second link into place with one hand. His other was straining mightily to keep the mill from rolling till both sides were level.

"Smarter'n I thought," he growled when we were ready to go again. I knew it had to be his strange way of saying I'd done a good job holding Old Jack.

The rest of the way we made it without anything worse happening than Delphie Doll's shoulders getting grabbed raw by the harness. When we'd backed the mill up to the biggest cane pile, Eb poured stockdip on her sores and cussed out the world while we waited for the tardy Bode Jenkins, first on the list, to report for work.

# 9

Bode Jenkins came whistling through the brush behind us in a straw katy and blue relief shirt, thumbs in his overalls bib. "Green, he's bringing in the team and wagon from New Hill way. Surprised he's not here yet," was his greeting.

Eb, with a pleasant welcome his made face showed he didn't mean, hitched Old Jack to the pole. He fixed a cigarette and leaned against the mule's belly, his eyes on the creek.

Bode Jenkins put kindling in the pit and motioned me to help carry the big cook pan to the bridge. We had finished washing it when Green drove in.

Without giving him time even to tether the team, Eb called, "Bring on your buckets there, let's go!" in the same tone he'd talked to me coming home.

Green jumped from the wagon, and wound the checklines slow around a sycamore sapling. He looked at Eb like he hadn't heard clearly and asked, "Mean me, Eb Holt?"

Eb, slapping the mule's rump into motion, called, "Yeah, you. Get your finger out of your ass and your mind out of Arkansaw!"

Green's answer was a fast trot forward, a bucket in each hand.

Till Nate Brice got us on relief back in Pelper County, we'd used mainly store 'lasses, all winter long. Sometimes we'd mixed it with soft lard to eat on biscuits or cornbread. Other times, we'd spoon it from the plate, to save our precious bread. When there was no bread, between meals I'd stick my fingers in the big white crock that sat in the kitchen corner and lick my fill, if I didn't get caught first. Waking in the middle of the night with hungry insides, I'd tiptoe to the crock. Once, I misjudged the distance and stumbled, sinking my arm in past the elbow. It had taken the rest of the night to lick myself clean. Then there was the time some stray cat Mom had been mothering went mousing, only to fall in and drown. Nate

Brice, for two bits, had traded the rest of the crock to a neighbor for his pigs, who likely ate the cat and all. Another crock from the store had replaced that one. So, up to now, 'lasses was something store-bought. I guess I'd never spent a thought on how it was made.

It was like a spelling match in school, there was that much teamwork to it. Bode, soon shirtless, fed the long stalks into the gears as Eb, stripped to his jeans, took turns shoveling the cane closer to Bode, yelling at the mule when he slacked his pace. Old Jack, whether or not he worked faster than the men, outsweated them both. Beady drops from his rippling shoulders made a wet little path on both sides of the tiresome circle in which he walked. Green, for the most part, squatted to watch the buckets slowly fill. When he stood up to change a full one with an empty, it became his habit to watch me before bringing the bucket to me at the pan. Twice the dangerous pole almost smacked him across his chest. As he poured each bucket of black-green juice into the cooker, I had to keep the ladle busy fanning away hungry flies.

"You get old enough to have big titties like Opal, Goldy Lark, I'll marry you," he'd tease under his breath.

"Wouldn't have you if I was paid," I finally snapped, hoping to shut him up. He answered by pulling my plait and winking.

I kicked at him and looked up to see Eb Holt watching us.

Before it was time to cook, Eb had lighted the coal oil fire. "Best chance you'll ever have to earn your salt, Goldilocks," he told me. "And cut out the funning while you're at it." He stopped to watch Green wipe sweat from his face. "County's got a rule against playing house at 'lasses time. Everybody save Bode and Ilish Trout lives it right."

I got so mad over that I stirred and stoked till I thought my arms would fall to the ground.

Eb sometimes used Bode's pitchfork to reach under the mill and clear out the twisted, split cane stalks gathering there. This was a fast tricky job that had to be done in time to Old Jack's movements without stopping the mule. Standing in place, Eb would duck, fork, and then pitch the gathered twisted stalks into a heap about twenty feet from the mill before he had to duck again. This pummy pile, as he called it, would be burned for stove kindling when dry.

At noon I was shaking so from the hard stirring I couldn't eat the plate of rice Aunt Ilish brought down. I laid down on the bridge after wetting myself from head to toe in the creek, a safe distance from Green Jenkins, while the men ate. They smoked after that, and again I tried to eat. Back stirring, I tried a third time, only to decide it was no use; the shaking wouldn't stop. The weather got hotter and hotter, and the fire didn't help. The growing pummy pile danced in front of my eyes. I was fighting such dizziness I worried about falling in the scalding, bubbly juice.

I hadn't known Eb was paying me the slightest note. Truth is, I'd have been more apt to think the other way round, for after growling at me for tempting Green Jenkins, he'd bent down at the mill to say something to Green that most likely had to do with Aunt Ilish and Bode. Whatever, it had caused Green to double his fist at Eb and snub me from then on. So I was surprised when Brother Dossie showed up late in the day to beg a jar of the first batch (for Aunt Cloma) and hear Eb tell him no.

"Goldilocks, she's petering out on me. You earn a jar, I'll give you a jar, by hell."

"It your 'lasses, Eb, or Brother Bode's?"

"Half mine, if I don't take the money. No matter how you look at it, you'll be dipping into some of my share. I'll let you have a jar, provide you work."

Brother Dossie's nose twitched. "What you mean I should do?"

"Get them stalks on the pummy pile, then spell Goldilocks so's she can rest and sleep. The cooking done, you can take your jar, beat it back up through the brush."

"The Lord helps us who helps ourselves," Brother Dossie said, rolling up his shirt sleeves and taking the pitchfork.

I stretched out in some tall, dried grass on the bank, rolled over once, and went to sleep.

It seemed well past midnight when I woke. The fire was still bright, and I could see Eb hunched over the pan, stirring. Bode and Green Jenkins were asleep between me and the fire.

I went over to Eb, who stopped to light a smoke.

"Guess you think I'm not much good for anything," I said, reaching for the ladle.

He beat me to it. "Reckon I know a wore out mishling'n I see one."

"I just got so weak . . . "

"No reason not to. I know who's been up both day and night tending Pop. He told me. I could see you'd had all you was able to take without sleep."

"Ain't you tired yet?" I watched the sweaty hair making spit curls on his chest.

"Nope."

"Well, let me know when you are." I dropped down several feet from the fire and took up a supper biscuit.

No sooner was I settled than he motioned me forward, saying, "Reckon I'm now ready to snooze." He slapped the ladle into my hand. "Stir slow, one hand at a time; won't tire you out so fast." He tweaked my plait exactly like Green Jenkins had done. "Might even put hair on your chest, like mine."

I worked till daylight alone, thinking of Eb Holt and the funny way he had of saying and doing the most kind, and unkind, things.

Aunt Ilish called our attention to the black, heavy clouds overhead when she came down to get water for Old Jack. "Looks like our prayers could finally be answered, praises be."

Eb pretended not to have heard. Turning his back to her, he took out his cigarette makings. He sang,

> Oh, it ain't going to rain no more
> So how in heck can I warsh my neck
> Since it ain't going to rain no more?

till Aunt Ilish dipped her bucket in the creek and started back to the house.

By breakfast, we had Bode's 'lasses crocked and loaded. Green and me had finished scrubbing the sticky cooker for Doc Helton's (bought) crop, and Bode had headed home. Eb, at the bridge on his way up to eat, called to me, "Let's go, Goldilocks," then, "Dammit, what in hell's this?" loud as he could.

Tired as I was, I didn't right away realize what sounded like rocks pelting the cooker was actually heavy drops of rain. Green Jenkins must not have been as numb as me. He took off after Bode, and, after a minute, I followed Eb and the mule.

Listening to the hard banging on the kitchen's sheet-iron roof, I downed my two lard-smeared pieces of sad bread in the doorway, watching the rain hitting the dust.

"Such a welcome to so many prayers at such a wrong time, such a bad time," Aunt Ilish kept saying as she ate.

Eb Holt drank his coffee in silence.

Hardly was the ground wet than here was Brother Dossie on his knees by the mudhole, his face skyward. "Oh, Almighty God, You have strengthened our faith in You from this minute on," he screamed over and over.

Eb waited by my side for him to finish.

"It'll slack up, stop, afore we get done eating," he said when Brother Dossie was inside. "Since you claim to've caused it, Dossie, stick close, help us work in the mud."

"Oh, you poor lost unbeliever," whispered Brother Dossie. He reached into the pan of biscuits on the table, lifted out four and stuck them inside his shirt. "I thank you, Good Lord, for this bread. It ain't every day me and Sister Cloma get something this good to eat. Amen."

Aunt Ilish reached out to touch Brother Dossie's muddied hand. "You're welcome, Brother Dossie. Thanky yourself for helping to bring this good rain," she said.

# 10

Theron Copeland slid sideways, fighting the swirly mud with every step up to the house. "What can you do, Eb?" he asked while still in the yard. "The rain rots my cane, I'll be hurt bad."

"Never heard tell of anyone caning in hard rain," Eb told him.

"Ain't no way to cover the buckets and juice while it's pouring so," said Bode Jenkins, who'd come back to help.

"Can't keep your cane from rotting in weather like this," Eb said.

"Can't cook with it coming down this hard," said Doc Helton, coming inside.

"Well, fix yourselves for rain nigh the rest of the week." Aunt Ilish touched her chest. "I can feel it right here, same way I feel a lot of things. Like this storm. Late last night, I told Milt so. Rain afore noon, I said."

Doc Helton took off his glasses and blinked. "Philco radio's report from Jeff City said the same thing, minute afore I left home."

Eb belched, rubbed his bare belly. "Ten minutes time, it'll stop, I say."

"What if it don't?" Doc was plainly worried. "Storm could flood folks out, radio said."

"It does, I'll get me a bottle and sleep it out." Eb studied us each in turn. "What's the rest of you aiming on?"

"Son." It was Milt from his bed. When Eb went into the front room, we heard Milt say, "My pop, remember, was a 'lasses man. Back in the September flood of '13, we. . . . "

Not much later, we were going again. Bode Jenkins had spaded a deeper trench around the cooker to keep the rain from running into the fire. Eb, Green, and Doc Helton had creased a piece of sheet iron from the barn roof into a tent-like shelter over the pan. I had the mule harnessed and was feeding Doc's cane through the mill and also watching the bucket. Green finally spelled me there when he got done helping cover the pan.

Bode mostly stirred, standing in the rain, the smoke under the new tent being unbearable. Eb worked the pummy pile and drove the mule at a steady pace, which wasn't very easy with Old Jack treading mud past his fetlocks. I kept feeding for Doc, who'd had to take off his glasses in the pouring rain. Eb told me to, for Doc's sake, because without his glasses he was nearly blind, and one wrong guess would gnaw his fingers to bloody pieces. Doc stayed behind me, keeping his pile moving up.

Lucy Lee Copeland's father, Theron, drove in with several old quilts to cover his cane. He jumped Eb as if the rain were his fault, yelling what was he going to do.

"Dammit, Theron, I'm doing the best I can!'

"You're not working my cane," Theron Copeland growled.

"Bode's got his done and he's sticking round to help out Doc. Why don't you quit bellyaching and do the same?" Eb was so riled his voice shook. "Doc's radio says the storm's a doozy. Only way to beat it's work night and day."

"How can we nights, Eb? We'd have to, to save us."

"Hell, we got lanterns, ain't we?"

"When do we sleep?"

"That's your worry. I don't aim to!"

"The mule hold out?"

"We'll all drop dead talking of work long afore Old Jack tires out."

They had their head together for a minute before Theron Copeland began loading his cane on his wagon. Three more wagons holding several men and boys came to a stop on the hill. Three men jumped Eb as one.

"I don't give a good god damn what you do!" Eb shouted to be heard above the rain, falling harder now. "You can't pitch in to help your neighbors and yourselves, load up and go home. You're slowing me down. Stay with it there, Old Jack. Little mud don't scare us none!"

Loud voices made me turn to see the Vestman wagon brake to an unsteady stop behind me. The entire bed was covered with a tarpaulin lashed at the sides with twine. The men gathered around him before he even lighted, probably wanting to blame him, too, for owning the mill, I thought.

"You got a radio like Doc's. When it said rain, why didn't you tell Eb Holt so's we could get our cane to shelter?" said one.

"That damn radio's been saying rain nigh every day for the last three year. All I hear on it goes in one ear and out the other," Urch told him.

"You still had some warning we didn't," Theron Copeland reminded.

"Why, you're all a bunch of Bible-reading, corncob-pipe-smoking old women, ever last one of you!" Urch's voice cut like a whip. "Don't take a smart man to see Eb's doing the best he can for everybody. There ain't a one amongst you who's not been in my store this past week saying Eb was taking money this year astead of a share, to bury his pop proper. With Milt Holt laying up there dying and every damn one of you owing him favors that date back some of 'em thirty years, favors he wouldn't let you pay back, how's about thinking of him now? Your cane can be saved, there's enough of us here. If Eb says so, I say the same!"

"What do we eat on, Urch?" someone called.

"When this storm started, men, I loaded up enough grub to feed an Arkansaw army. It's free for the taking. We can eat in the rain, sleep and cuss in it, if we get mad enough. But, by hell, we won't let it ruin us, will we?"

"You just ain't talking shit!" Eb called back.

"All righty then, let's go. All of you know what's to be done." He eyed the group. "Where's Brother Dossie?"

"Gone home, 'way back," Green Jenkins said.

"Well, Green, you go get him. He says one word, tell him at first snowfall and he comes to our doors with his little bucket, visiting, they'll all be slammed in his face if he don't chip in. Bode, you get up to the house and tell Burt Troat to get his weak back down here or I'll come up with a rope and drag him down. Theron Copeland, you pile for Doc. Doc, get your glasses back on, take you a rest. One of you take Green's place at the bucket. You, there, work the pummy pile. Hold it there, boy, whoever you are." He was speaking to a boy I didn't know either. "How's about you getting down in the mud up to your belly button and spell the feeder there?"

Somebody grabbed the cane from my hands and I slid on all fours out of the mule's path to the nearest wagon, mud from my knees down. The rest of me was sopping wet. It was almost impossible to see with the rain running in a steady stream down my eyelashes.

Onion Creek had swollen so the water was over the bridge. I stopped halfway across to rinse most of the mud from my overalls that had been Milt's, and realized it had been what seemed a week since I'd seen him last. The ache in my arms had worsened since I stopped work. Funny, I told myself, I hadn't noticed it lately. But if Eb could do this to give Milt a good burial, I'd be back down soon.

A hand raised me to my feet and I turned, hoping to see Eb. My skin crawled at seeing the jagged scar my teeth had left early last year on Nate Brice's arm.

I jerked free and took a step backwards. "What do you want?"

"I come to see the little girl I raised," he whined.

Sour puke that wouldn't come all the way up settled in my

throat when I saw this mean, whiskered face and whiffed the dirty clothes he wouldn't have had to wear if Bree were still alive.

"I don't even want you to look at me, Nate Brice." My head was making its sizzle sound again.

He bit his lips and went up to the house, careful not to touch me again as he passed.

Aunt Ilish spent a long time with him on the hewn log, leaving me to care for Milt, dog tired or not. I watched the man who'd taught me to hate as he kissed the woman who'd showed me how to hate more, and I thought they should have long been married to each other, they went together so well.

# 11

The men labored four days in the driving rain, Eb working them as hard as he did the mule. They took turns sleeping in Urch's wagon under the tarp. During the day, most staggered up the hill to fall into either my bed, Opal's or Burt's. Several of them bedded down in the barn. A few slept in Old Jack's shelter, Eb among them. When he felt the mule had gone his limit, he'd ride him up to the house, where both would grab a few precious hours sleep. During all that time, neither had much more than three hours rest in twenty-four. The workers fared better by a few hours' time, though all soon resembled Burt Troat in their beards and their smell.

My biggest job, discounting Milt, was constantly getting hot coffee across Onion Creek. By now the water was three feet higher than the bridge, and the men crossed with the help of Urch Vestman's rope tied to a post oak tree on either bank. The force of the water was such that I could only cross higher upstream by riding Eb swimming Delphie Doll, one hand clutching the coffee pot, the other holding onto the saddle horn for my very life. Looking back, I don't seem to have feared the muddy water swirling around my waist. I knew Eb was waiting for coffee on the low side and Milt needed me on the upper, and that was what most likely chased away all fear.

Opal was stranded at Doc's. I breathed easier knowing she was that far from Eb Holt. There was something passing between them that I didn't care to think about long. Poor Milt was out of his head often, calling for Jane Bell to bring his pipe. When he was himself, he worried if maybe Eb wasn't pushing the mule too hard. I told the biggest lie of my life by saying all the horses were taking their turns at the mill. The truth was, none but Old Jack worked, as Green Jenkins had taken all the other horses and mules except Delphie Doll home to their dry stables. Aunt Ilish stayed at the table most of those days in a mad silence. Whatever her thoughts were, she didn't tell.

On the fifth day it suddenly stopped raining about nine in the evening. Milt and my aunt were both asleep, and I stood on the high bank watching the men, who'd finished not fifteen minutes earlier, packing up by lantern light. The mud was so deep they couldn't get out until tomorrow, maybe the day following. Green Jenkins and the younger boys had been sent home to bring back the mules and horses at daylight, and the men who were too weary to walk home crossed over to stay all night at the house. Theron Copeland and Bode Jenkins were among those who left. Milt woke from his doze to greet his company like a little boy at Christmas seeing Santa Claus. He was the happiest I'd seen him since my first day here.

While Aunt Ilish, at Milt's side in the green bed, pretended sleep to get out of work, I fixed eats for the men. It was well into the night when they finally had their fill of coffee, fried bread, and some pork and beans brought by Urch Vestman. They commenced yawning and stretching out everywhere in the three rooms till there was no place left for me. I looked at Urch Vestman flopped on my devonette and Eb snoring in the rocker. I thought of the barn, then remembered Burt Troat would be there. The kitchen had men sleeping everywhere but on the table. The back room was full. The only dry place left was the hewn log on the house's north side, where the sheet-iron roof hung over it a foot or two. Somebody's big bare feet headed west, somebody else's pointed east. I took the space just my side that was under the washtub hanging on the wall.

I awoke to bright sunshine over the bridge coloring the soaked cedar trees with a golden glow.

A day and a half later, when the last of the water-logged wagons were pulling out, those loaded with fresh cane and dry wood were driving up at the creek.

Not a man whom Urch had tongue-lashed failed to give Eb a hand. The 'lasses crop was finished without a stalk of cane going sour. Milt smiled proud at the kindnesses his neighbors paid Old Jack, whose strength, like Eb's, was beyond question.

Before Eb went home to look after his house and pay a younger Jenkins boy for feeding his pigs, he got drunk. He spent the better part of an hour in the rocker, trying to coax Milt into singing, "It Ain't Going To Rain No More."

No matter to me that Burt Troat called Eb weak or that Aunt Ilish thought him a mule's ruby red rear end. I could still see him sliding barefoot in calf-high mud, driving a pack of whiners, more man than the whole of them together ever would be.

And every inch of him measured a foot tall.

# 12

By Aunt Ilish's word, the pummy pile took longer to dry that year than usual. Even then, the green kindling didn't always catch when the coal oil poured on it was lit. There was no such thing as spare paper on the place to use.

"Easier for you, looks like, to pull the newspaper off of the walls or burn up the Lynch Bible'n to cut dead kindling wood," she complained one day at breakfast.

"Ask Goldy Lark for some of the papers she rattles under her head all night," Burt butted in, on his way outside.

"You got papers in your sack?" Aunt Ilish asked me.

"Some grade cards and lessons I got E's on back home," I told her, surprised she hadn't looked for herself long ago. "And there's—"

She jumped ahead of me into the front room and to my devonette, where she grabbed my floursack and untied the end. Shaking it hard, she watched as my keepsakes, among them the paper Miss Emmer had given me with an A on it for memorizing

"The Cloud," and Eb's letter to me he'd written for Milt, dropped a few at a time to my bed.

"You sure that's all, Goldy Lark?"

"You won't find the money that letter said I had coming," I answered.

"Well, I found that out night after you moved in here," and she gave the sack another shake.

The pink silkies, which Opal, unknown to me, had hidden with my things, fell at my feet.

Aunt Ilish picked them up with her bare toes and slung them on my bed. "They're yours, reckon," she said, hands on her hips.

I thought it best to nod yes.

"Nate Brice buy 'em for you in Pelper County?" She spat on the hewn log, eyes flashing fire.

"Urch Vestman give 'em to me," I said.

She stuck her face close enough for me to catch her tobacco breath. "Why?"

"He said I was fifteen and pretty and they was a pretty."

She gave the floursack another rough shake. The *Missouri County Gazette*'s 1921 story of Harley Farker's death, which Mom had so often talked of having but hadn't let me see till just before her passing, landed atop the silkies. Aunt Ilish picked up the yellowed paper and read:

"Harley Farker of St. Louis, who came to Missouri County in November, 1919, died this week at the home of his wife, what's her name, at Onion Creek. Services at New Hill read by Reverend Dossie Lynch. Burial at Rard Cemetery. In addition to what's her name, he is survived by a week-old baby, Goldy Lark." There were a few more lines 'bout the law being unable to locate two of Harley Farker's sisters said to be living in St. Louis. If anybody knew their exact whereabouts, let Jessie Red McKay know.

Aunt Ilish picked up Milt's letter, my note from Miss Emmer Cox, and the other papers. "I'll use this as need be, starting with this." It was the newspaper story she held to my face.

Don't, Aunt Ilish, I wanted to say. That piece of paper's the only thing I've got of Harley Farker, it's all of him I ever will have. But the look in her eyes wouldn't let me, for I could see she wanted me to beg.

"And this." She held up the silkies.

I didn't open my mouth.

Gritting her teeth, she flounced to the kitchen and lifted the stove lid to throw in the paper and the silkies.

Opal flew into a temper fit when I told her that night at the bridge. Finally tired of cursing my aunt, she stretched out on her belly and cried like a hurt baby. "My silkies! My pretty pink silkies! Eb never got to see 'em on me! And I won't never have another pair so long's I live!"

Her words on my Eb Holt made me feel sure, that so long as I lived, I'd never again lie for her sake.

# 13

I was busy with breakfast dishes the day Eb Holt showed up guiding Urch Vestman's woodsaw behind Old Jack and Delphie Doll. "Well, Goldilocks," he greeted me inside, neither glad nor mad, "I reckon we got to hit the ball again, you and me. How's Pop like the 'lasses Bode Jenkins left him?"

I said it upset his innards so, I'd quit feeding him any.

"It being Bode's, I could've told you that." He growled at Burt, who was eating molasses thick with butter from a spoon. "Tell your pretty cousin there to put on his woodsaw clothes. Tell him he's got a whole minute to get in the notion."

"My back's not up to no cross-cut saw, Eb Holt," Burt said.

Eb helped himself to coffee. "Suit yourself. Cold weather comes, you'll stay in the back room with the door shut, freezing your big ass off, on account of I aim to be here to see to it you do."

"Ain't Goldy Lark help enough?" asked Aunt Ilish.

"I already got a job for her," Eb said.

"Well, you get Brother Dossie then."

"I care lesser if he freezes."

She was clanging her telephone a minute afterwards.

Eb Holt had the sled I'd helped him dig out of the mud behind the barn earlier, when Brother Dossie Lynch puffed into the yard. He let us all know, first off, he'd been busy praying for Missouri County at Aunt Ilish's call. But since it meant his winter wood, surely the Almighty would understand just this once. Burt seemed to have caught on it meant something to him, too. By the time I was garbed in Milt's old overalls and relief shirt, and a pair of his big work shoes on my feet, my cousin limped a lot less.

Burt Troat chose to walk to the woods rather than ride with the three of us and Old Mame. Brother Dossie rode on the sled's back end, kneeling in prayer. I hunkered almost under Eb's long legs, ready to grab one, if need be, on the bumpy ride to the woods.

And the need did arise once when we hit a rock that almost tipped the sled on its side. Brother Dossie, so deep in prayer, didn't notice. He hit the ground still praying. I looked back in time to see Burt bring him back to himself with a jab of the axe handle to his shoulder.

Just beyond the Lynch property line, on land said by Eb to belong to nobody, we halted. Wordless, Eb pointed to a dying post oak, and in a short while he and Brother Dossie had felled the tree. Burt, whining, chopped off the limbs as the other two sawed through the middle to make a proper fit for the sled. The second tree Burt had to help down. He swore with every zing of the saw. They lifted the two logs on the sled, where Eb lashed them with log chains wound tightly near each end.

"I want two more this size done by time we get back," he told Brother Dossie and Burt. "Let's go, Goldilocks."

"Just who in hell you think you are, Eb Holt?" Burt Troat growled, taking a step forward, his long arms fastened on the axe handle.

Eb picked up the checklines. "Your boss, looks like to me."

"Couldn't Goldy Lark take the logs home alone?" Brother Dossie asked. It was plain he didn't like the hard work any better than Burt.

"Got to show her how, first load," Eb said. "Gee up there, boy," he told Old Jack.

"Well damn you anyhow!" and Burt threw the axe with all his might at the nearest tree.

"Oh, come now, don't be a bad boy, Burt." Eb's face was beet red despite his teasing. "You like Arkansaw razorbacks, don't you? Bend your hurt little back a time or two and Santy Claus Eb might give you a bite of tenderline, come Christmas."

Eb walked on the high side, the checklines slack, warning me that if I didn't do likewise, the logs could loosen and mash me to a greasy spot. The hill leading down to the creek was the dangerous place. I was to try to hold the mule back, but if the load got away from me, I had to jump clear. Old Jack could look out for himself. Crossing Onion Creek where the buggy passed over wasn't my problem, either. Give the mule his head, stay on the high side. Before I knew it, the load would be at the woodpile.

"I can't lift these logs alone, Eb," I said, when Old Jack had stopped in the yard.

"Don't have to." He loosened the log chain, put his foot in the middle of the first log and pushed. It rolled easy, and so did the other one. "There, now. See how it's done?"

I was so scared at the big trust given me I was shaking in Milt's old shoes. Yet I'd far rather have died than admit I maybe couldn't bring in the logs.

By dinner, I'd hauled in twelve loads without mishap. Eb Holt told me at the table not to come back for at least two more hours, the men were far behind me now. Uncle Dossie had had to pray twice, and Burt's back was worse by the minute.

In three days' time we had a log pile nearly as high as the mule's barn. Eb thought it would see us and my uncle through all of the winter. The sun had yet to show mornings before he had the woodsaw going, calling Burt to rise and shine, ordering my aunt to tell Brother Dossie the day's work awaited. Both men dragged to work each day like the breath they'd just taken was sure to be their last.

It took all three men to lift each log onto a platform where it got cut stove-size when pushed against the whirring saw blade. Eb worked that end, the most dangerous job; for if he failed to watch closely, it would take only part of a second to lose a finger, hand, or an arm. Brother Dossie worked next to him, helping shove the logs in place for the next cut. Burt stood third, at the end pieces, always the smallest part of the tree. My job was to grab the ends as Burt dropped them by my feet and pitch them into a different pile for kindling. This was about the same woodsaw job I'd done for Eb at New Hill.

As each pile of the biggest sticks of wood—which were intended for the front room King Heater—grew to the height of the woodsaw, we'd all push the rubber-tired machine a few feet backward. For if the pile got uneven and started to roll, somebody might be badly hurt before he could get out of the way.

By the second day we'd worked ourselves back to the rail fence and still had forty logs to go. Urch Vestman, visiting Milt while old Villie tended the store, called attention to the fact that if we went much farther backward, we'd be sawing under water. "Wasn't the 'lasses making enough of a wet time?" he laughed.

He peeled off his shirt in the chilly autumn air and set to work stacking wood against the mule's shelter, to give Old Jack extra winter warmth. As soon as he'd cleared enough to give us more working room, we pushed the woodsaw closer to the log pile. Urch worked by us until near-darkness, splitting the heaviest logs in two.

The next day Urch was back with his own axe just as the last log was done, a while after dinner. Seeing him, Burt threw the last end-piece to the ground and started for the house. "I quit for the day. I hurt; to hell with it."

"Get your stinking self way out of my sight," was Eb's unexpected answer. "But come daylight tomorrow, you have your bad back bent over to what me and Urch don't get at today." To Brother Dossie, panting like a thirsty dog, he growled, "Haul yourself home, too. With Goldilocks and Urch helping, I won't need you back till morning neither."

When they were gone, Eb asked Urch if he had a bottle.

Urch patted both hip pockets and grinned. "We get done, I'll help you lay on a doozy."

It was late when we finished by lantern light, not even having stopped at noon. While they ate, Eb and Urch took turns washing down their cold, greasy fried potatoes and sad bread with deep swallows from the two brown bottles. Everything that was just as usual to me seemed funnier and funnier to them both.

They were laughing so much that when the time came to hitch Old Jack and Delphie Doll to pull the woodsaw back to Vestman's, neither could figure out how to do it. Eb rode the mule, the lantern high above the harness, and Urch rode the mare. They had another big problem at Onion Creek. Both wondered if the six-feet-wide woodsaw could cross the three-feet-wide bridge. I ended this worry by running down and guiding Old Jack to the buggy crossing. Eb was so busy telling Urch some joke about this little boy so smart he'd shit his pants three weeks ago and his parents didn't know it yet, and Urch was laughing so, they failed to see me.

Going up the hill, they sang:

> I got a gal in Kansas City,
> Who's got a gum boil on her titty . . .

The last I heard of them that night they were having a loud but friendly argument over, of all things on earth, the gum boil's exact whereabouts, left titty or right.

# 14

The rest of the week I kept busy stacking wood and splitting kindling, sleeping only when Milt did. Next was the way overdue corn shucking. I loaded the ears onto the sled and Old Jack dragged it to the barn manger. The fodder I put in the barn beside the bed. There was no other dry storing place there since we'd pulled off the sheet-iron roof on the barn's other side for the 'lasses making.

On the Friday before Halloween came chinking day. That meant take the washtub, the mule, and the sled up by the corn-field, where the best clay dirt was, and bring back one filled tub at a time. It took a good part of the day to mix the dirt with the right parts of water to make a thick paste. What time left was spent chinking mud between the foundation rocks for more winter warmth. Old Jack's shelter I was told to pass. My aunt said the linoleum—which I now cleaned every day in Milt's stead—would keep the winter winds from blowing up through cracks in the floor.

Chinking done, I had to gather two washtubs of wild 'simmons (persimmons) before Old Mame got there first. The first frost had been last night, changing the hard, bitter orange fruit into sweet, mushy balls. These I stored in relief pokes under Burt's cot; most would be used for winter pies.

The next day, Saturday, Eb Holt came unexpectedly as Opal and me were finishing the wash. He was the friendliest I'd ever seen him, also the drunkest. He actually politely asked my aunt's leave to fill the three house mattresses and the mule's, with new leaves, a yearly fall job. He was so comical I had to turn my head and smile. But I felt like fighting when he asked Opal to come along with us. It made me madder still when Aunt Ilish, freshly dressed and combed, went to look for mail, telling Burt to tend Milt in Opal's stead, she wouldn't be long.

I had more reason to boil in the woods near where we'd got winter's wood. While I scooped up leaves to stuff inside the center opening of Milt's mattress, which Eb wanted filled extra full, Eb and Opal busied themselves sticking leaves down each other's backs. Once, Opal screeched he'd used a mouse instead, get it out this minute, get the scary thing out. As Eb reached down her dress back, she screamed, jumped and twisted so that their faces came within inches of one another's. For one awful minute my heart turned over in tortured fear they would kiss. Opal, instead, stepped back to slap at him in play. He returned this with a whack to her rump. They rode the back end of the sled on our way home, their backs to me, whispering something Opal said I wasn't old enough to hear.

When we got in, I sewed up Milt's mattress, made the bed, and helped Eb lift Milt from the devonette where we'd moved him earlier. Opal stood back and watched, patting her plaits. She made no offer to help, either, when the time came to load her mattress, Burt's, and Old Jack's.

"Cussed mule needs a mattress bad's I need another ball," complained Burt, who hadn't helped us either. He bit into a 'simmon, made a face, and added, "Hell, even a hog knows all mules stand up to sleep."

"That's how you know, then," Opal said.

I had one foot on the sled for the second trip when Eb growled, "Stay with Pop, Goldilocks. We won't need you this trip."

"Burt's here," I said.

He made a fist and pointed it at me. "You got something ailing your ears, maybe, dammit?"

I clamped my teeth together to keep from answering and went inside, making a big effort to walk with a light step.

Aunt Ilish, dress wrinkled and pieces of dried leaves sticking in her hair, returned soon afterwards. In the kindest tone she'd ever used to me, she said, "Take a poke and go into the woods ahind New Hill for wild grapes. I plan to make some grape-and-'simmon pies for Monday night. I'll make a grape for you, provide you tote home a full sack."

"Monday night? What for?"

"Pie Supper at the school they hold on Halloween. The kids put on a program and all the women take pies for the men to bid on. Monday buys schoolbooks. Eb Holt, he hardly ever goes, he can keep watch on Milt."

"Opal going, too?" I held my breath waiting for her answer.

"She ain't missed one yet," I was told.

I went up towards New Hill, hoping Eb and Opal had gone to the same leafing place as before so I'd miss seeing them. Knowing what they might be up to made me want to cry. The one good thing about today was, Monday night they wouldn't be able to do the same thing again.

Directly in back of New Hill I found a thick crop of blue grapes vining up a big oak. I was busy picking when Green Jenkins came around the corner of New Hill, dusting the blackboard erasers for Miss Maudie. He caught me holding the sack in front of my knees to keep him from seeing up my dress.

"What else they learn you, asides tree climbing, down home these days?" he greeted, with a big smile.

"Go on away, Green Jenkins. Eb Holt don't want me to have any truck with you."

"Well, since when'd he buy up this part of the county?"

"I want you to leave me be, too."

"Girls your size don't run the world neither." He gave a wise wink. "All you're good for's to make it more fun for us men."

"I reckon you take after your gooser dad." All the hate I could raise went into my words.

He laughed. "Well, you're like your Aunt Ilish and look how good her and Pop's got on all these year." He ducked when I spat at his head and then added, "And from what I hear whispered on Bree Lynch, Pop didn't throw rocks at her neither."

"Likely he wouldn't throw rocks at anything in a skirt. Nothing to brag about," I said, picking faster.

He watched me several minutes with his Bode eyes and then asked, "You coming to the Pie Supper, Goldy Lark?"

"No."

"You bringing grape pie?"

"No."

"What color paper you wrapping it in?"

I didn't answer, so he turned and ran back to the school. In a short while he was back, jangling a key on a chain. "Get here early so's I can see the color of your paper," he called up. "You bring grape. I don't never bid on nothing else."

"I'm bringing 'simmon." My arms ached so from the sack's weight I was sure I would drop from the tree.

"Just like I said, Goldy Lark, bring 'simmon. Only kind I ever bid on." He whistled himself round the corner of New Hill and out of sight.

# 15

A big orange harvest moon was peeking over the foothills Monday night, partly lighting the way for my aunt, my cousins, and me. Burt Troat walked ahead of us, holding the lantern behind him for Aunt Ilish mostly, who was worried about getting mud on her pretty white high heels, a present at one time from Evelyn Helton, Opal said. She wore a long-sleeved pink tunic dress with a bow at her throat. I'd seen it often in the dresser and wondered why she never wore it, but had never guessed it was being saved for a special time such as tonight.

Opal and me, the cold hard rocks stinging my bare feet, she cussing the times a sharp rock gouged through the worn soles of her last winter's shoes, carried the pies. All three were grape, as it turned out, Burt having downed the 'simmons while he unseeded them earlier. Opal's pie was wrapped in green crepe paper, my aunt's in a pretty pink that matched her dress. Mine was dirty white, an end piece left over from the flowers Aunt Ilish said she'd placed on Henry Troat's grave last Decoration Day. Opal's had come from the part used for leaves. Aunt Ilish had told us it wasn't any of our business where she'd got hers. What mattered was it matched her dress, and it did to a T, didn't it?

Opal complained with every step she took. One reason was her blue government dress. "Mom's got her nerve, doing up the way she is when I got to wear this." Another was her need of new winter shoes. "These goddamn rocks, they're like stepping on icicles. Asides, I'm too old not to have a Sunday pair of shoes, too." Yet another gripe was the color of her pie wrap. "Goose-shit green! Who'd ever look at it twice? Nobody there'll bid on it, Goldy Lark." Still, I knew that, beneath it all, she was mad that Eb Holt hadn't come in my stead. She let me know that when a jagged rock drew blood on the side of her ankle.

"Shit fire and save matches, Goldy Lark Farker! Why couldn't you seen to Milt, like you're supposed to, and let Eb Holt come? Leastways, he'd hold my arm and guide me round these bastard rocks."

"He didn't want to come," I said.

"You don't know your ass from a hole in the ground," she snapped. "How in hell could you? You're only fifteen."

New Hill was lighted from a lamp on the teacher's desk, and a welcome fire was crackling in the stove. The school was as crowded as the day Hollyhock Jenkins found faith. At the door Aunt Ilish turned to take the three pies, in order to better push her way to the rostrum. "Letting herself get seen," Opal griped.

Where there had been talk and laughing at our entrance, a quiet now filled the school as Aunt Ilish went forward to a table built specially for tonight. Whether they watched Aunt Ilish because Milt lay dying and she dared go to a celebration or if it was because of her beauty in the pink dress, I couldn't have said.

Opal's temper fit reached its height when Aunt Ilish started back to us. She flew to stand on another side of the room, leaving me to be likened to my aunt. Burt, meantime, had joined a bunch of jostling grown boys at the back of the room, one of whom was Green Jenkins.

Miss Maudie stepped to the rostrum, rang the bell for order, and asked that all those standing be seated on the floor; the program would begin. Opal, I could see, had settled on the knee of a C.C.C. boy. Bode Jenkins, nearby, offered his spare knee (one was holding Virgie and baby Elmer) to my aunt, but she had the mule sense not to notice. Instead she picked the lap of Nate Brice, who, though he directed his invitation to her, was gawking hard at me. I pretended not to know him and dropped to the cold floorboards without looking behind me. The someone I bumped turned out to be a pale, blank-faced Hollyhock Jenkins. She was so thin, I saw, she might also have been dying from consumption, like Milt. She didn't seem to remember me.

Lucy Lee Copeland, her red hair hanging in sausage curls, her eyes on Green Jenkins, started the program with "A cool October brings the pheasant . . . "

Doc Helton's younger girls sang about Autumn next. The Jenkins kids, including Green, acted out a short play following that. One of the younger girls held up a dead tree limb and said, "What am I? Can you say?" The others answered, "A dogwood, asleep till Spring, for I am Mother Nature in my Autumn dress come to protect you in your long nap under Winter's snow." And so on, till it was Green's turn. He was so busy looking at me he forgot his part and just threw down his hands and went back to Burt.

The little Copeland boys ended the program with a song.

Urch Vestman, in his suit of clothes complete with necktie, auctioned off the pies. Holding the pie above his head, Urch would sing-song, "And this one smells like dried apples, so it must be dried apples and you all know who makes the best dried apple pies and how much'll you pay?" Virgie Jenkins' had one of those. It sold for a whole dollar, bought by none other than Bode. Miss Maudie Troat's, also apple, was bid on by Burt and Doc Helton. Burt outbid him by a nickel, the going price being $1.25. Theron Copeland bought Evelyn Helton's, a pumpkin, for $1.30. Doc returned the favor to Theron by paying a whole two dollars for Mrs. Copeland's gooseberry pie. The money went into a shoe box on teacher's desk.

Opal's was the first in our family to come up. While Urch

showed it I saw her nudge the camp boy, who offered a quick $1.50. There were no other fast bidders.

"Aw, come on now," Urch teased. "A delicious big grape pie like this going so cheap, that's like voting Republican, plain low down." The crowd cheered. "Can't anybody offer me a nickel, a dime more!"

Another camp boy on the other side of Opal bid $1.60.

Urch shook his head. "Can't let this one go, boys, for less'n two. That's what I'm bidding myself. Who'll beat me a dime?"

The boy Opal had nudged went to $2.15, and he followed her out the door for his prize. Opal's face as she flounced by had a look that plainly said, "There, mine cost the most, and I guess you all know where to kiss."

As life willed it, Aunt Ilish's pie followed Opal's. A great number of bids went up, but Nate Brice's high of $1.75 won. His walk to the rostrum drew heavy clapping from the men, for a reason I could fully understand. As my aunt and my mom's second husband went out the door to eat by the light of the lanterns, strung here and there in the trees, I happened to notice the face of Virgie Jenkins. She looked like a hen froze in the middle of laying an extra big egg. That made the first and the last time I ever saw her show any feeling of any kind toward Aunt Ilish.

I could tell when Lucy Lee Copeland's pie was up for sale by the way she blushed and tried to give Green Jenkins a hand sign. Thumbs in his overalls bib, he leaned against the wall, pretending not to notice. I knew then he actually was waiting for my pie. Urch Vestman himself bought Lucy Lee's pie for $2.00.

My own pie came up next and it was then down to Hollyhock Jenkins and me, the only two teenage girls left. I died a thousand deaths when Urch Vestman held my pie up, hoping anybody but Green Jenkins would buy it.

And then Urch Vestman was speaking to Green Jenkins and the few camp boys left, "Now, New Hill needs your money to buy books with and if there's a one of you down there dying to eat with a pretty girl, who'll be first to bid on this yummy pie and what am I bid?"

My heart stopped beating when one of the camp boys stood up. "A dollar here," he said.

Green Jenkins jumped to his feet before the boy set down again and raised the bid to $1.50.

"$1.55," another boy called.

Green bested him by a dime.

"Aw, come on, boys," Urch said.

When Hollyhock Jenkins stood up and slipped outside in a hurry, I saw all eyes land on me.

"Well, I'll give you $2.00," called Green Jenkins.

"Sold!" Urch told him. "Now let's eat."

While Green paid, I forgot the pie in my run for the door. Green overtook me on the path home, caught me in his arms and kissed my mouth, slobbery kisses that tasted like wet spit. I couldn't believe his skin: soft like a baby's, with no beard at all. Even with my eyes clamped tight, he was still Green Jenkins; he could never hope to be Eb Holt.

# 16

Green Jenkins walked me down to Onion Creek, sharing his coat, asking that we stick to the old rule that said every time either of us stubbed a toe, we had to kiss. It came to three times. His kisses still tasted exactly like wet spit.

I dropped beside him on the woodpile. "Say what you want to in a hurry, Green. I can't stay long."

"Goldy Lark," he started, "marry me. I can take care of you all right. I'll turn eighteen, few weeks time. We can go down to Arkansaw and tie the knot without anybody's say-so but ours."

"I'll have to see." Close to laughing, I hadn't the meanness in me to tell him I had my heart set on somebody I had to have or not live.

"Goldy Lark, I can't wait. I got to get your true blue promise tonight."

"Ask Lucy Lee Copeland," I said, kind as I knew how. "She's crazy for you, Green."

"Lucy Lee's fine to play house with. It's you I want to marry, Goldy Lark."

"You do that with Lucy Lee?"

"Look, Goldy Lark. Pop laid down the law and Theron Copeland, he laid down the same one. Us Jenkins kids can't walk home with the Copeland's after school, all acause of a goddamn gooseberry bush or two. One day at school last year, I looked real good at Lucy Lee and I liked what I saw. So I said how's about meeting me tonight after dark at Onion Creek, right at the damn gooseberry patch. We been meeting there, whenever I want her, ever since. Ain't my fault she's gone moon-eyed. I never did promise to marry her, like I'm asking you, believe me."

I said I did.

"Since I met you, Goldy Lark, I ain't been back there so much. I don't want Lucy Lee Copeland that way anymore. I don't want her any way. You're who I want the rest of my life."

I stood up, shakier than before at what I'd heard, and started inside, Green following. He caught me at the kitchen door.

"Don't," I said when he reached for me.

"Will you see me tomorrow night, Goldy Lark, at the bridge? You don't, it might be too late. Pop's signing me up with the C.C.C.s to get me away from here."

"Away from Lucy Lee?"

"No. From Goldy Lark," he said.

"What's Bode got against me?"

A match flared in the yard. "You got born, you little bitch!" Eb Holt lit his cigarette and I realized he'd been there all along, listening. He started toward the mudhole, walking slow.

"Be seeing you," Green called. He was already at the corner of the house.

"You ever show your hide 'round here again sparking, Green Jenkins, I'll beat your ass, I swear it!" I could tell Eb was cold sober. "And you Goldilocks . . . " He grabbed my arm and wrung it so hard I nearly cried out.

"He just walked me home, Eb. He bought my pie." I was suddenly afraid of him. "We didn't do anything wrong."

He loosened my arm to slap me so hard my teeth hurt. "And that's not the half of it. You ain't going to."

I held back tears, making no reply.

He slapped me again. "God damn you, why'd you have to be birthed looking like Ilish Troat?"

"Eb, we just kissed," was all I could say.

"You so damn dumb you can't tell he's got a bone for you? You get knocked up, by hell, you'll still not get him," he promised and shoved me with all his might.

I landed in the cold mudhole, the rock step cutting into my knee.

Eb picked me up and brushed me through the kitchen door. "I ought to killed you with my bare hands the day I went to Rard to get you. Who in hell'd ever miss another hot-assed Lynch?"

I cried myself to sleep when he left.

Eb's next visit to Milt brought word that Green Jenkins was set to marry Lucy Lee Copeland in Rard on Saturday morning. She had left school the day after the Pie Supper when she'd puked at her desk. Bode Jenkins and Theron Copeland had ended their long feud by agreeing that the wedding between Bode's son and Theron's daughter take place soon as could be. Lucy Lee, Eb said Urch Vestman guessed, was probably four months on the way with another mouth to feed, as Eb put it, on government relief and Vestman credit.

# 17

Uncle Sam in Rard had sent Milt a heavy shirt to wear in bed, so one morning Aunt Ilish dug deep in the back room rag box and pulled out his old winter coat. "Here, Goldy Lark. Milt won't need it again, it's yours now. Can't have you catch your death of cold when I need you so bad to help me."

One look at the ragged gray coat that Milt had stained so bad and most of its buttons missing, and I guess I turned up my nose without noticing.

"Heap sight better'n the coat your brought on the train, which was no coat at all," she snapped. "Now you forget it ain't clean and girly fancy and hie yourself up to the store. Get Milt's medicine on your way back at Doc's."

"Aunt Ilish, couldn't you get me a girl's pretty coat from the relief?"

"Talk Urch Vestman out of one, if you want it so bad." Her eyes flashed fire. "Well, you got some silkies from him, free of charge. Don't cost nothing to try for a coat."

"I'd sooner be cold," I said, remembering Bree and some of the men she'd slept with to keep us from starving to death.

"We'll see," I was told.

At the rock marking our property line, Old Jack shied at Brother Dossie Lynch, bundled up against the chilly winds, stepping from behind a tree. Without even a greeting, he asked how often I went to Vestman's store.

"Twice a week, guess. Sometimes I don't get past Doc's, though. Milt needs a lot of medicine these days."

"Can you ride to Vestman's each time from now on?"

"I guess so," I said.

"And don't mention it to nobody, not even Sister Ilish. What I'm doing's a powerful big surprise."

I promised.

He reached behind the property rock and drew forth a dirty floursack he showed me that held a goodly amount of coins. "Fifty whole dollar here, Goldy Lark. I want you should swap this for paper money."

"I will, but what if Urch asks what they're for?"

"You tell him, come the first spring robin, I'll commence the great church I've built in my head all these year, and I need bills handy. Tell him not to tell on me, now."

I tied the sack to the saddle horn. "You'll have fifty dollar waiting each time I go by?"

He nodded. "I hollowed out under our property rock and covered the hole so's it won't show. You just stick your hand in, it'll be there. Coming back, if I'm not here, leave the bills in the floursack, poke it in the hole. I trust you to do this for me?"

"You must've thought you could, else you wouldn't have asked me, first place."

Urch Vestman said it was high time Brother Dossie started his big church, and don't worry, he'd be the last to spoil somebody's pleasure. He was alone in the store, for which I was thankful, as things turned out.

I'd put the money in my coat pocket, gathered up the coal oil,

Harper's Homespun, salt, and Brother Dossie's sack, and was almost to the door when Urch called me back.

"Goldy Lark, if it's any of my business, how's come you got on a pair of shoes I sold Milt two year back?"

"They fit perfectly good." (My toes reached halfway to the tips.)

"Pretty good ain't good enough for old Urch. Set down, I'll get you something more your size."

"Urch, I ain't got no money," I said.

"Well, now, can't I give you a Christmas present early?"

"Aunt Ilish burnt the silkies," I told him.

"Why'd you tell her you had 'em?"

"They fell out of my things."

"Well, I can't send you back in them old shoes. I don't care what she thinks," he said, reddening in the face. "You give me Brother Dossie's money, I'll sell you some warm gear. You tell him I said if he's too lazy to come out in the cold, you need warm gear to go out for him. Tell him what the people giveth, Urch Vestman taketh away, you hear me?"

"I can't do that," I said. "He'll . . . "

"He tells on me, I tell on him. You tell him so."

He laid a pair of boy boots nigh my size on the counter. A red winter shirt and a pair of boy's blue jeans followed several pairs of long ribbed socks.

I handed the sacks back, saying, "Milt, he don't have no socks and he's laying cold's ice. I'll take mine in his size."

Wordless, he added up for my things and took the amount from Brother Dossie's bills. He wrote "Paid in full" across a piece of paper with my name on it, stuck it in his pocket. "Case anybody asks," he said, "I was paid." He pointed to my new gear. "You can wear it home, Goldy Lark."

I pulled the blue jeans on over my clothes, wriggled into the new shirt and slipped the boots over my icy toes. Putting on Milt's old coat, I took up Brother Dossie's sack and headed outside. My hand was on the door knob when a pair of long ribbed socks were laid on my shoulder.

"Already took out for these, Goldy Lark. Just forgot to tell you so," Urch called.

He was lying, I knew, but my feet were so cold I couldn't argue. At the rock, I found Brother Dossie waiting. He took my story with a funny smile. "See it don't happen again," he growled and ran into the woods, cradling the money sack to his heart.

Aunt Ilish didn't let me off so easy. She wouldn't believe me when I said Urch had given me my clothes, and I couldn't tell her about Brother Dossie's money without breaking my promise to him. She accused me of having Pelper County money hid back, like she'd felt all along.

It ended with her riding Old Jack up to Vestman's before I could unsaddle him. Urch must have told her the same thing I had. Because, for a while, she let me be.

# 18

Before mid-November, Milt suddenly worsened, causing me to spend one whole night at his side without closing my eyes once. The next noon, someone screaming brought me to. My first thought was that Milt had died and it was my aunt carrying on so. The sounds, though, were coming from the back room.

I jumped up, pushed the door open and ran in to find Burt pinning Opal's arms to the bed. Aunt Ilish stood over her, lashing her bare back with the mule whip. Each time it cut her flesh, Opal screamed in pain; her cries going unheard, save for me.

"You aim to tell me what you done with the money, Opal?" my aunt screeched with each crack of the whip. "You aim to say or don't you?"

"That hurts, Mom! Piss on you!" Opal screamed back.

"Opal, if you had to diddle, why didn't you get a tap like the one I got in Rard?" Her eyes were crazy wild.

"Uncle Sam wouldn't give one to a single girl, that's why. Even when I said it was for you, he still wouldn't."

Aunt Ilish snorted. "Me with my man laying in there half dead and you tell a person like Uncle Sam I've wore out my tap diddling him? Damn you, Opal, all the way to everlasting hell!" The whip cracked again.

"Don't, Mom, I can't take no more! I'll tell, I'll tell!"

"That's more like it." My aunt, puffing hard, dropped down on Burt's cot and reached for her chew. "Leave her be, Burt. She's learnt it don't pay to try to put something over on somebody smarter'n her."

Opal, tears flooding her face, crawled halfway from bed and began feeling for her clothes. "Under the barn manger, Mom, on Old Jack's feed side. In a fruit jar. I hid it all not spent on sodey pop."

"Get yourself back to bed, Opal," my aunt said. "I ain't even started with you yet."

"What's Opal done?" I asked.

"Nothing, Goldy Lark, nothing at all." Aunt Ilish looked very tired suddenly and almost her age. "She's just going to have a baby, that's all."

"Fugged every boy in the C.C.C. camp, I'd bet my balls, at two bits a ride." Burt sounded a little ashamed of his sister not charging more. "First little bastard to come into the world with three hundred and seventy-two daddies, now that's really, truly something to be proud of."

"Well, it ain't about to come into this world," snapped his mother. "I don't know much else right now, but that much I'll swear to. Saddle the mule, Goldy Lark, and hie up the hill. Tell Urch to give you a pair of shoes in Opal's size, winter ones. Stop off at Doc's on your way back and say Opal's caught grippe, she'll need a few days abed. And get Evelyn's big Monkey Ward catalog while you're at it. You don't have to blab I finally got the means to buy me a new dress." She spat at the closed door. "A black one, for Milt's funeral."

"That all, Aunt Ilish?"

"You get me a hot warter syringe and all the fixings. Tell Urch it's for Milt's hung gut. You say anything else, you'll answer to Burt, you hear me?"

Opal was crying when I left.

On my return, Milt was a big worry. He lay deathly still, his hard breathing from throughout the night now a natural rest. Too quiet for a man whose every breath might well be his last.

"Forget him," my aunt answered when I asked. "It's Opal I'm busy with now."

"Didn't Milt even wake up to eat?"

"Didn't give him a chance to. Melted down four times his medicine dose while you was gone, Burt helped me spoon it down. Milt, he won't know from boo what's going on."

"What's to happen?" I asked.

"Your only job's to get me a tub of warter heating up and see to it nobody, and I don't care who it might be, gets closer'n the bridge. Give 'em any reason you think of. Well, go on. You know how to lie, don't you?"

For a long time I hunkered against a rock on the low side of Onion Creek, my hands over my ears in a vain try to shut out Opal's screams. What Aunt Ilish and Burt were doing to her, I could pretty nigh guess. I'd heard Mom and Nate Brice talking once about a single girl in the family whose father had made her lose her baby by flooding her insides with hot water. The girl had died soon afterwards. My heart leaped at the thought Opal might not be here to wear her new winter shoes I'd just brought from Vestman's. (Maybe they'd fit me.)

When Aunt Ilish finally called me, she said, "You go in there and get a good gander at what'll happen to you, too, if you get a mind to mess with a boy you ain't married to," and I found Opal asleep, pale and quiet as Milt. The black bruises covering her thin shoulders could only have been caused by Burt's powerful arms pinning her to her bed. The hot water syringe had been pitched with her new shoes atop the rag box, the long terrible tube partway hid under the mattress. I kicked it out of sight, not daring to ask if Opal's life was fading away, and set to work on all fours mopping up the still-steaming spilled water.

At sundown, both Milt and Opal were awake, he hungry for the supper I'd fixed of soup and cornbread. The extra doses of medicine didn't seem to have bothered him nearly as much as they had me.

I took Opal a plate of eats, only to have her reach out and heave it against the wall above the rag box. "Tell that God damn sum bitching baccer worm who calls herself human, I said if she ever looks straight at me again, I'll cut out her heart, if I can find it, and make her precious baccer worm little boy eat it raw. You tell her I wanted my kid, no matter who its daddy was. You tell her she ought to killed me while she had me down, acause she just let me live to become the biggest whore this here county's ever seen."

"Opal," I whispered, so close to her I could smell the stockdip on her back cuts, "who told?"

"Nobody. She heard me puke mornings. Oh, damn her to hell and back!" She settled on her mattress and cried hard. "Now she's took my baby and all my money and, asides that, Goldy Lark, all my pretty storebought soap was out there, too." She wiped at her nose. "No more pink silkies in my life and now never again all the sodey pop I want!"

Before bedtime, there was certain signs she was no longer in the family way.

Aunt Ilish paid Urch Vestman for Opal's new shoes before sending off her order to Montgomery Ward. The funeral dress she bought with my cousin's sin money came around Christmas, a bright yellow lace with a satin sash at the waist. But the coat she'd ordered to go with it was all black. Just right to wear to Milt's funeral over the pretty new dress.

# 19

Eb Holt had been helping several neighbors with their hog butchering. As planned, before, he would move in with us for the winter, bringing his own pigs for us to kill and eat. He was usually finished by the first part of November, but it was past Thanksgiving when he rode in driving his two Arkansaw razorbacks—one that Burt Troat had stolen last July, and two others that were all white. Deaf to my aunt's whining he put up fence rails and turned the pigs loose to run in the yard, saying tomorrow we'd butcher. The hogs headed straight for the mudhole, causing a bigger stinking mess.

Eb paid no mind to my aunt's complaining. Having put Delphie Doll to winter in the barn on the bed side, he left as quick as he'd come. He stepped into the yard a while later carrying two homemade rabbit traps and a steel trap, and the rest of his things in a floursack on his back. He pitched the sack on the devonette by mine, then, seeing Milt was asleep, he said he'd stay till Milt's passing, like it or not. He almost smiled at me when I said we'd had rabbit traps just like that in Pelper County and I knew how to bait them and pull out a caught rabbit feet first. "I'll tote a big hickory stick, too, to kill 'em with, you want me to help you," I added.

"You can't hit the hide. Ruins it," he said.

"I hit the back of their heads," I said.

"Shows you got a little sense, Goldilocks. Them hides bring in a quarter apiece."

The steel trap was just for red foxes, he told me. "You come get me and the rifle, if we trap one. They're mean, bitey little shits, but their hide brings in a dollar apiece."

He had all three traps in place before dark. "Rabbit ones close to the creek, up by the field. Steel trap's near the mouth of Onion Creek. Pop always thought a red fox family lived there. I put in some sad bread while I was at it, though I won't have time to check 'em till butchering's done, reckon."

"Ain't you afraid Aunt Cloma'll step on the steel trap?" I asked.

"I just told Dossie not to let her out alone," he said.

He stayed outside most of the rest of the day, sharpening his two butcher knives on a whetstone kept in the barn and cleaning Milt's rifle. Twice I called him to supper; twice, no answer.

I went out for night wood before dark and saw Eb on the woodpile, watching his hogs walk through the mudhole. It took ten trips to stack enough wood against the front room wall nearest the kitchen stove to keep Milt warm all night. I don't think Eb Holt even knew how many times I passed by, he was so busy with his own thoughts.

Opal, her face older than her age nowadays, came up the path behind my aunt on my last trip, her head wrapped in a floursack. She had on a dirty, torn coat that had seen many winters, most of them on Aunt Ilish's back; it was a lot like the one of Milt's I wore, though a better fit. Aunt Ilish, wearing her brand new coat, went around to the front door rather than pass the hoggy mudhole. Not Opal. Seeing Eb, she stopped to smile.

"Opal," I heard him say, "you still true to me?"

"I dream of you night after night," she kidded back, a little of her old self showing.

"Bet a pretty you don't dream the kind of dreams I do about you."

Supper done, Eb Holt made for the rocker with his bottle to go on what my aunt called a "sinful toot," soon telling us all to go to hell and stay there. "You first, ripe pussy, afore I send you there," he told Opal.

She laughed. "You're a little bit late, Eb Holt. All my life, I ain't been no place else."

# 20

I was awakened many hours before daylight by the tip of Eb's rough boot jabbing my rump. "Show life, Goldilocks. Hard day ahead."

"Look, I just go to sleep, Eb. Milt coughed so—"

His big hand whacked my head. "We get done butchering, I aim to take you up to Doc's, get your ears looked at."

I got up wearily and pulled on my new shirt over the old relief dress I slept in. My new boots and jeans I hadn't removed, one reason being that I had but one quilt, with Milt needing so many; another was that I had to get up many times during the night, for the house would become freezing cold if I let the fire die.

My first chore was breakfast for all, the watering the mule, the hauling more water for dishes, and still more in the two borrowed tubs I helped Eb carry up to start boiling on the stove. The members of my family, for the most part, crowded the fire. Opal was waiting for time to go to work, my aunt and Burt for daylight. While Eb built a fire in the yard by the strongest cedar, I tried to call Brother Dossie on the telephoney to help, but I got no reply. I figured he was too busy guarding his church money and counting it into fifty-dollar piles to bother.

"Save Old Jack's horseshoes," Eb said when I offered to go to the cabin. "He won't help, he won't beg meat. Be more for Pop and me that way."

He stood by the fire till daylight grayed over the ridge, then called for Burt to hop to.

"See this little piece of rope, Burt Troat?" He used the same tone you would to a three-year-old. "See that razorback rooting there by the step? Well, you take this little piece of rope, you tie it around his neck like you'd had practice, and you lead him down to the bridge, where you tie him up. Wait there for me and Goldilocks to bring the mule, that one with the harness on," for Burt was still watching the hog, "and a knife and the gun. Do like you're told and I'll give you a choice of shooting him or cutting his throat. What's your pick?"

I never asked why it was my fault the pig flopped in the water when he died; I was beginning to learn that the less said about anything these days, the better. Burt's aim, clean between the eyes, had stunned the pig enough for Eb to leap astraddle and with one plunge cut three-fourths of his throat. Icy water splattered us all when he bit bottom. Eb, cursing at me, dropped the bloody knife in time to catch a hind leg as the carcass bounced. In two seconds flat, he'd fastened a log chain to the pig's ankles and would the other end of the chain to Old Jack's harness.

Eb called to leave the knife and gun, we'd be back. Old Jack strained hard to bring the body up the steep creek bank. The pig was a sick mix of muddy, bloody hair by the time he was dragged into the yard.

To make matters worse, I almost forgot to shut the rails behind me, and the second razorback, who likely felt his hanging doom, had three feet through the gate to freedom when Eb threw a rock, turning his path in time. The rock whizzed so close to my head it all but cut another part in my hair, this one on the side.

Several boards borrowed from the barn's side a while ago had been placed near the fire. It took all three of us to heave the carcass onto the boards, where it was splattered with two tubs of boiling water. Burt and me got sent back for two more tubs while Eb and my aunt dropped to their knees and commenced scraping away hair with the butcher knives. We put the extra two tubs of water on the outside fire to have handy. When the pig was completely naked, we hoisted him with the log chain to the lowest, thickest cedar limb.

Eb, with one hefty whack, axed his body open. I had to nearly stand under him with a tub to catch the smelly, smoking innards.

They'd be washed and stuffed, probably later tonight, with the sausage ground by Vestman's hand-cranked grinder.

More boiling water was then splattered inside and out, more was used to clean the boards, where we's lay him for Eb to cut up. Burt's and my running path to the creek for more water caused several other problems. One of these was that I couldn't do many things at one time. I caught Old Mame feasting on a half bucket of the pig's innards seconds before Eb looked that way.

I put her in the house to stop at least one more quarrel.

Aunt Ilish and I carried the quartered meat in to the tablie when the men went down to kill a second pib. So, rather than trust a now-sleeping Old Mame not to wake up and help herself, I tied her with bindertwine to the hewn log. My next chore, having helped fill the tubs again, was to watch the remaining guts to see that no late flies got near. The first pig's gorey head had been slung, nose up, in the bucket. It's creepy dead eyes followed me, no matter which way I turned.

Near dinner time, I cut three sticks, jabbed the hog liver and heart on the end of one, and roasted them over the fire for the others to eat as they worked. Butchering was akin to 'lasses making in that, once started, there was little slowing till done. Where we'd had the rains to fight before, the sky was now heavy with snow clouds and strong puffs of winter winds were blowing in from the north.

"Be lucky if we finish afore them clouds get overhead," Eb said, lighting the second smoke I'd seen him take all day.

"You worry too much over nothing. Won't snow till I get the last bit of lard ready to render out," argued Aunt Ilish, spitting to one side as she spoke. Some of the tobacco juice came flying back to sting me in the eye, but she was too busy to notice.

I took Milt some fresh liver and a heart when Eb told me, paying no mind to the dog, who'd broken her string and was sneaking past. Milt mumbled he wasn't hungry. He turned over wearily, saying maybe tonight. Eating the meat from the stick, I brought him a pill and begged him to swallow, which took a long while.

Back at the fire, I spied the dog gnawing on the first pig's nose the same second Eb saw it. Eb jumped to his feet, grabbed the hog's head and threw it at the dog with all his might. "Well, God damn you, you starving cooner, eat!"

Old Mame, who knew how to duck too, grabbed her prize and commenced to drag it behind the house.

"Feed the mule," Eb told me. "You can't do anything else right, looks like."

I fed Old Jack corn nubbins with one hand while my other hand fanned at flies that weren't there. Having replaced the mule's bridle, I asked Eb how Old Jack could drink, since there was no empty tub.

He pointed to the creek. "Whole lot of warter just down the hill yunder."

"Won't kill him, he's drunk it afore," my aunt butted in.

"Well get him down there, dammit. Can't you hear?"

On my way to the creek I smiled to think that for once my aunt and Eb Holt were of one mind. What next?

It turned out Old Jack didn't mind cold creek water nearly as much as Milt thought he did.

During the scraping of the third pig, Milt let out such a yell that even the howling winds couldn't drown him out. Eb reached his side ahead of me, but he was unable to turn Milt over with such sticky hands. I turned him easily, however, for Milt weighed so little now, and then brought him a rag from the washpan for his burning forehead.

"You want Jane Bell, Milt?" I asked. "She's right here in her rocker shelling peas."

"Tell her to touch me, I hurt bad."

I touched his cold cheek. "Can you feel her now?"

Both his sweaty hands fastened on mine. "Don't leave me, Jane. Don't ever go away and leave me again." And he sunk down, fighting for breath.

Eb looked from his father to me. "I reckon nobody's all the way useless, are they, Goldilocks? Don't you get off that bed again 'less I say so, hear me?"

My head propped against the wall, I got the longest sleep in several weeks that day, Milt not stirring again all the while. It was past dark when I awoke. The others, now including Opal, were still hard at work. I could sees her standing between me and the mule's window, stirring something on the stove. Burt, from where I could hear, was grinding the stuff for sausage or head cheese at the cabinet. An argument came up between Eb and Aunt Ilish about where to store the meat. She favored the barn. He pointed out that if her little Burt wouldn't eat it, the dog would. Then what was wrong with it under one of the back room beds, say, Opal's? The dog again. No, she couldn't be tied up; she'd howl, and that would bother Milt.

"You had a smoke house ahind the woodpile when I went into the C.C.C.s," Eb said. "What happened to it?"

"Little Burt got cold that winter and burnt it," Opal said.

They finally decided the only smart answer was to hang the meat from the roof rafters of Old Jack's room with bindertwine and bob wire, and all of us take turns watching the window.

Now that the sausage-cooking was going on, the whole house held a delicious smell, and my hungry insides growled so the leaves rustled beneath me. I faced a choice of eating and being blamed wrong for something that had happened while I slept, or playing smart and keeping quiet. In a very short while I dozed off again.

Sometime in the night Milt brought me up with a sharp pull at my sleeve. I fixed him some oatmeal on the front room stove, which was still burning bright, telling me someone had been up till only a short while ago. Milt ate a few spoonfuls, took his medicine, and settled back, partly clear-headed, to ask what had happened yesterday.

"We butchered Eb's hogs. That means sausage and tenderline for breakfast; meat cracklings in a day or so."

"That all, Goldy Lark?"

I told him about the dog stealing the hog's head, expecting him to smile. Instead, he looked at me funny and said, "You mean nobody come?"

"Eb's here to stay. He's asleep in the rocker." I didn't add that Eb had said last night that he hated us all too much to ever sleep in a Lynch bed.

"Ilish here?"

"She's sleeping on the devonette, Milt, so's I can stay by you."

Next he was worrying about Roosevelt winning the coming

election. "Don't want him to beat my man from that town called Kansas."

I couldn't find the heart to tell him the election had been held over a year ago, 1936, and that his pick had lost. "You know it's snowing out, Milt?" I could see the white flakes piling up on the window rags behind Eb's head.

"I wet myself," he answered.

We kept up this way of talk till the pill got the best of him.

When I was sure everybody was asleep, I sneaked down into the kitchen. I was able to find the breadpan on the pink cabinet with three biscuits still on it. The skillet, with melted hog grease nearly to the top, rested on the nearest stick of wood. I ate faster than even Burt, dipping the bread into the delicious salted grease until I finally had my fill.

I crawled back in beside Milt and slept like I'd just been born.

Morning showed three feet of snow had fallen in the night. My aunt's last two old hens were found on the hewn log, frozen stiff.

Eb Holt started off the second day of his life with us by having an argument with Aunt Ilish over what we'd eat for dinner, chicken and relief noodles or tenderline with sop and sad bread. Old Mame brought peace by helping herself to the two brown leghorns while my aunt was boiling the water to clean them in.

# 21

The long cold winter had started with the first snow, and from each day until Christmas the weather dropped a degree daily, according to the thermometer at Vestman's store. Onion Creek completely froze over. When there wasn't snow to melt, Eb had to chop a hole in the ice above the bridge to get drinking water for us and the animals.

Christmas Day, because Milt asked it, Eb stayed sober. Brother Dossie, bearing a jar of gooseberries, came to visit. Save for a fast blessing for the fruit given Theron Copeland by the Good Lord, then passed on by him, and now received by us, he hadn't much to say. If Milt's sickness bothered him, it didn't show.

"Say," Eb asked Brother Dossie on his way out, "how's come you didn't get hungry enough to help us hog-butcher?"

"I was praying so that day, I forgot to eat. Clean forgot," Brother Dossie said.

"Hope your prayers get you through the winter, acause the meat you ain't going to get from me won't," Eb told him.

Opal, regaining some of the color she had lost during her nightmare, sat tight-lipped throughout the day. I knew she'd welcomed some of the camp boys at least twice in the barn bed. Aunt Ilish was also using the barn for her business with Bode Jenkins and Nate Brice. Nothing short of a miracle had kept their paths from crossing at the same time.

Burt Troat, as it happened, had bumped into Brother Dossie Lynch at the creek. He came running in to tell his mother that Brother Dossie had promised to baptize him—providing the creek wasn't frozen over and Burt could stand the icy water—Sunday next.

"Hallelujah!" cried my aunt. "So you finally believe in Brother Dossie, praises be!"

Burt laughed. "That'll be the day bulls have titties. It's to get Miss Maudie back sleeping with me I want. Tired of coming in my hand."

"Miss Maudie aim to give me half her teacher's wages a month when she's back under my roof?" Aunt Ilish asked.

"Split her sixty dollar a month, you and Bode," Burt said. "All I want's her ass."

Taking the dollar Eb had finally paid me for working the cane crop and helping with the schoolhouse woodsawing, I rode the mule to Vestman's a few days before Christmas. I'd searched through the store for a present for Milt and finally found a shiny star for Old Jack's bridle. Urch had set it in place with bright copper brads, making it too fancy for words. Milt couldn't have been happier. He wasn't satisfied with just seeing his present, he had to know how it looked on his mule.

And so, Christmas morn, I led Old Jack in, expecting my aunt to throw a temper fit. She surprised me by standing quietly aside, watching tight-lipped as Milt petted his mule and blubbered his thanks.

But I knew she hadn't let it pass that easy when she followed me to the woodpile to say, "Eb Holt, he gives you a hard-earned dollar acause he feels sorry for you, and you don't show the sense of a bedbug, you throw it away! Well, you happy now, Goldy Lark? You feel good about it, huh?"

I didn't dare smile and show her just how good I did feel. Eb had bought Milt a new pair of long johns. He helped me wash Milt's newest bed sores and salve and change him. His sad, teary blue eyes that met mine over Milt's skeleton body, nearly tore my heart in two. Doc Helton, on the lie of listening to Milt's chest the week before, had lifted Milt to turn him over. He told me and Eb later that Milt's weight was less than ninety pounds, if he judged right. "I don't see how he's held on this long," he'd said. There wasn't much he could do about the stinking bed sores. At least, a heavier dose of medicine would keep Milt from knowing his backside was blood-raw from new bed sores coming on each week.

So that Christmas, for one short minute, Eb Holt and me had been of one mind without a word passing between us.

I'd thought the bridle star and the underwear were the only presents bought, but I turned out to be wrong. Going outside for nature, Opal tied a bright yellow scarf round her head, offering no reason for having it. She didn't have to tell me it had been passed on the sly by Eb, for I'd seen a tip of it sticking out through his shirt when we'd washed Milt.

I felt a sinking sickness inside me the remainder of the day; I had had the fool notion the scarf was meant for me.

The following Sunday Brother Dossie, without a congregation, braved the cold to baptize Burt Troat in near-zero weather. Miss Maudie, her clothes and a few books in a floursack, hugged Burt when he was back on the bridge, shaking "like a dog shitting peach seeds," as Eb Holt described it. Aunt Ilish pitched a quilt in Brother Dossie's direction and knelt in several inches of snow to offer thanks for Burt's salvation from the fire and brimstone of damnation.

"I could smell your pureness from up here," Opal told Burt, when, hanging onto his wife, he came in to get warm.

Even Eb had to drunkenly agree that Burt Troat had been made clean in more ways than one.

While the others had dinner, I tried to help Miss Maudie get settled by sweeping a place under Burt's cot for her few belongings. I was on all fours trying to bring out all the dust—for the back room hadn't been swept right for a very long time—when Burt entered. He put his heavy shoe on the back of my neck and shoved my nose down near the dirt.

"What you poking under my bed for, Goldy Lark? Expect to find gold, maybe?"

I got free and managed to stand. "I was sweeping up."

He grabbed the broom. "Any sweeping under here, I do."

Backing away, I bumped into Eb leaning in the doorway, fumbling with his cigarette makings. "What's your hurry, Goldilocks? Ilish Troat's little boy lay a hand on you?"

"Go on, Goldy Lark. Say what I said," Burt dared.

"He didn't touch me," I said, trying to move past.

Eb caught my arm. "And he ain't aiming to, are you, Burt Troat? Leastways, till I tell him he's got my say-so. You got that down, Burt Troat?"

Burt's answer was to throw down the broom and take Miss Maudie, clothes and all, to bed.

# 21

Right after Christmas there was another letter from Miss Emmer Cox. "Dear Goldy Lark, please keep your promise and write me. I'm very lonely now with Roy at Lotoe College and Freeman gone most of the time. I miss you very much and hope you're well and happy there. Merry Christmas."

I tore her letter into little pieces and watched the wind carry them away. I truly hoped never to hear from her again. The times I would remember Pelper County, I wanted only to recollect Bree. There was nobody else I wanted brought to mind.

Most days now I hadn't time to think of anybody but poor Milt. He had worsened, becoming a helpless baby at times. Hard coughing caused him to mess his long johns at least once a day. Even with the two new pair I'd got at Vestman's, it was very hard to keep him clean and dry. When Eb let me tend the traps in his stead, I was glad to get out in the fresh air, away from Milt's bad smell.

I carried a stout club to the rabbit traps, also sad bread, in case we had caught one and I had to re-bait. If there was a rabbit, I'd club it and bring it down to the woodpile, where Eb's big knife was stuck under the tarp to deep it dry. After I'd cut off the rabbit's head and feet, I'd slit its belly and leave its guts on the ground for Old Mame, then pull off the hide easy. Eb would then nail the hide tight to a board before hanging it over my devonette wall to dry. Some man from Rard would come to Vestman's twice monthly to buy the hides.

"Holler extry loud if there's a fox trapped," Eb would say when I'd leave to check the three traps.

Always dreading to go back to the house again, I'd take my time at the rabbit traps. They were made from hollow logs about twenty inches long, with a board nailed across the back end. The front had a frame on all sides of the door, with a trigger to let a little door fall down fast when the bread was touched. Unable to turn round and try to push the door open, a rabbit was easy to pull out by its back feet and kill. The dumb thing would just lay still and watch you, not fighting back.

Nearing the steep trap, my heart always beat faster. If there was a red fox caught, it wouldn't die easy. He might chew off his trapped leg, I knew, and come after me, thinking I'd caused his pain. Sometimes some small animal stole the bait without hitting the trigger. The times this happened, I had to lay on more bait without triggering the trap, and I didn't breathe easy until I was back in the yard.

Eb had hid the steel trap behind two tall rocks, causing me to be nigh on it before I saw it. That and a bad head cold was why I couldn't know the trap was sprung the morning I almost walked smack into a snarling skunk. I saw it the minute it saw me. In one eye blink, we were back to back, me running, him spraying. The last few inches of my plaits caught some of the spray; Milt's old coat took the rest.

Likely Eb smelled me coming; he was on the path with the rifle before I got halfway home. Holding his nose, he called, "Get some warter on," when he ran past me.

147

Aunt Ilish started gagging at the sight of me and wouldn't let me in the house, so all I could do was stand outside in the cold, stomping my feet to keep warm, thankful my eyes didn't burn too bad and that I couldn't smell at all.

"Run down to Bode's for some lye soap and a jar of maters," Eb ordered my aunt when he got back home and they had a tub of water heating on the stove.

"I-I-g-got some from Virgie last week," Aunt Ilish, still gagging, said.

"Open 'em. Then let's get this tub on the floor and you get some big rags to dry her off. Find me the damn scissors quick!"

"They're in the devonette," I said. When Eb had found them, he said, "Unplait your hair and get your ass over here."

"Now, you ain't aiming to do what I think, Eb Holt," my aunt stopped gagging long enough to say. "A woman's crowning glory's her long hair, the Bible says."

"It ain't when I have to sleep in the same room with her, Ilish Troat," Eb said.

"N-No, E-Eb." Gagging again, she was trying to take the scissors from Eb's hand. When he finally shoved her hard against the wall, she said, "Oh, I wish my Burt was here," and she commenced wringing her hands as she gagged.

"You don't care nothing about Goldilocks' hair, Ilish Troat," Eb told her. He set the filled water bucket atop the stove. "Now dry up, dammit, and stay out of my way."

Eb quickly sawed off my long hair with the rusty scissors, blew the loose hair from my shoulders, and growled, "Get in the kitchen, take everything off. Throw 'em out the door and I'll burn 'em with your coat."

"E-Eb, not her c-coat! I can't get her another'n now!"

"Goldilocks," Eb called me from outside, "wash the rest of you afore your hair. I'll stay out here till you're done."

My ears and neck were freezing cold for the first time I could remember. I got out of the tub after washing myself and bent over to rub the homemade soap on my head. After scratching it good, I dipped my head in the tub twice, dried myself fast and pulled on my clothes before I called Eb. He rubbed the jar of tomatoes into my hair hard before throwing a warm bucket of water over my head. I smelled just fine to me and thought I must smell good to Aunt Ilish, too. She was no longer gagging, but sitting by the front room fire, and she let me crawl under my bed covers to get warm.

"Ain't nothing I can do about Meadow Lark's turning over in her grave when she knows this," she said over and over.

Eb Holt called me "Boy Goldilocks" when he saw me with my hair dry and starting to curl. Burt Troat laughed loud when he got back from Vestman's, slapped his thigh and asked, "Who tried to cut off your head and missed?" causing Aunt Ilish to tighten her mouth and shake her head.

It was Opal who really surprised me by saying, "Why, Goldy Lark, you'd be right pretty if you didn't look like your Aunt Ilish." Several times before bedtime, she touched my hair, then reached up to feel her own plaits. I thought she must be real jealous of me, and it felt good to think so.

Since we burned the lamp all night in case Milt needed me fast, I got up once to feed the fire, glancing at myself in the looking-glass as I passed the dresser. I had become prettier since moving to Onion Creek, I saw with happy feelings; no two ways about it. Now I looked a lot less like Aunt Ilish, I swear it, and a lot more like my Bree, save for my darker complexion. Thinking I'd look like this when I was finally somebody, I smiled at myself noticing that my mouth was pretty, too, for the first time. Thinking maybe Eb Holt would fall for me now, I finally crawled back into my bed.

Both Opal and my aunt were late coming back from Helton's the next day, and we'd already started eating when their angry voices sounded from the bridge. Aunt Ilish came in first, mad as a wet hen, with several scratches on her face and a black eye, to boot.

"That little bitch's just let Evelyn Helton help send her to hell!" she screeched, taking her place at the table. "Not only that, Evelyn Helton took a dime out of my week's dollar, too."

I saw what she'd meant at Opal's entrance. For not only was my cousin's face scratched and bleeding, her hair had been bobbed exactly the same way as mine.

"I'll be damned," said Burt and Eb together.

Aunt Ilish pointed a long finger at Opal. "That's the one who's damned, right there! Oh, I could see the bad signs on you all last summer, Opal."

"I thought you'd like it," Opal smiled.

Eb, eyeing Opal, said, "You look just like little Bree," and gave her a big wink.

"I said we don't say that name in this house, Eb Holt!' Aunt Ilish was on her feet, doubling her fist like a man.

"That might be what you told Boy Goldilocks," Eb said. "Me, I can say anything I want to, wherever I am," and he laughed.

"Not in my house," she screeched.

Eb swallowed the bread he was chewing and said, in her tone, "I'll be out of your house the day Pop dies, Ilish Troat."

"Goody. Take Opal and Goldy Lark with you."

"I never get that drunk," he laughed.

To make things worse, Jessie Red McKay came one Saturday with a brand new pair of boy jeans, a heavy shirt like Milt had on, and a brand-new boy's sheepskin coat from Uncle Sam's relief office.

"Heard tell you tangled with a polecat, Goldy Lark Farker." Noticing my bobbed hair, he added with a smile, "Why, girl, bet you're nigh's pretty's my daddy used to say your little mommy was."

This so riled Aunt Ilish she made me do Milt's wash before bedtime and hang it by lantern light across the rail fence in the falling snow.

And then I saw my Eb Holt reaching into Opal's bloomers as she trimmed his hair with Evelyn Helton's new sharp scissors, and the sizzling pain returned to my head.

After that, even with my new warm clothes on, the house felt colder and the long nights even longer than before.

# BOOK THREE

# 1

The March weather's warming brought down Brother Dossie Lynch. Without even giving him time for a prayer, Eb told him, "Next time you hear the telephoney jangle, it'll mean Pop's gone, so you get here quick. I'll be in need of you."

"Wanting me to pray that Brother Milt's soul's in Paradise," Brother Dossie said sadly, wiping his whiskered chin.

"No," Eb growled. "I'll want you to help me get his body to the undertaker at Rard."

Brother Dossie cornered me at the barn when I was getting dinner raisins to ask if I'd taken the money left earlier that morning under the rock.

I said I had.

"That was the last I need. Now, you pray for Brother Milt's soul," and he went down the creek path.

During the worst of the weather, Jessie Red McKay had brought our relief down by car as far as New Hill, where he'd stacked it against our mailbox. Eb and Burt had taken turns sledding it down to the house with the mule. The March thaw meant long, hard trips to Rard, so on the month's first good relief day, a Friday, both Aunt Ilish and Burt offered to make the ride. I harnessed Old Jack and steadied him till my aunt and Burt were in the buggy seat and Opal and Miss Maudie in the buggy bed. Miss Maudie would get off at New Hill for her last day of the term, and Opal would get off at Doc Helton's. I knew all four were going much too early in order to get away from the terrible rotten smell of Milt.

I went inside to find Eb Holt tearing the inside back room door from its hinges. The last of our winter wood, including all the kindling chips and the cane pummy pile, was now long gone. Milt, so yellow and smelly, lay shivering under almost every spare quilt in the house. There was only one thing to be done, and so I shouldered the axe and followed the buggy's ruts as far as No Man's Land.

By noon I'd cut and toted home several armloads of wood. On my last trip I noticed that Milt was peacefully asleep. Eb, pulling a batch of biscuits from the oven, asked how many I wanted to eat.

"I ain't hungry," I said.

"You take three or four anyhow, stick 'em in your pocket. Cut close to the road and wait there, you hear me, for Vestman's wagon to get back from town so's you can load up the wood and come home with the others. When the wagon's unloaded, you take it back up to Vestman's, bring the buggy home."

"What if you need wood sooner?"

"I won't. You just do's I say."

I chopped fast and without eats. I just couldn't choke down a bite for thinking of poor Milt suffering so. Vestman's wagon, also bringing back Miss Maudie, returned from town soon after I heard the term's last school bell being rung.

"Hurry up, Goldy Lark," Aunt Ilish called as me and Burt loaded as much of the wood as would fit in the wagon bed with the relief: "There's something bad happening at the house; I can just feel it here in my heart."

"Tell her Bode's likely been up and she's missed her daily fugg," said Opal.

Burt grinned wide. "Well, I didn't get all I wanted last night myself. Miss Maudie, she was awful busy with grade cards."

"There's always tonight for you," Opal told him.

Burt climbed up into the wagon seat and took up the reins. "Ain't that right?" He grinned and added, "Well, girls, looks like the wagon's full. Guess who's got to walk home, now."

"Go play with yourself," Opal told him.

"May God forgive them both for such sinful talk at a time like this," Miss Maudie whispered into the air.

We were almost to Onion Creek when my heart rolled over at the ringing of my aunt's telephone. I knew it was Eb Holt calling the news of Milt's passing to Brother Dossie Lynch. Milt had passed away four days before my birthday, about sixteen years and two weeks from the day Harley Farker died.

# 2

Eb met us at the mudhole, his weary red eyes and whiskered face turning to one at a time. "Well," he finally said when nobody spoke, "he passed on peaceful, spite of all he's gone through. Go in and see him, if you want to."

We all stood back like bashful children afraid to join in a game, except Aunt Ilish, who dropped to the ground to pray.

"You taking him out tonight?" Burt soon asked.

"When the wagon's unloaded," Eb said.

"I'm going back up to Doc's," Opal said, almost in a whisper. "I can't stay here and see Milt go out; I'm not that big. I'll see if I can stay at Doc's till funeral time."

"You need help building his coffin, I can drive a nail," Burt offered.

"Done got him a storebought'n put back at the Rard undertaker. It's all paid for with 'lasses money. Aim to sell Delphie Doll to get him a fine suit of clothes. Pop's going to have a right good funeral, like he give my mom."

"When is it?" my aunt asked, rising and dusting her knees.

"Monday, early's we want it. On his own say-so."

"You mean Milt come to afore he died?"

Eb nodded. "Goldilocks, if you don't want to go in, how's about getting the grub and wood unloaded afore dark?" He turned to Aunt Ilish. "What you got in mind to do?"

"Go to Brother Dossie's till funeral time. I don't like to be in a house where the Death Angel's just been. You go with me, Burt."

"You go by yourself. I'm taking off to Bode's with Miss Maudie."

"Can't you stay and help Goldilocks till I'm back?" Eb asked my aunt.

"I got worries enough of my own," answered Aunt Ilish, heading down the path after Burt's wife. "Goldy Lark, you put down in the Lynch family Bible about Milt's going and what took him. And you get all that smell out of the house tonight, you hear me?"

"I'll wait and help you and Uncle Dossie load him," Burt said.

"Don't touch my poor pop, Burt Troat, you ain't fit to. Just haul ass out of here!"

Scarcely was Burt out of sight than there was Brother Dossie puffing up the path in such a hurry one of his overall straps hadn't been hooked yet. "Oh, God, have mercy on poor Brother Milt's soul. When did it happen, Eb?"

"Quarter hour ago maybe, no more. Come on, Goldilocks, I'll give you a hand on the wagon."

I watched silently as they carried Milt's quilt-wrapped corpse across the bridge and laid it carefully in the wagon bed. Eb took up the checklines and started Vestman's horses and my uncle steadied the body. The lump in my throat grew bigger with each turn of the wagon wheels.

Inside, I got the Lynch Bible from the dresser. "Much loved by his son, Eban Milton, and almost like a father to me, Goldy Lark Farker," I wrote after the particulars of Milt's death, and signed my name.

I spent a long time looking at the empty bed trying to cry, but no tears would come. Milt was gone forever, like last winter. But so was his pain. The only thing I could do for him now would be to ready the house for the company that would be coming to pay him respects. I started by dragging his smelly mattress onto the ash pile, where I burned it along with his pillow.

Next I buried his plate, cup, spoon, and spit pan in a deep hole I dug by lantern light close to the creek banks, throwing in with them his bed sores salve. His other medicine and some old clothes he'd worn toward the end and his forehead rags, I pitched on the hot ashes. Soon they were nothing, too, like Milt.

Despite my scrubbing everything he'd touched, the house still smelled of sick, sick Milt. I fixed a fire, heated a tub of water, poured in the better part of a bottle of stockdip, and set to work scouring all three rooms. When each piece of furniture had been washed fully, even Milt's old warped fiddle, and that dried off, I dumped the tub of water on the back room floor. Using my aunt's worn buckbrush broom, I swept the steaming water into the front room, next to the kitchen, then to the mudhole. The only thing left to do now was wait for Milt's body to be brought back home.

Old Mame, all this time, was hunkered on the devonette, whining pitifully, her sad eyes looking from Milt's empty bed to me. I stooped once to pat her head. "He's gone, and he ain't coming back," I told her. "He's dead and gone and I feel bad's you do."

The empty, stripped bed bothered me the more I thought about it. Suddenly, I remembered Opal's mattress and that the coming company would need a place to sit. With a lot of struggling, I got it on the green bed. I covered it with the best quilt I could find that hadn't been near Milt's face. Opal could help me fill her a new mattress after Milt's funeral on Monday.

Wondering if Aunt Ilish had some floursacks for a mattress tick and knowing I'd be in bad if she didn't, I told myself I didn't care and sat down by the dog to wait. It hadn't yet come to me to be afraid of being alone in a House of Death, as Aunt Ilish had called it. I'd just been doing a job for the sake of a man who'd have done no less for me.

It was Old Mame's actions that first got me jumpy. By then she was shaking so much I'd ordered her outside. She refused, instead jumping into my lap and licking my face. Her whining grew to nearly a howl. At this time I blew out the lamp and settled into the darkness to wait for Eb. A thousand times I imagined Milt's tortured coughing and the rustle of the bed leaves when he turned over to find his spit pan. Soon I could all but see him shaking hands with Harley Farker, saying, "I done the best for Goldy Lark I could down there." I wondered if Harley Farker would tell how much it hurt when Old Nance's shoes tore out his innards, and if he'd ask about Mom and me.

A loud noise at the woodpile, that of someone falling against the chop block, sent me hurrying for the rifle and to aim it where I judged the kitchen door to be. Only after thinking maybe I'd dreamed the noise did my heart stop pounding long enough to make breathing easier.

Then, without warning, the kitchen latch was lifted and a being I couldn't see padded inside, the feet stopping at the water bucket. My hair stood on end at the heavy breathing from this something I felt could see me, though it was formless to my eyes. Old Mame, in her sorrow, had neither barked nor entirely stopped her whine.

When I knew I couldn't stand it any longer and live, I cocked the rifle and aimed the barrel straight at where the water bucket must be. I shut my eyes, ready to shoot.

Amid the dog's whine and my chattering teeth, came the pitiful: "Little Nonny died today. I can't find her no place."

I caught my breath only after I was at the telephone, calling Aunt Ilish to come for Aunt Cloma on the run.

# 3

As Milt's coffin rested on New Hill's right side rostrum, Miss Maudie led the congregation into "Will The Circle Be Unbroken?" in a voice choked with tears. I sat on the aisle side nearest the coffin, Eb Holt between me and Opal. Next to her was Burt, and on the far end sat Aunt Ilish, dry-eyed. From time to time she quieted Aunt Cloma, who probably cried because Brother Dossie, at the pulpit, cried for the church brother he had lost.

Most of the hundred and fifty-some people passing (according to Sheriff McKay's account, which would appear later in the *Missouri County Gazette* I read at the store) were strangers to me. Urch Vestman was the first I knew. He halted suddenly, his reached hand seeming to fight the desire to touch Milt's shoulder. He covered his face with his hands instead and staggered from the aisle to the back of the room.

Fat old Villie was next. As he waddled past us, he turned his piggy head in a hateful glance at me before stopping at the coffin. There, he dropped to his fat knees and snorted into a red bandana.

Doc Helton, holding sniffly Evelyn, got up from the right recital bench and went to see Milt's body, the girls following in a line. I'd seen tears standing in Doc's eyes when he was unable to ease Milt's suffering toward the end. Now he stood quietly, and after a minute's time, led his family back.

A well-dressed man from the government office passed after the Helton's. I knew who he was because Opal had told me beforehand he attended the funerals of all the county people on relief in order to report straight back to President Roosevelt himself. He must have had a different name, but I knew him only as Uncle Sam.

Behind him was Sheriff Jessie McKay in his brown outfit. Two deputies I didn't know, shiny badges on their shirts, stood a few steps back. McKay's badge almost looked like a button on his broad chest, the pistol butt sticking out from his pocket a toy capgun. He bent to lay something on Milt's shirt. I couldn't think why he had done so until I remembered how, yesterday at the house, some unknown woman had told Evelyn Helton, "Milt was a deputy, I forgot." And Evelyn Helton had whispered, "Don't you recollect it was him who always caught Ilish's first husband, Henry Troat, for stealing Vestman's seed corn? And how Milt arrested Burt Troat twice for trying to buy a car under Milt's name when poor Milt couldn't even write his own name?"

The singing had long finished when the Jenkins family passed. Miss Maudie got in line behind her mother and lifted her little brother Elmer from Virgie's arms. Virgie, I saw then, was far along the way to another baby. Maybe it was on purpose that, when Green Jenkins walked by with a waddling Lucy Lee, he touched my shoulder and looked down to meet my eyes. Whose face was saddest, his or Lucy Lee's, I couldn't have said. And when Hollyhock Jenkins stopped to see Milt, Brother Dossie lifted his eyes to give her a glance she didn't return. She broke the line to race to Virgie's side and help Bode lead his crying, praying-aloud wife back down the aisle.

Life had willed that Nate Brice follow Bode. Such a hush then came over the crowd, the awful silence lasting until Nate had passed through the door. I knew it was one of my aunt's lovers following the other that had caused the stillness. I'd heard several men in our yard during the last three days joking over who'd be the first, Nate or Bode, to sleep with Aunt Ilish after Milt's funeral.

Between strangers, I saw the Theron Copelands and a great many of the C.C.C. boys whom I was sure, Opal could call by name. I could tell by the way my aunt was looking that she didn't know most of the people. She was giving them her frown that said the whole business was holding up other fish she had to fry.

The line moved very slowly, as was to be expected from the size of the crowd. About the last twenty or so were soaked to the skin from the hard spring shower that had started without my notice. It was not beating so hard on the sheet-iron roof that it almost drowned out the women's cries.

Women who maybe never saw Milt Holt twice in his whole life could stand there crying at his passing, I told myself, while here is his widow, dry-eyed these past few days.

The line finally came to an end without me realizing it, I was so deep in thought. The four pallbearers, Urch Vestman, Doc Helton, Theron Copeland, and Jessie Red McKay, had gathered at the rostrum, two on each side of the coffin. Since the funeral service had been preached earlier than the singing, Brother Dossie now called for a prayer that ended with, "Blessed are the mourners, for they shall be comforted."

He then called Aunt Ilish's name as the one "who's been called upon to bear the worst, having to bury her good husband and God joined together with her in this very church."

Aunt Ilish got to her feet wobbly, not being used to the white high heels she hadn't worn since Halloween, and went to stand before Milt's body. I saw her stiff, straight back slouch in a fair try at sorrow, her thick black plaits hanging below her small waist under the new black coat. And then I remembered Opal screaming for her life in the back room and found myself wondering for a few seconds why she hadn't died that day and left Eb Holt for me.

When Brother Dossie thought the one with the "heaviest heart, asides his son," had looked long enough, he called Eb's name. "Brother Milt's grown son by his first wife, good Jane Bell, who sold his mare, one of his few earthly belongings, for clothes for his father to wear to the grave," got up from the recital bench to quickly walk to his father's remains. He might have been Milt standing there, save for his dark hair; he looked so much like him it choked me.

And then Aunt Ilish's own "two poor children" by her first marriage to Henry Troat, "who thought as much of Brother Milt Holt as they did their own father," went forward, each to stand at the side of my aunt. Burt was wallowing in his mouth a thick bite of Harper's Homespun he'd pulled from Aunt Ilish's dress front when we were at home. Opal was scratching one of her thighs through the stiff, pink lace dress, with floursack piecing tacked to the hem to give it a decent length, that Evelyn Helton had lent her just for today.

Aunt Cloma followed my cousins to the rostrum, carrying little Nonny in her arms. The shelf bearing the words "Missouri Farmers Association" in giant red letters had been folded where she judged the baby's head to be in the blanket.

My ears were pounding when I heard Brother Dossie say, "And my poor little orphan niece, Goldy Lark Farker, last August taken into Brother Milt's home to be raised as one of his very own."

I stood, shaky, and went for the last time to look upon a face I'd never seen in life. The Rard undertaker had filled out and colored Milt's cheeks to a pinkish tan that hadn't shown during our short acquaintance. He'd shaved him and combed his hair to show a clean white scalp that hadn't been Milt at all. He'd dressed him in a snow-white shirt, a black coat, and matching pants with a shiny black belt. On his feet were a pair of brand new shoes. His old fiddle rested against his chin. He smelled like the orange I'd got from Bree in Pelper County one Christmas long, long ago.

# 4

Milt Holt's coffin was hauled to Rard in Vestman's wagon, Brother Dossie and old Villie riding in the bed while Urch drove. Eb kept Old Jack steady behind them, sharing the buggy seat with Aunt Ilish. Opal and I sat in the buggy's back end with our feet dangling over the road. Old Mame and Aunt Ilish walked behind us, just ahead of Bode Jenkins' crowded wagon that held Burt Troat and the Jenkins family.

"Goldilocks, you get out and walk a ways, let your Aunt Cloma have your place," Eb told me at the store. He'd had to brake fast when a wheel loosened on Vestman's wagon and Bode Jenkins almost ran into Aunt Cloma at our sudden stop.

I tried to talk Aunt Cloma into getting up in the buggy bed. I even tried to lift her up, with Opal's help. She shook her head no. She clawed Bode when he tried to get her into his wagon, and screamed loud when Brother Dossie dropped her easy in Urch's.

"Leave her be," he finally said, setting her down in the muddy road rut.

Aunt Cloma wiped her nose and her eyes on her dresstail and smiled once when she was back in place alongside Old Mame.

She was so pitiful sliding in the muddy rivulets, slowing up the long line, picking out rocks from between the toes of her left foot, having lost that shoe somewhere along the road. My heart pained when I saw her little Nonny fall in the mud. She picked her up, brushed her blanket, and hummed her back to sleep, keeping in step with the dog.

Opal and I both smiled when tired Old Mame, much smarter than Aunt Cloma, jumped up between us for the rest of the ride.

It was a long way to the graveyard. We traveled slowly and the rain pounded us every inch of the way.

Ever since coming to Missouri County, I'd wondered what I would do upon seeing my father's grave. Likely fall to my knees and have to be dragged screaming from the graveyard? I'd done that when they buried Bree. But it would be several hours after Milt's burial that I recollected having stood almost at the foot of Harley Farker's grave and thought only of Eb Holt and done nothing more than hold him tight, our tears mixing with Opal's on his shirt. It should have bothered me then that I felt nothing for Harley Farker and maybe never had cared. But I did hate Opal with all my heart for even touching my man.

"Rest in peace, Pop, rest in peace," Eb whispered to himself as we walked from Milt's grave. The crowd had stepped aside to let Burt, Miss Maudie, Aunt Ilish, and Brother Dossie pass ahead of us. To one side, Sheriff McKay was pulling Aunt Cloma from the fresh muddy mounds of a little Nonny she suddenly remembered once being laid to rest there. I didn't see Urch Vestman at the time, though as Aunt Ilish reached the gate, old Villie jumped in her path.

"Mishling!' He twisted up his hateful red face and spat on her shoe. "Mishling! Mishling! Mishling!"

She lifted her head several inches higher and walked faster, paying him no mind. Old Villie couldn't let well enough be. He nearly fell over Eb Holt's feet in order to block Opal.

"Mishling!" The single word was almost a scream.

"Well, bust a gut!" Opal shot back, going past.

A woman's scream caused me to look backward in time to see old Villie fall in the mud. I saw Doc Helton run to his car and Sheriff McKay slide through the mud from Milt's grave. Urch Vestman was running from the same direction, his pair of checklines used to lower Milt's coffin into the ground flopping over his shoulder. Soon Doc Helton, carrying his black bag, dropped to the mud at Old Villie's side.

Bode Jenkins, leading Aunt Cloma by the hand, pushed his way clear to join us at the buggy. "Old man had a stroke, Doc says." He looked from my aunt to Miss Maudie. "He don't die tonight, Doc says he'll be paralyzed, sure, the rest of his life."

Old Villie didn't die. He was meant to live and become every bit as helpless as Milt Holt had been towards the end.

"Mishling" was the last hateful word he ever spoke.

# 5

Because he was too drunk to make it home, Eb Holt stayed with us four days after Milt's burial. Hunkered in the rocker, his eyes seldom leaving the green bed, he cried like a lost little boy. I helped him to the doorway, where he'd go pee in the mudhole. I cooked his meals and wiped up the messy floor afterwards. I covered him as he slept, made trips to Vestman's for new bottles when the old ones were dry. His tears I wiped away with the floursacks I was sewing into a new mattress for Opal's bed.

The day Eb sobered, he stood by the kitchen door looking at us all a long time. "You know Pop came to, right afore he died." His fingers shook as he rolled a smoke.

"You told us that," Aunt Ilish said.

"I got the old Holt place and his dog and buggy," Eb said.

"Wouldn't have 'em as a present, long's I got Old Jack," said Aunt Ilish.

Eb's answer was a smile.

"By right's that mule's mine," said Aunt Ilish, and up went her long, pointy finger. "Four dollar of my hard-earned money Milt paid for Old Nance after she'd kicked Harley Farker to death."

"Pop, he didn't look at it that way, Ilish Troat. He felt Goldi-locks was entitled to Old Jack. So long's she feeds him his biscuits and heats up his warter, he's hers."

I looked from Eb to the others, just waiting to see who'd speak next. It was Opal who said, "Pay Goldy Lark back the four dollar so's she can get a train ticket away from here, and you keep the mule." (So she didn't like me around Eb any more than I liked her around Eb.)

"She ain't got no place to go," Aunt Ilish snapped.

"My Farker kin in St. Louie Jessie Red McKay spoke of—" I started to say, but was silenced with a, "So that's what I get for taking you in from the world's cold! You'll take the money mentioned in that Pelper County letter Brother Dossie got and look up the Farkers! Well, look up the Farkers! Just leave me and my mule and take your ruby red rear and go!"

"There ain't no money, Aunt Ilish, you know that."

"Then you're pretty damn piss-poor, Goldilocks," Eb said.

"Say what you're trying to say," Aunt Ilish told him.

"The mule's mine, Goldilocks. Pop word-mortgaged him to me for the C.C.C. money your train ticket from Pelper County cost," Eb told her.

"Sucking hind tit and hind tit run dry," Opal laughed.

Eb turned to me, "You got any questions?"

"Yeah, I do," Burt said. "What'd Milt leave me?"

"The relief," Aunt Ilish snorted. "Tote in some for supper."

"What about me?" Opal pretended a whine.

"He left you me," Eb said.

Aunt Ilish bit off a hefty chew and wallowed it in her jaw a while before saying, "That mule leaves this place, Eb Holt, I'll have Jessie Red McKay after you afore you get home, and I just ain't talking to hear my head rattle there."

"Pay me for what Goldilocks' ticket cost me, he's all yours," and Eb went outside to harness Old Jack and ride home in the buggy that held all the mule's belongings, even his water tub. Nobody made a move to stop him.

Remembering his mother's rocking chair, which Eb had forgotten in his temper fit, I started to run after him down the path.

Aunt Ilish stopped me with that pointy finger. "First chance in all these year I've finally got it to myself. You leave it be."

It was soon to be Eb's good luck he left the chair behind. For soon it would be the only reminder of Jane Bell Holt he had, besides her grave.

# 6

Milt Holt was buried the day before I turned sixteen. The next day, Bode Jenkins rode Aunt Ilish in the barn and I saw Nate Brice waiting his turn at the woodpile.

On the twenty-sixth, Eb Holt, Old Jack, and Old Mame surprised Aunt Ilish and me with a visit. "You may's well know right now I come to say I'm marrying Opal in a day or so, Ilish Troat," was his greeting. It nigh stopped my heart cold.

"I got eyes, I know it," she said, and she bit off a chaw.

"You aim to sign for her right nice like, or do I take her down home with me to live in everlasting sin?" Eb smiled and dropped to my devonette.

"I'll sign," she said. "You're welcome to the little bitch." She turned on him with a temper usually saved for me. "And I hope ever last kid she brings into this world she can rightly claim belongs to you."

Eb laughed. "Just acause you lost your cherry at ten . . . Aw, hell, what's the use? I'll have Old Jack ready to start out for Rard sunup Tuesday. You be set to go."

"Set and waiting." Aunt Ilish opened the front door. "Now that your spoke your business, hie off my property. I've heard the last sass from you I aim to."

"Eb took out a bottle and had a long drink.

She watched him a minute before slamming the door. "Thought

maybe you'd quit swigging when Milt died. How's come not, it got the best of you?"

"First guzzle I've had since I left here after Pop's burial. Reckon as how I'm about over it now." Eb wiped his mouth with his hands. "Day a man moseys forth to get into this God damn family, lawful, of his own accord, guess he's entitled to one good, long snort. How you think Burt's apt to like it, having me for a brother-in-law?"

"It's a free country." She spat in the hearth pan.

"What's he going to say about Opal's being knocked up?"

Aunt Ilish almost choked on her chew. "Opal's in the family way?"

"What do you think I was doing in the barn Christmas, asides looking for a warm spot to lay your hot ass girl, when I come on you and Nate Brice swapping chaws without using your hands?" Eb was really enjoying himself. I was dying inside.

"You and Opal in the barn Christmas?" And I didn't even know it and it happened on my own land, she should have added.

"Baby'll be here late September." He took another drink and pretended to study her head. "That a gray hair I see there, Gramma Ilish Troat?"

Wordless, she flopped to the bed and shut her eyes.

Burt and Miss Maudie had been visiting at Bode's most of the day. Upon their return, Burt took the news with a fit of laughter.

"Always claimed the day my sister got herself a white man, I'd do something big. Recollect, Mom?"

Before Aunt Ilish could try to stop him, he'd unbuttoned his over-alls fly, opened the kitchen door and was pissing in the mudhole.

"Oh, my God!" Miss Maudie covered her eyes in shame.

"It's a good thing I don't plan to live here, Burt Troat," Eb's face was purple. "I'd yank that thing, the prettiest part of you, from your pants and shove it down your God damn throat."

Burt laughed at him from the kitchen. "Going up to meet Opal, Mom?"

"No, son." Aunt Ilish's voice was tired. "She can look out for herself now, reckon."

"I'll fetch her myself." Eb was trying to rise. Finally able, he staggered outside.

High spring winds were sweeping down the front yard from the north when Eb and Opal returned late. Arms entwined, they entered the kitchen as one. Eb was sober by now, and Opal seemed both dreamy and sad. A piece of dried buckbrush hung on the back of her old coat.

"They all in bed, Goldilocks?" Eb asked me.

I nodded, put some warm bread on the table. "Have been since dark."

Eb suddenly grabbed Opal by the yellow scarf she'd worn every day since Christmas and pulled her against him, his mouth meeting her parted lips. She returned his kiss with shut eyes, straining to push closer, groaning at each tightening of his arms. When they finally loosed one another, he sat down to gawk at me.

"Bed's a good place for you, too, Goldilocks," Eb told me.

"I got dishes to do," I said.

"We'll do 'em for practice, huh, honey?" An arm around my cousin's backside, he spooned up some butter beans. "Hie your ass to bed," he growled at me.

Less than half an hour afterward, Green Jenkins came banging on the door to tell Eb his old house in the hollow had just burned to the ground. "Dad smelt smoke first and come running to Copeland's to get me. We couldn't tell if it was brush afire or what, ashes was choking us so. Though since it was in your direction, we hied there. House was too far gone even then for warter, them old wood shingles went up like paper. Tried our best to save the barn, couldn't. Grainery and smokehouse went up with it. Wind blowing so took us a good hour to beat out the burning buckbrush, guide a path down to Onion Creek for it to burn itself out. You leave your stove burning, Eb, when you left today?"

"I wasn't home today, any time," Eb said in a funny voice. "Stayed last night at Urch's, had breakfast, my dinner both there. Come straight here from there. What's that you got?"

I saw Green hand him a battered coal oil can. "Pop found it near the house. Name's been plumb scratched out. He said if you didn't leave your stove afire and he was you, he'd go for McKay. Looks like somebody burnt your place apurpose."

# 7

It was high noon the next day when Jessie Red McKay came with Eb and Bode Jenkins. The sheriff lowered himself onto the devonette, motioned that we all sit, and looked from Burt to my aunt to Miss Maudie to me. He took a wallowed chew of tobacco that was wrapped in a red bandana from his shirt pocket and put it with the coal oil can at his feet.

"Anybody pass by here yesterday going towards Eb's?" he asked my aunt.

"They could and me not see'em," she said. "I don't watch the creek path, you know. Whoever done it could've gone down Bode's or Theron's road at New Hill, too."

"Bode didn't see anybody pass." Sheriff McKay looked at Burt. "Neither'd Theron Copeland; I asked him. Anybody going on horseback would've had to pass Bode's or Theron's or here. Since he didn't, then he went afoot."

Aunt Ilish took a bite of Harper's Homespun. "Well, don't ask me if I saw somebody sneak through all the buckbrush, acause I didn't."

"Way I figured," the sheriff, still watching Burt, rubbed his nose, "the man new Eb was gone, where he was, and that he wouldn't be back in time to catch him at it. Anybody you know of got it in for you so bad, Eb, they'd burn your place down?"

"Just Burt Troat," Eb said.

"Now, you hold it right there, Eb Holt!" Aunt Ilish was on her feet.

"Set back down," Burt said. "I don't want my pretty step-brother turning into my pretty brother-in-law so bad I'd cut his guts out if I had a good chance, but burning down a man's place, that's damn ornery, even for me. Pass me a chaw."

"What'd you do last night, Burt?" McKay asked.

"Nothing," Burt said, biting off a chew. "I left your place yesterday, Bode, with Miss Maudie. We come straight here, had supper, went to bed. I got three people to prove I didn't leave. Two more can swear I was sound asleep when Green told us, Eb

Holt, you and Opal. You yourself, Eb, run in swinging the lamp to wake me up. By hell, you prove different."

"I was gone from here about four till after nine," Eb said. "A whole five hour. What you done during then I can't swear to."

"Well, Mom and Miss Maudie can swear I didn't set foot outside after dark. Goldy Lark, too."

"He didn't," Aunt Ilish said. "I went to bed but I didn't sleep till Opal come in with Eb from Doc's."

"You swear to that, too, Miss Maudie?" McKay asked.

"He didn't leave," she said, her eyes on Burt.

McKay turned his green eyes on me. "He step out the front door after dark, Goldy Lark Farker?"

I shook my head no, looking him straight in his eyes. "No way he could. By dark, I had supper cooked and all my chores done, except dishes. So I stayed at the table after they all went to bed, keeping eats warm for Opal and Eb. Burt didn't come out to the kitchen. Front door was bolted. I'd heard if he'd gone out that way."

"You sure now?"

"The back door don't open all the way on account of the beds and the big rag box. There ain't a way Burt could've got past me."

"And he didn't, not even for a minute or so?"

"He didn't get out of bed afore Eb got him out," I said.

McKay rose and picked up the coal oil can. "No name on it. Cans in these parts all alike. So I write down fire by person or persons unknown. All I can do, Eb."

"Let me have five minute outside with Burt and it won't be another Almy Copeland thing this time," Eb said.

"You can get in trouble saying a thing like that." The sheriff, seeing Aunt Ilish was about to speak, had hurried to beat her to it.

"Lots of things I got left to lose in a court of law, I'm pretty piss-poor, McKay, or ain't you heard?"

"Forget it, I say. All got here's a chew any of a hundred men or women—" he glanced at Aunt Ilish—"could've dropped at the fire and a coal oil can that could be mine, for all I know. Fighting won't get you anything but a stay in jail."

Old Mame growled low to tell us company was coming the same second horse hooves sounded on the yard rocks. Urch

Vestman ran in without knocking, seeing none of us but Eb. "Look, now you come stay with me, I got room."

"Like hell, Urch." Eb went to set in the rocker. "Burt, he burnt down mine and Pop's birthplace to spite me, reckon. Well, I got good news for him. I aim to stay put right here against time I can build back."

"This ain't no place for you, Eb," Urch told him.

Eb rolled a cigarette, shaking fingers showing his temper. "Come Tuesday, you know, me and Opal Troat's to get hitched. I meant to take her down home to live. Now, looks like we'll stay here, me, her, and her loving mom and Goldilocks, happy ever after."

"You ain't running me and Miss Maudie off, you bastard," Burt said through clenched teeth.

"Like I told you," Eb said, blowing smoke, "Tuesday I get married to Opal. Wednesday morning, bright and early, Burt Troat takes his big ass and his woman out to the barn to live. He won't set food in here, wintertime or summer, save to eat."

"You're not human, Eb Holt!" Aunt Ilish screeched. "They'll freeze out there in this blowy weather. Asides, it's my place, not yours. Sheriff, can't you—"

"Sounds good, till he can build back," McKay said, turning to me. "Well, now Milt's gone, what you aim to do?"

"She can stay here," Aunt Ilish answered for me. "She's more help'n Opal ever was."

"That what you want, Goldy Lark Farker?"

"I'll stay on," I said. Catch me leaving here and handing Eb Holt over to Opal without a fight.

"Reckon that's settled then," and McKay took his leave.

Eb opened the door to flip his smoke into the mudhole. "Dish up dinner, Goldilocks," he said, acting like me and him was the only two on the place.

Long after dinner was over, Burt and Aunt Ilish stood by the mudhole, looking at each other with worry.

"There's no law in this here county," she kept saying. "Ain't no law here atall."

She was wrong there. There was a law and I had to get word to him before Tuesday so Opal would be in jail for whoring and couldn't marry Eb.

# 8

"That's like asking me to cause snow in July, Goldy Lark." Urch Vestman dumped the coffee he'd just ground for me into a small poke, fixed the end, and laid two Harper's Homespun twists alongside.

"I just asked you to tell Jessie Red McKay Opal's a camp girl. Ivy Helton, too. Opal said so."

"Why d'you want me to tattle?"

"She's aiming to marry Eb Holt," I whispered.

Urch laughed in my face. "It is going to snow in July, ain't it?"

"I didn't think you'd make fun of me." I was near tears, like I'd been all day at thoughts of losing another love.

"Listen, Goldy Lark." He put a big poke of cornmeal with the other things. "I can't go to the law and say a thing like that against my neighbors, even if it's true. Why you ask me to?"

I looked him in the eye. "I want to marry Eb myself."

"So that's how the wind blows." Urch shook his grayed head. "Few year time, you know, you'll be cleaning him, like you done Milt. Happens to drunkards, hear tell. You want that?"

"Eb'll quit when he's mine. I'll see to it."

"How's come you don't want a man who'd be better to you, give you things a pretty girl wants? Goldy Lark, I mean me," he said.

Thinking he was funning me, I said, "You was Bree's boyfriend, Urch."

"You think I'm too old, don't you?"

Rather than hurt his feelings by saying yes, I picked up what I'd come for and headed for the door. Urch was moving faster. I thought that meant he'd open the door. Instead, he stretched his arms wide to block my way.

"If I tell McKay and he catches Opal with the camp boys and Eb still don't want you, will you marry me then, when Pop dies?"

I don't know what suddenly made me think he was still afraid of old Villie, paralyzed and unable to talk but still boss of the house. I couldn't help thinking if this hadn't been so several years ago, what else kept him from marrying Bree and fist-fighting the old man for his share of the store? Whatever the truth, my head started to sizzle and I knew I had to get out of there while I could still see the door.

"Skip it, Urch," I managed to say in a steady voice. "I'll hitch a ride to town with the mailman tomorrow, go see McKay."

He dropped his arms to let me pass.

Jessie Red McKay saved me a town trip by being on the path as I got a bucket of water just before dark. I figured he had gotten word from Urch about Opal sleeping with the camp boys for money. That's why, this being my last chance to stop Eb's marrying her, I right off cut loose with all I knew.

"Well, I'm dommed," was McKay's answer. He looked at me for the longest time, then added, "Here I come all the way out here to ask you—well, never mind it now—to tell you, no, ask you, reckon, why you don't write to your Pelper County school teacher. She wrote the office she's worried acause she don't hear from you."

"I don't want to write to her," I said, wanting him to ask what I knew on Opal. If being with the camp boys for money was against the law in one county, it must be in all other counties, too.

"You got a good friend here like this Miss Emmer woman?" he asked.

"I don't want a friend." I just wanted Eb Holt.

"Well, now, don't you think you've got a friend out here?"

"Acourse," I said, "Old Jack."

McKay stood up to dust his backside and put on his hat. "You write to that Miss Emmer, anyhow. She's worried over you."

"I ain't got three pennies," I said, my chin rising.

"Well, now, tell you what." His big hand reached inside a pocket to pull out some change. Having sorted it, he held out three cents to me. "Buy you a stamp, now."

I shook my head. "I don't take money from men; Opal does."

"I know you don't." He smiled and put the money away. "Well, I'll write to your Miss Emmer, tell her what you just said."

"What about what else I just told you?"

"Only heard one thing, Goldy Lark Farker. You don't want to hear from this Emmer Cox, I'll tell her so myself."

I caught hold of his big arm and pulled tight at his turning aside. "You can't let Eb marry Opal! He's mine! Can't you hear me, I said he's mine!

He loosed my fingers one by one, bent down to face me, and said, "That drunkard's doing you the biggest dom favor anybody'll do for you, Goldy Lark Farker, if he marries your cousin. Take my word for it."

He tipped his hat and hurried away, causing my heart to give a giant grasshopper jump that brought on a nigh blinding head sizzle.

# 9

Hunkered on my devonette the night of Eb's wedding to Opal, I held my hand to my mouth, wanting to die. Opal, who didn't love Eb like I did and was carrying another man's baby, lay curled in his arms in the front room bed, groaning in her sleep. She must have been covering her face with his because I couldn't hear his snores. Not ten minutes before she'd been screaming in the same way Bree had when mating with Nate Brice.

"Kiss me, Eb, or I'll scream! I love you, love you!"

Eb had kissed her, I'd heard him doing so, yet she'd screamed anyway.

Burt's heavy breathing in the back room doorway had become faster with Opal's excitement. And Aunt Ilish, pitching her body on Opal's bed, ordered there by Eb, was surely in need of Bode Jenkins or Nate Brice or any man. Miss Maudie, I could only guess, was praying with covered ears.

Save for my heart's knotting inside me with every beat it took, it had been pretty much a usual day till the newlyweds got home. Burt had spent the better part of his time whittling, grouching to Miss Maudie over anything and nothing. Twice he'd napped on the cot they shared. Upon each awakening, he'd called her and we'd stopped house cleaning while they mated. I'd taken myself to the woodpile at these times, thinking hard.

I'd tried to hate Opal more and I'd tried to hate Eb. I'd also wished, too late now, for nerve to tell him what I'd told Sheriff

McKay. Maybe it was best, though, I hadn't; he'd likely married her anyway after calling me a liar, and hated me the rest of his life. I happened to glance toward the back room, and noticed that many of the foundation rocks below Burt's cot was loose and several inches out of line with the others. Last winter's thawing snow couldn't have melted the chinking that much, what with the sheet iron roof's overhang. The clay mud, on closer look, had been chipped away to loosen the rocks.

My mind still on the wedding, I carefully re-wedged the rocks in place and went back to my thinking.

The house was spanking clean and supper was waiting, when the buggy came from Rard. Eb lifted his bride—who carried a bed pillow, their wedding present from Urch—high in the air before putting her down. Aunt Ilish, who'd been made to ride in the bumpy end bed, spat at the mudhole to show her hate of the wedding.

Miss Maudie hugged them inside, whispered a prayer, and took the pillow into the back room. They stood a minute in the door, watching me like they expected a happy word. I turned my back to feed the mule a biscuit I knew I wouldn't be able to choke down.

Setting for super was a nightmare. Opal, Eb's Christmas scarf bright over the red dress from Vestman's she wore, kept one hand over Eb's. "I love you," she must have told him twenty times over.

"Marry in red, wish yourself dead," Burt said on his way outside.

"Marry in yeller, always smell her," Eb called after him.

"My dress was that color," Miss Maudie said sadly.

"Mine was pink, both times," said Aunt Ilish.

"Marry in pink, your love will stink," Opal said back.

The dishes finished, I took the lamp into the front room, leaving the newlyweds at the table. Aunt Ilish sat in the rocker; for the first time since I'd met her she did not have her bedtime chew. I went to bed at once, and so did Miss Maudie. Soon Aunt Ilish, too, peeled back the covers of her bed and climbed in, not bothering to take off her new dress. Burt passed by while she settled.

Eb came in first, his chest hair showing through his open shirt. Opal, her skirt wrinkled, was a step behind. Seeing my aunt in bed snoring much too loud to be asleep, seemed to anger Eb. He jerked the covers from her and pointed to the back room. "In here's as close as I can stand to smell Burt."

Aunt Ilish, wordless, rose to obey.

Eb had the lamp out before she left the room.

"Throw my wedding present in here, Ilish Troat." I heard Eb's pants hit the floor as their pillow whizzed through the room.

"I put it under my head or my ruby red rear?" Opal asked, louder than need be.

For a very long time they whispered and giggled, the dried mattress leaves sharing their secrets. Inside the stuffy back room, the others also squirmed and turned.

Finally Burt commenced mating with Miss Maudie, which stilled the other two beds. At long last, Eb claimed Opal, my throat thickening with each whack of the bedstead against the wall. A song Bree had sung to me years ago began to run through my head. The words "I wish I'd have died when a baby and never grew up to love you," caused hot tears to sting my eyes.

At daybreak, Burt, his few clothes gathered in his long arms, took Miss Maudie out to the barn to live. Aunt Ilish followed them in silence through the door, failing to glance toward the Lynch family bed where the new keepers of the house slept safe in each other's arms.

# 10

That day, for the first time since Milt's funeral, Brother Dossie Lynch visited. Barefoot despite the chilly winds outside ("There's some of us meant to suffer for His sake"), he settled at the table, downed his coffee with one swallow, and mumbled something about mercy and forgiveness.

"You mean me?" Eb asked. "For not letting you hitch me and Opal? Me knocking her up afore us marrying? Or throwing Burt Troat out of his own house on his fat ass or him burning down my place or what?"

"Maybe," my uncle said, "I meant something altogether different."

"I'm all ears," Eb hugged Opal tight. "Up to last night, though, I had a peter, too."

Brother Dossie didn't laugh. "Folks saying Burt burnt you out don't make it so by them saying it. You telling me Opal's in the family way don't make it so, neither, 'less I know for myself. I guess when I've gone on to Glory Land, you'll hear talk of me that might seem different, provide you don't look at the whole truth."

"You sound like you're readying yourself for the Death Angel, Brother Dossie. You got a feeling doom hovers close? Well, you ain't a young man anymore, you know." Those were my aunt's first words all day long.

Brother Dossie's eyes filled with tears. "Sister Ilish, I had some powerful heartaches all these year to put up with."

"We all know it ain't been easy, with Sister Cloma and all," Aunt Ilish said.

"Ever since little Nonny died—"

"Nonny didn't have much to do with it. Sister Cloma, she was so simple the day of her birthing she likely squalled when she was fed and tee-heed when she was hungry."

"I spent twenty-three long year up there, living the clean life of Jesus Christ, and fighting black sin the few time it showed its ugly head. I never thought of Sister Cloma as a woman after we lost Nonny, most of that long, lonesome time. She was just a lamb I sheltered in the dark of night."

"You could've took her to the Lotoe Crazy House," Eb reminded.

"What God hath joined together, let no man pull apart," said Brother Dossie, the tears falling faster.

"What's your bellyache, then?" Eb asked.

Brother Dossie sniffed. "Mercy. That's all I ask for now, a little bit of the milk of kindness God himself seeped into the hearts of all His people."

He arose, his hands feeling for the door. He staggered down the path like a drunk man, leaving his heelprint in the puddle of mud.

# 11

We learned the reason for Brother Dossie's strange actions on Saturday. Just at dinner, Bode Jenkins walked with Jessie Red McKay to ask had we seen Hollyhock in the last few days.

"She went looking for spring flowers yesterday," the sheriff said. "Not been home since."

"Made only about the fourth time since her baptizing she'd said more'n boo to any of us or been out of the house longer'n five minute," Bode said.

Opal entered from the back room, fluffing her bouncy bobbed hair. "Why, I seen Hollyhock yesterday'n I went to work. In the path by our property line, with a floursack."

"It full of flowers?"

"How'd I know? The end was tied."

"Say anything to you?" McKay asked.

"She didn't get a chance. Brother Dossie, he comes running through the brush toting two floursacks. He led her down toward Bode's. I thought he'd found her out lost, was taking her back home."

"Let's see what Brother Dossie's got to say," the sheriff said. He led the way up through the cornfield, Bode, Aunt Ilish, and me behind.

The Lynch cabin door stood propped wide open with a rock. Scattered around the room was his collection of books, save for the Bible, which lay in the center of the empty money tub in front of the cold fireplace. On the table by the plate of untouched beans was a note.

"Lord, help us who can no longer help ourselves," it read.

All we could do that minute was look from one to the other, not knowing what to do. I guess we all thought of the whirlpool the same second, Jessie Red running first. There stood Hollyhock Jenkins, with her arms stretched skyward, saying something I couldn't hear above the water's gurgle. It turned out to be "Bringing In The Sheaves" when Bode led her from the water's sound.

"You go on, Bode, take her home," Jessie Red told him.

Bode passed within inches of me on his way downcreek, his eyes so full of tears he stumbled several times.

I found Aunt Cloma, naked save for her sunbonnet, close to the buggy crossing, her poor body blue from the cold. Every so often she'd stick her wooden baby in the cold water.

"In the name of the Father, the Son and the Ghost," she'd say before bringing Nonny up.

It was Aunt Ilish's sudden notion that Aunt Cloma be taken to the Rard Courthouse and declared hopeless. From there she'd go to the Missouri Crazy House at Lotoe.

"May's well take her now, soon's Goldy Lark gets her clothes on her, seeing how your car's up there handy at New Hill and all," she told Jessie Red.

"Dom, Ilish! Does it have to be done today?"

"They ain't going to think any lesser of me sending her off'n they will over what Brother Dossie's done."

"Reckon not," he agreed.

"When we get to Urch's," she said, "I want you should stop and go in with me. I got to be the one who tells the county what Brother Dossie's done. They can call me any name that suits their fancy. But when I walk out of there, that'll be the last talk about Brother Dossie I ever hear."

Aunt Cloma had never had any reason to run from me. Now, without Brother Dossie on hand, she hung by my side. She refused to leave without me for the walk up to New Hill. She trusted me so much I was even allowed to carry little Nonny when she tired.

At the school I expected she would get in the sheriff's car and take her last leave of me. But she was afraid to ride in the car, with or without me by her side. She was so scared even Nonny in the back seat by me couldn't coax her in. Sheriff McKay tried driving a few foot away, hoping she'd follow after her baby and me. All she done was wait on the school steps for our return.

Jessie Red McKay finally brought a long length of bindertwine from his car and tied it to the back bumper.

"No, don't!" I begged when I knew what he had in mind.

"I ain't got a choice," he told me. "If I tie her up and make her go in the car, she'd likely be dead afore I got to Doc's. Poor old thing's bound to be starved. I'll buy her a poke of candy at Vestman's, get her so busy she won't notice she's been tricked."

I shut my eyes so I wouldn't have to see him tie one of Aunt Cloma's hands to the car with a loose end of the bindertwine. The other he left free to carry her baby girl.

"Goldy Lark, hie home now," Aunt Ilish called from the car's front seat. I could tell from the way she worked her jaws she was ready to spit big.

The last picture I keep of my Aunt Cloma is her silent race from side to side of the road in a jerky try to stop the pull of the car. She was in the right side rut when I saw her loose hand jump to her eyes. Aunt Ilish's flying tobacco juice caused her to drop little Nonny in the dirt, where the baby finally died.

# 12

The week after Brother Dossie's shaming us, Opal had gone to work only to be told by Evelyn Helton she wouldn't need her anymore if we couldn't pay the church money back. At Eb's try to dry her tears with a kiss, she'd said, "Go away. Forever."

She wasn't the only one wishing so. But I meant it.

And Eb, drunk, had laughed her words away.

I hadn't realized how hard Aunt Ilish had been hit till early one Saturday Bode Jenkins came with a jar of peaches and was told no, right in front of me.

"Life's already got me where the hair's short." My aunt swiped at a pretend tear, sniffed a hard sniff. "It gets any worser, I'll be apt to set myself down and cry."

Before Bode had time to get home, she'd changed from sorrow back to her usual self. "Goldy Lark, tell Eb Holt, don't you ask him, I said hitch the mule to the sled. I want it ready'n I get back from the barn with Miss Maudie's school key."

"Goody, goody, Goldilocks," Eb laughed when I told him. "Maybe she's moving up to New Hill, boo hoo hoo."

"Well, tee hee yourself, Eb Holt," Aunt Ilish said from the doorway. "But you won't tee hee long. Come with me, you'll see, you'll see."

As usual, she was right. Several hours later, Eb and I were too tired to laugh. Not only had we made many trips to the schoolhouse, we had loaded, unloaded, and stacked Brother Dossie's books, with little help from Aunt Ilish. Then, dragging tired, I had to ride Old Jack up to Vestman's.

"You tell Urch, tomorrow being Sunday, he can spread the word today to Missouri County and half of Arkansaw he'll auction off all of Brother Dossie's books at noon. On the school steps. He's to say the money took in can go towards still building a wilderness church, right here at the mouth of Onion Creek, if they want to. They can have the land free. It's all up to them."

It turned out to be a very good notion, with Brother Dossie's name drawing a funeral-size crowd, most of them just looking. But one wasn't, a white-headed woman Jessie Red McKay brought. Miss Madge Kellison was in charge of the Rard Library. She bought the whole collection to donate to the town. The money, even more than last fall's Pie Supper made, was to be kept in the Rard bank in Urch Vestman's and Doc Helton's names. It would be used as the people wished. They voted by a show of hands to think on Aunt Ilish's offer of free Lynch land for a new church.

My aunt was resting on the kitchen step when I got back from the sale with Burt and Opal. Hearing from Burt that the congregation would have to talk over the offer of free Lynch land, she gave her head a quick shake. "They'll never find a better place for their church, and they know it. Why, even when I'm gone with the Death Angel, they'll be other Lynches on the land," she said sadly.

Her hand went to her dressneck for her Harper's Homespun. "They'll always be somebody here to care for the land and the church, they forget that. All us Lynches, for the most part, was caring folk when it come to the land."

"You tell her it won't be me and my little bastards," Opal said to Burt. "Must be you she means."

Burt grabbed his mother's tobacco twist from her hand. "Not me," he said, taking a bite. "Reckon, Goldy Lark, it's you she's got in mind."

"Looks like it," I said, trying not to think too hard that where Eb Holt lives was where I'd be, for fear they'd read my heart.

# 13

On a late April night Opal called to my attention how old Mame had failed to show up for supper.

"Probably out after a squirrel," I said.

"Else, laid down in the woods and died. Old Mame's awful old, you know."

Eb stepped down from the front room to seat himself at the table. His eyes on his fingers, he rolled a cigarette and lifted the smoky lap globe to light it. "Dog come home for a day or so, Goldilocks?"

"Seen her myself," said my aunt from the rocker.

"Wasn't talking to you, Ilish Troat. Old Mame seem sick, Goldilocks, or puny?"

"She eat some biscuits, last time I seen her, Eb."

"Wasn't ailing, then. Look, you saddle up Old Jack and fetch me the lantern. I'll mosey down to the old homestead, see if she's sleeping there. You never get to go any place much. Come on along."

"Don't this county have enough to talk about on us without you dragging out a girl old enough to sleep with, your wife's cousin, to boot, this late at night?" Aunt Ilish asked.

"Anybody sees us, I'll say it was you," Eb growled.

At the edge of our property, I climbed from the quilt to let down the rails, then put them back when Old Jack passed through. The only light for a long way was the lantern's glow. It cast creepy shadows that danced on the buckbrush and trees as the mule trotted along. Suddenly, to our left, I saw lamplight through the trees across Onion Creek and knew that it would be Theron Copeland's place.

"Where's the gooseberry patch Bode Jenkins and Theron Copeland was feuding over?" I asked.

Eb laughed for the first time in many days. "Theron give his part to Bode the day Green shotgun-married Lucy Lee, I heard tell."

"Urch told me yesterday when I went to the store Lucy Lee had her baby a few days back. A boy." I waited for him to speak, and when he didn't, added, "And Virgie's baby's due sometime soon, looks like."

"Something, Bode riding his own wife," Eb snarled, making me sorry I'd ever opened my mouth.

Bode Jenkins' big old house stood within thirty feet of Onion Creek. Hearing his dogs, Bode had come to the front porch, and when we got in the yard, his wife, kids, and cooners all gathered around him on the porch. Eb reined in, asking if they'd chanced to see Old Mame.

"Kids see her go back and forth pert near every day, Eb," Bode said. "My cooners bark, I come out to look. Didn't see her today, come to think. You kids happen to?" None had. "She sleeps down at the old place some nights, see her going back to you some early mornings. Acts old and tired."

Virgie had come to the porch's edge, her swollen belly showing in the lantern light. "You folks hear any word on Brother Dossie, Eb?"

"Sheriff would come here first, Virgie."

"Well, I keep hoping, praying, all the time. What he done to my Hollyhock. . . . "

"The money's gone, Virgie, he'll crawl back. Ain't that what McKay said?"

"He won't crawl when I get through with him." Bode's face darkened as he spoke.

"I just can't understand Brother Dossie's doing a bad thing like that, Eb. And my poor Hollyhock, she's never been all the way right in her head." Virgie wiped at her tears. "Eb, how's my Miss Maudie?"

Eb scratched his head. "Don't want to worry you any, both of you, but she don't eat enough to keep a bedbug alive and last night—well, I just wish you'd come up to see her."

"Come morning, we'll look in," Bode promised.

"You hear Green and Lucy give us a grambaby boy?" Virgie asked.

"Don't seem to make you look any older," Eb kidded.

Feeling someone's eyes burning my back, I turned to see Green Jenkins coming through the bushes. After a good gawk at me, he turned to eye the quilt I was on and grin up at Eb.

"Say, now, where you two heading for?"

Eb jerked the bridle reins so hard the mule reared. "To hell, if we don't change our ways," he said low as we left.

What had been the Holt house, once standing the same distance from Onion Creek as ours, was now only a square of blackened foundation rocks holding a scattering of ashes the winds hadn't managed to blow away. The barn Eb told me his grandfather had built had one lonely charred board standing. Part of a smokehouse leaned against the ruins of a grainery. The lone building was an outhouse, standing behind what had been the grainery, its door ajar.

"He did a right good job, didn't he, Goldilocks?" Eb sounded ready to cry.

"Burt Troat didn't leave the house that night, Eb, less he crawled out through a crack," I said.

"I ain't calling you a liar, Goldilocks. He didn't leave home either the day Almy Copeland got raped and her throat cut and her asshole tore up with bob wire. Then Pop told me once he heard Ilish accuse Burt of being outside long enough to do it. You heard about that, reckon."

"Burt told me his first day home from jail."

"Black ass bastard would."

On our way back Bode was on the porch as we passed his house. "Didn't find the dog," Eb called, flanking the mule.

"You sure didn't stay long," Bode answered.

"Didn't aim to, you old nosey sum bitch," Eb said, out of Bode's hearing. "Ilish Troat's likely told him me and Opal's on the outs these days. Best he use his bald head to figure out if I had a bone for someone, it sure's hell wouldn't be kin. Whoa!"

Eb halted Old Jack so fast he nearly reared, alighted and took the lantern over to Onion Creek, motioning me to follow. He reached inside a homemade wooden box in the water and handed me a fruit jar of cold milk. Holding the lantern high while squatting on the creek bank, he pulled handfuls of little green onions from the ground. After swishing them in the creek he bit off the heads one by one and, when finished, handed them to me.

"Here." He opened the jar. "Better us have it'n Ilish Troat."

The only way to drink the oniony milk, caused by the cows eating the wild onions during daytime hours, Eb whispered, was to dip one in the milk and chew it good before you drank. In this way we emptied the jar in a short while.

"Ain't the first time I stole milk from Bode," Eb laughed low. "Way, way back, I was hurting for some and our cow wasn't fresh and there's a cow of Bode's, her calf penned up close by. So I milk the cow, let the calf in to her. Guess Bode always thought the calf got on its own. Leastways, he never come after my kids. I ain't let on to a soul till this minute. Now, don't go blab on me."

He filled the empty jar with water, put the lid on loose and crooked, laid it back in the box.

"Now the nosey sum bitch can think the lid loosed itself, for all I care," he said, picking up the lantern.

We walked to the Lynch property line, me leading the mule. Eb opened the gate and closed it after we got through, but instead of re-mounting Old Jack he took the lantern into the brush. I held on to the mule's reins, shivering in the chilly night air, and waited for Eb to go nature. I finally wound the mule's reins around a tree trunk and jumped up and down to keep warm.

"Goldilocks," Eb called after a long time, "come and see what I got."

I stepped through the brush into the lantern's light, wondering what on earth he'd found. My mouth dropped open at seeing his man part poking up through his open fly. "I got a bone for you, Goldilocks," he said in a quivery voice.

"Eb," I whispered, "you're Opal's man."

He grabbed my arm and clamped it tight. "You go back to the mule and get the quilt, I said I aim to fugg you."

"Oh, Eb, I can't!" One reason was knowing what Aunt Ilish and Burt would do to me if I got knocked up, the other was that it was the wrong time of the month. "Eb, I just can't!

He slapped me with his other hand. "I got a quarter, if that's what it takes. He stood facing me, breathing hard.

"It's the wrong time for me," I finally had to admit.

"Acourse it is." He moved closer, his hand feeling for my straddle. I stood still to let him find out what he wanted to know. "Aw shit, wouldn't you know it?" followed his hand pulling away fast. Then, just as quick, he took my hand and laid it on himself, saying, "More'n one damn way to skin a cat."

"Eb, if Opal ever found out . . ." I was shaking so hard with happiness at the thought he'd even want me in any way, I couldn't finish what I'd meant to say.

"Who's aiming to tell, you or me or the mule?"

I hadn't time to answer before he was holding me the way he'd done in my dreams so many times, kissing me better than even Roy Cox had, his face whiskery hard and a little bit hurtful. When he started moving against me, I knew what to do with my hand. He quickly quit kissing me to hold tighter, and whispered "Goldilocks, I love you." His body jerked wildly. As he finished in my hand, my name changed from Goldilocks to Opal.

After that, the only thing to do was wash my hands in the creek, dry them on my dresstail, and follow him home.

# 14

Bode and Virgie Jenkins visited Miss Maudie at breakfast. My aunt, seeing them go in the barn, picked up the coffee pot and two cups and went out. "You go up the creek a ways and gather some wild onions for dinner," she told me at the mudhole.

My feet led me straight to Brother Dossie's place. I stopped at the closed door of his cabin in the shade of the sycamore before going to watch the rock give birth to Onion Creek. I was still shivering inside over last night with Eb, tasting his kisses all over again, feeling his arms wild and strong, feeling his wanting me. I looked at the wild onion shoots shoving up through the soil and smiled, remembering our feast of them and the milk meant for Aunt Ilish. I came back to myself when I saw a blacksnake slide into a hole, and knelt for a closer look. That's how I happened to notice fresh dog tracks in the dirt. I followed them around a big rock to Eb's trap. There I found Old Mame tied to a cedar sapling with just enough bob wire length to allow her to wet her face. Her mouth was muzzled with another length to keep her from barking. She was whining low, trying to call me, probably had been for a long time, but the water's rush (and Eb Holt) had drowned her weak cries.

Dropping to her side, I petted her and tried to undo her binding. The wire was so tight I saw it would have to be cut. I saw something else, long wide footprints that could only have been made by Burt Troat, that caused the hair to rise on my head. A hunk of hard fried bread lay nearby.

So Burt Troat had tied the dog here to aggravate Eb. He'd surely meant her no harm. Else, why bother with feed and water? If I told Eb either him or my cousin would die in the yard down home. The less said, then, the better.

I gathered the wild onions and raced home, trying to forget the dog's sad cries. The first good chance I got I'd return to cut her loose.

That same afternoon, I saw Bode Jenkins head for the bridge, where Aunt Ilish just happened to be filling the drinking bucket. She brought up a jar of gooseberries an hour or so afterward, but not the water.

The very next day, she surprised us all by putting on her new yellow dress and plaiting her hair for the first time that week. "Well, don't just stand there with your mouths wide open, you might swallow flies. Anything wrong with me snagging a white man if he's over twenty-one and willing?"

"You can't marry Bode Jenkins, Ilish Troat. He's already took," Eb said.

"I ain't marrying Bode," she snapped, eyes blazing. "I aim to live the rest of my life in Brother Dossie's cabin with Nate Brice. When I come down here, it'll be just to see my Burt and get me some relief eats. Goldy Lark, you put my things in a floursack. My tap, in the second dresser drawer, lay that in afore my pretty pink dress."

"Aunt Ilish, I don't know what you mean," I lied.

She put her hands on her hips. " 'Oh, tee hee and fish farts, cousin. Don't you know what this is? It's a tap!',' " she answered in Opal's voice. Then in mine, " 'Oh, Opal, that little round thing keeps Aunt Ilish from havin' a kid? What's the funny little long thing for?' " Without blinking, she went back to Opal's voice. " 'That's her glue gun, Goldy Lark. She didn't glue the tap in, the way Bode goes at her, she'd cough it up through her teeth when she comes. Tee hee hee.'

"Oh, yes, Goldy Lark, I heard you both looking it over, not long after you come here. I sneaked back to the house for my tap because I didn't want you two to know I was there. I stood on the hewn log less'n a foot from you and neither of you dreamed I was around." She stuck her long finger by my face. "So like I say, sack up my tap."

"Goldilocks to live with you?" Eb asked.

"Nate feels like he fed her long enough. Anything else you want to know?"

"Yeah," Eb said. "Nate being so old and you so little, who'll help you lift him on and off?"

"Ask her why she's taking Aunt Bree's leavings, Eb," Opal said. "Tee hee hee and fish farts, that's scraping the barrel pretty damn low."

"I never heard tell of the one she just mentioned, and you can tell her so, Eb Holt," Aunt Ilish bristled. She stuck a twist of tobacco down her dress front. "You tell her Nate's life's insured for a thousand dollar and Nate's old. He's to give me his farm when he kicks the bucket, too. I can sell it and get lots of pretty money, maybe enough to get me off of the relief."

"Best you keep Nate's place, since you got only one share of Lynch land," Eb told her. "There's Opal and Goldilocks and your little boy Burt and—"

"Anyone tries to give me one inch of this damn place, I'll tear off his big toe and beat his ass with it," said Opal.

"You feel that way, too?" Aunt Ilish asked me.

"Well," I said, watching her eyes narrow, "I was born here. I wouldn't mind dying here, reckon."

We both held our heads a little higher as I spoke.

Doc Helton's visit to Miss Maudie with my aunt and Burt also at the barn gave me a chance to sneak upcreek to free the dog, the rusty scissors hidden in my shirt. Burt would never know but what Old Mame herself broke the wire. My heart turned a flip-flop at finding the place empty. I never saw Old Mame alive again.

I got back to the sight of Burt Troat on the woodpile, biting his fingers so hard they bled.

"Bode made Miss Maudie leave him, on Doc's say-so, she'd

die if she didn't," Opal was happy to explain. "Burt, he thinks she'll put in for a devorce any day now."

Why, I asked my heart in bed that night, couldn't it have been Eb and Opal instead?

# 15

I had my second talk with Nate Brice when I'd gone to the store for Eb's makings and Urch Vestman gave me my aunt's yearly order of a dozen brown leghorn baby chicks. Urch said Aunt Ilish, wanted to keep them at the cabin of course. I went up the creek before stopping at the house, carefully balancing the box on the saddle horn.

I got down from Old Jack to set the peeping chicks in the yard. Two knocks on the door brought no answer. I'd re-mounted the mule when Nate Brice, rubbing sleep from his eyes, stepped through the door.

"Brought Aunt Ilish's chickens," I said and started to turn Old Jack.

He caught the bridle with his hairy hand, jerking the mule to a stop. "That all you got to say to the man who was like your own pop to you most of your life?"

"Turn my mule loose, Nate."

A look of pain shot across his weathered whiskered face. "I'm old and gray now, Goldy Lark, not so spry's I used to be, but I was pretty good to you. You and pretty Bree always had a good living. Don't you remember, Goldy Lark?"

"Acourse Nate Brice. A lot of things. The way you knocked Mom round. The time you got in my cot. Your bastard this, bastard that. I remember way too much to stay here and listen to you whine."

I jerked Old Jack loose and left.

Luck would have it that I met Aunt Ilish at the cornfield. "How's come you're hurrying so? Nate try to hug you or worser?"

"I'm late," I said, flanking the mule.

By the time she reached the cabin, Nate Brice's itchy feet had led him to other places unknown to us. In a sneaking hurry, the same way he'd left Bree. No goodbyes to your face. I'm gone, tough on you; that was Nate.

I almost pitied Aunt Ilish, she tried so hard to cry when she came down to get eats. "Not married a month and so soon after Brother Dossie's shamed us and he does this to me." She touched her face and groaned loud. "Feel like I could crawl off to some deep hole and die there, I loved him so much."

"Means he made her come twice," Opal laughed in her mom's face.

"Dry up, Opal."

I jumped at the sound and sight of Burt Troat by the mudhole, a hateful gawk aimed at his sister, Opal.

"Her tooth hurts," he snarled. "It's hurt her nigh a week. What she needs is a mayapple poultice for it and no sass."

"There's mayapples up by the road in No Man's Land," I said the same second Burt said, "Goldy Lark, you get the hoe."

Aunt Ilish showed me how to boil the mayapple roots the same way Meadow Lark Lynch had, then, "knowing I ain't welcome in my own home," went out to the woodpile to wait till I was done. A hefty chew of her twist was resting atop the bad tooth, another of my Indian grandmother's cure for toothaches, she said. If the mayapple didn't work, it might take the smoke of a cigarette, held in her mouth as long as she could hold her breath, to deaden the pain.

"That don't work, I'll be apt's not to ask Eb Holt for a snort of what he takes for toothaches, forgive me, Lord," she said, taking the bucket holding the hot mayapple juice.

"I'll carry it home for you," I offered.

"Home, Goldy Lark?" She turned on me so fast I could feel the wind from her dress. "What you mean, you'll take it to my home, Goldy Lark? Ain't this my home, Goldy Lark, huh? Ain't it, huh? Ain't it?"

"Look, I didn't mean—" I tried to say.

"Yes, you did. You mean to do everything mean to me, all of you," she said, starting for the cabin.

I couldn't believe it when Jessie Red McKay brought me the surprise news that Nate Brice, in case of his death, would pass all his earthly goods to me. The Brice farm deed, plus his life insurance policy for $1,000 made in my name, had been left in the sheriff's keeping at Rard.

"I won't touch anything Nate Brice ever breathed on," I told Jessie Red McKay, when he came to Onion Creek.

"Any change is up to him," he said.

"Don't I have no say so about it?"

"When Nate dies, you can always turn it over to your aunt."

"I'd sooner the mule," I said before I thought.

Aunt Ilish heard the news from Bode Jenkins instead of the sheriff, which made things all the worse. I went tearing up through the field at her trouble ring on the telephoney and met her, Bode at her heels, starting out at a hard run for me, screaming my name with every step.

"First it was my mule you took!" Hands on hips, she faced me, her eyes fire red and her mouth crusty at the corners with tobacco juice. "And now, now, it's Nate's land and money when he kicks the bucket! What'll you do to me next? Try to turn me out to the poorhouse, away from the old homestead I was birthed at?"

"I won't take what Nate Brice wants to leave me," I said. "I don't want it, I didn't ask for it. And I didn't ask Milt for Old Jack. He won't be mine anyhow till I can pay off Eb Holt, and I can't pay off Eb Holt acause I'll never have a dime to do it with."

I stopped to catch my breath. "You think if I had any money coming from Pelper County, astead of buying Old Jack back for you, I'd hide it?" I asked.

Her black eyes narrowed. Other than that, she didn't move.

"Aunt Ilish, look . . . "

She still faced me, panting hard. I stood nigh helpless as a bird hypnotized by a snake. Like it or not, and I didn't like it a bit, Aunt Ilish could sometimes do that to me.

Bode Jenkins put his arm on her shoulder, but she shook him off. "What's she aim to get from you, Bode?" She was still facing me. "Your boy? Green, he wants to leave Lucy Lee for her, you told me so yourself, and twice you've made him go back. How's come, Bode, huh? Your Green, he ought to go real good with Milt's mule and Nate Brice's land and pretty money?"

"Green's notions to marry me, if he's got any, are all his and none of mine," I told Bode.

"And Eb Holt, he takes her down to his old home place to diddle her, and here's Opal's belly about to bust. Gives her what Opal ought to get!"

She was close to breathing fire. "And you know what else, Bode? Urch Vestman give her pink silkies and a pretty red shirt and blue jeans and boots. Everybody and his brother gives Goldy Lark pretties and she ain't smart enough to know they all want to jump on and ride. She thinks it's all acause they like her so!"

I know I would have knocked out her aching tooth and ten more with it, and jerked out all her hair if Bode hadn't pulled her from my sight. That made the first time I had to wet my head in Onion Creek to get the sizzle to stop.

# 16

We didn't get to Rard Graveyard on Decoration Day. Aunt Ilish's toothache wasn't any better than her temper, and the hard spring showers would have ruined the crepe paper flowers I'd helped make the past week. By Tuesday, the showers got harder and oftener, and the toothache worse.

"You'll play hob," Aunt Ilish snapped at me when I offered to lay the flowers on family graves in her stead. "Last time you and Eb got left alone, you went at it like dogs the second you was out of sight. I'll make sure it don't happen again, bet your last dollar on that."

Face afire, I handed the letter for her I'd found in the mailbox and said, "Eb says we'll go when the rain slacks up. He'll get a tarp from Vestman's to keep the flowers dry," and turned to go.

"It being relief day," was her answer, "we'll get Urch's wagon, too, to hold the eats."

Eb and me had the buggy dug out of the mud and washed, and Old Jack hitched when my aunt came down the path. Eyeing the two quilts I'd put on the buggy seat for her to lay on and rest when we got in the wagon, she sniffed.

"Looks like I got here just in time to stop you two," she said, climbing up in the seat.

I sat in the wet buggy bed alone till we got to the store.

Once we were in Vestman's wagon, with the flowers covered with Urch's tarp just in case, the sun came out and the sky stayed clear till dark.

I helped Aunt Ilish carry in the flowers to the Lynch family corner while Eb tied Vestman's horses to the big iron gate. Instead of standing by my father's grave, I stood between his and Milt Holt's. If I cried, which would my tears be for, I wondered. Milt, I decided, seemed the most real. I had touched him and he'd touched me. Harley Farker was just a faceless man who'd died a hundred years ago, if he'd ever lived at all.

Eb was in tears at his parents resting place before he even found time to kneel. "Oh, God, Pop, I'm worser off now'n I was a year back, a whole lot worser. Oh, God, Pop, I hurt so," he was whispering to Milt's grave.

I walked away to let him be alone and went farther into the Lynch family corner just as Aunt Ilish started towards my father's grave and those of Eb's parents, three flowers left in her hand. I studied the names on the markers, from my great-grandfather on down. Irishman Joshua Jeremiah Lynch, schoolteacher, and Annie Lynch, his wife and loving mother of Harvey. Farmer Harvey Lynch, beloved husband of Cherokee Meadow Lark, beloved father of whore Ilish and whore Bree. Jailbird Henry Troat, first husband of Ilish Lynch, father of jailbird Burt and whore Opal Troat Holt, wife of step-brother Eb (Eban) Holt. Between two plots, likely meant for Brother Dossie and Aunt Cloma, was the tiny grave of baby Nonny Lynch.

Sadly, I thought of Mom. Bree Lynch Farker Brice, whore, mother of Goldy Lark Farker, beloved wife of Harley Farker, second (and hated) wife of Nate Brice, husband number three to her sister, Ilish Lynch Troat Holt Brice. I hoped Miss Emmer Cox, who said she'd forgiven Bree and had no reason to forgive me, would remember her grave today.

Maybe it was a hovering angel, if I had one, who wanted me to straighten out the lie I'd told Sheriff McKay about seeing the first Sheriff McKay's grave when I'd first come in last summer. If it was, I found myself at the old sheriff's marker without knowing how I got there. Wilford, his middle name, caught my eye instead of his birth and death dates and, that's what I planned to mention next time McKay mentioned his father.

I returned to the wagon as Eb was blowing his nose. Aunt Ilish lay in the wagon seat, holding her jaw and groaning low. We headed to town for the relief, getting to the courthouse just as Uncle Sam was ready to close.

Jessie Red McKay overtook us in his big black car less than a mile from town. "Going to New Hill's school meet to keep order. The three school directors, they're hiring a new school teacher tonight," Eb explained.

I knew then Miss Maudie Troat wasn't coming back.

"Reckon that one, she's cut off her nose to spite her face by divorcing my Burt and not wanting to schoolteach again this year," Aunt Ilish raised up to say. "Bode, he's apt to plum starve this year, with all the mouths he's got to feed, and no schoolhouse pay."

I thought it best not to answer, and I guess Eb did, too.

A full moon was overhead when we reached Vestman's store. No light shone inside the store, but on the house's front porch old Villie Vestman was in his wheelchair being tended by Louise Helton. At Vestman's barn, Eb exchanged their team and wagon for Old Jack and the buggy. When the relief was in the buggy, we started down the school road home. Even the bumpy rocks didn't rouse Aunt Ilish, finally and thankfully asleep.

At Doc Helton's, his younger girls were screaming at each other in a game of "Ghost." Evelyn was at an open window, sitting doing something I couldn't see.

"Buying some new dresses; Evelyn's all set to teach next year in Miss Maudie's stead," Eb said.

"Now how do you know that?" I asked.

"A little brown birdie told me," he grinned.

In the schoolhouse yard, a wagon, a buggy, and two saddled horses were tied under the post oaks. the bumper of Doc Helton's car was touching the steps; Sheriff McKay's was directly behind. I could see a gathering of men inside, only a few of whom I knew.

"Deputies. School meet outshines even the Pie Supper," Eb said as we trotted past. "Miss Maudie won't come back and Theron Copeland's got no girl to teach, so both Bode and Theron, two of

New Hill's directors, they'll go against Urch Vestman, third direc-
tor, argue over Urch's choice to teach. Urch, he's already been
paid twenty dollar or so by some girl's pop or some woman's
husband, and offer 'em twenty apiece to go his way. Good fist
fight or two, hour or so, New Hill's got a new teacher at sixty
dollar a month. They call that buying a school."

"Sounds wrong to me," I said. "Couldn't they just pick the
smartest and let her teach?"

He looked at me. "Wrong, now that's a funny word for Ilish
Troat's kin to use."

I gritted my teeth in answer.

"Nobody's honest when it's time to buy a school, not even Doc
Helton. He's been trying to fix it with Urch for Evelyn to teach,
even if she's only been one summer to college. Sixty dollar a
month ain't something a man can turn his back to easy."

I know, I thought. That much money was all the money in the
world to me.

Eb left me and Aunt Ilish at the bridge with all the relief eats we
could carry up to the house while he took the buggy to leave at the
crossing. Leading the mule, he brought up the rest, most of which
would be stored in the back room. Aunt Ilish and Burt took their
share and started up to the cabin, I thought. Planning to clean the
mud from my shoes by scraping them on the hewn log, I almost
stepped on my aunt before I knew she was there.

"You want more eats, you know where they're at," I heard Eb
say while my back was turned to the house.

"I don't, Eb. I just want to ask if you'd mind me moving back
in. Lonesome up there with Nate gone. Guess I don't rightly have
to ask, this being my home and all."

"Guess you rightly do have to ask, Ilish Troat, it being my
house now and all. The answer's no." I could hear him strike a
match with his thumbnail. "I like you up there just dandy. Wish
to hell you'd take your damn family along."

"Just acause you and your woman fight. . . ."

"Don't call Opal my woman, Ilish Troat. A woman shares her
man's troubles and his bed. No, Opal ain't my wife, we're just
hitched, that's all. And you know what else?"

"I don't care what else. She's your worry now."

"She ups and tells me last night she wants to divorce me when the baby comes. You want to hear the rest?"

"I done said I didn't."

"Now she's got the fool notion I'm fugging Goldilocks, just like you put in her head."

I heard loud coughing and guessed she'd choked on her chew. "I never done that, no such thing. Look, Eb, just for a spell. I'll do your warsh, cook."

"Goldilocks does it right fine," Eb told her.

I was in the front room when she said, "Goldy Lark sharing your love, too, Eb? That's why Opal wants free?"

"Why, you fugging old whore!"

Opal's sudden scream of, "Look out, Eb!" caused us all to turn. Eb's move was fast enough to catch the two-by-four Burt had ready to bring down on his head. All in one motion, Eb had yanked the board from him and sent him flying out the door, himself not far behind. I was at Aunt Ilish's heels when she got in the yard.

Burt was in a crouch, wiping blood from his nose. "I've had a bellyful of you and your God damn bossing. I aim to kill you right here, Eb Holt!"

"Oh, no, you ain't, you fat ass bastard." Eb spit on his thumb and formed fists. "You ain't, on account of I aim to kill you first!"

So the pinching sores that had been festering between Eb and Burt for several years had finally come to a head.

# 17

Where Eb Holt needed weight, Burt Troat was clumsy. But Burt's unbelievable arm length made up for Eb's extra height, so all things considered, and both sober, it was a fair fight. Eb got in the second punch, too, one that sent Burt staggering against Old Jack's barn, a loud "Uhhh!" sounding when his back smacked the building. Before Burt got his balance, Eb was on him, thumping his face with both fists. Burt's head rolled from side to side like a copperhead snake being put to death by a dog. He evened it by reaching up to pin his powerful hands on Eb's throat and squeeze with all his might.

With those hairy hands so, he pulled Eb to his feet. Funny sounds bubbled from Eb's mouth, his arms dangled useless, his color changed to a dark red. I was fixed to call him a goner, and there was nothing I could do, it was all happening so lightning quick, when he somehow found the needed strength to break partway free. He poked Burt in the eye with his thumb. Burt screamed, loosened his hold and his Eb full in the face the second his knee shot toward Eb's belly. Eb staggered against the woodpile, cussing with each breath. They both regained their footing at the same time.

The next second both were at each other again, Eb's big shoes savagely pounding Burt's shins, Burt trying but unable to knee Eb. When my cousin tried to get his hands on Eb's throat again, Eb hit him in the mouth, sending blood spurting down his face. Burt halted to wipe the blood from his chin. Seeing it covering his hand seemed to worry him, because he stopped just long enough for Eb to send him sprawling.

Eb astraddle Burt and actually holding both big hairy hands with only one of his, pounded his face into the dirt. The fight ended with Eb kicking and rolling my cousin all the way down to the bridge and shoving him under water to bring him to.

"Mom, get me Brother Dossie's shotgun. I aim to kill him afore daylight, I swear it," Burt said when able.

"No, son. I'm going to the cabin and bolt the door, live out the rest of my days longing for my old home. You're smart, so'll you." My aunt helped him on the bridge. "We tried. Eb Holt bested us, that's all. You can stay the night with me."

"I live here, I stay put." Burt limped toward the barn, blood still running from his cut mouth.

Aunt Ilish pulled out her tobacco and took a chew, then headed upcreek, walking like an old, old woman.

Throughout the fight, I'd stood with rooted feet. Not my aunt. She'd circled the men, screaming, "Kill him, Burt!" the times my cousin had the edge.

"Ilish Troat was on Burt's side," Eb said, washing the blood from his face and hands with creek water. "Who'd you want to win?"

"I wasn't worried for you once," I lied.

We found Opal at the woodpile, holding Milt's rifle.

Eb bent to touch her shoulder. "You love me so much, Opal, you'd killed your own brother for me?"

"Fish farts!" She moved from his touch. "I just don't like men fighting, that's all," and she took the gun inside. Eb following a foot behind.

A light swinging itself up the path caught my eye when I stepped outside for nature. Guessing it was Jessie Red McKay, and that he'd heard the ruckus from New Hill, I backed against the mule's shelter and hunkered down in the weeds. Calling my name low, the sheriff knocked easy above the open doorway. Not even Old Jack moved. At no reply save my thumping heart, he left the yard and went almost to the barn. I could still see him standing there, listening for one of us to move. So I stayed still as a mouse until his flashlight worked its way up the hill.

# 18

Many days of sullen silence had passed between Eb Holt and Burt Troat, when Opal was suddenly struck by hard belly pains. Somehow, me and Eb managed to get her in the buggy and up to Doc's. Evelyn Helton met us at the door. Her white face pinched with hateful lines, a plink pair of ear bobs on, she took one look at Opal and said Doc was away. "He was called down by Rard. Horse kicked a man. Guess you'd best try the doctor there."

Eb shoved his foot against the door to stop her from slamming it in our faces. "She thinks the baby's coming. We wouldn't make it, if that's the case."

"Looks like you'd best take her to Ilish for help, then." She sniffed. "I can't help her here."

Eb pulled two wadded one-dollar bills from his pocket. "Just atween you and me, Evelyn, I'd sooner my woman birthed our baby inside Doc's office then in the buggy out there in the road."

"Oh, come on in." Evelyn jammed the money into her dress pocket in a hurry and led us inside and down a hall. The room we entered held a high table, a desk, a devonette, and a chair. Snow white curtains covered the window at the side of the room.

Evelyn put a hand to Opal's forehead. "Lay on the devonette there. They pulling pains, Opal?"

"They're just hurting pains," Opal said.

"Well, lay still's you can till Doc comes. I got things to do," and she left us alone.

It seemed like we'd been waiting two hours when Doc Helton finally got home. Somebody from down Rard way had been kicked in the head by a horse, he said.

We lifted Opal up to the tall table and I was supposed to have Doc shoo Eb out but say I could stay if I turned to the window and stayed there.

"This baby coming early?" he asked when he had finished doing whatever he'd done to Opal.

"Acourse. I'm part Lynch, ain't I?"

"Look, Opal, I can't help you if I don't know the truth, so tell me if you've had a baby before."

I felt Opal's eyes jump to my back in quick fear. Then she laughed loud. "No, Doc, this makes my first."

"You feel scarred up inside like you had."

"I worked for you three whole year, Doc. Missed only two day last November with a sore throat and cold, in all that time. I ever look like I was nine month knocked up?"

He had to admit not. "All the same, they're there, the scars, and that's what you hurt from, the baby's not coming now. When did you first get these pains?"

"Close to two month after I was knocked up, reckon," she said. "At first, they was just pinging pains. Time Eb and me married, I hurt so bad I could varely let him touch me. He wouldn't leave me be and I couldn't stand hurting, so I told him if he touched me again, I'd divorce him. He did. So I aim to."

The pretty white curtains at the open window flapped against my face as she spoke and I halfway shut my eyes to picture them as my wedding veil when I married Eb Holt. I had to shiver at the beautiful thought.

"Here's some pills. Take one now and one at meals," Doc was saying when my mind got back to the room. "Go to bed and don't get up for anything, Opal, or I can't promise you'll carry this baby full term. You get your mom to help you."

"Damn my mom. I got Goldy Lark. Now, you tell Eb Holt to leave me be, huh?"

"I'll say so, till the baby comes," and he called to Eb.

Doc helped get Opal up in the buggy. As Eb took the check-lines, Doc said, "Funny cloud down by Ilish's place, Eb. So black, and smell it. Like burnt meat. Ilish doing the wash when you folks left, Opal?"

"Goldy Lark does it all," Eb answered for her.

Eb stood in the buggy bed to study the cloud. "Must be at Nate Brice's place, just ahind Lynch's. Nate's likely back and caught him a family of rabbits."

"I still think it's Lynch's," was Doc Helton's goodbye.

I breathed easier going down the hill. Eb whistled about his gal in Kansas City and Opal threw him a bone of kindness by letting his knee rest touching hers. I stood up in the buggy bed behind them, hanging onto the seat and touching Eb's shoulder (and burning inside with an aching need for him) the few times the buggy jumped on the bumpy road.

At New Hill we heard terrible screams to go with the black, meat-smelling cloud. All of us realized at the same time it was Aunt Ilish carrying on and that the cloud was hanging almost directly over where the barn had once stood.

We found Aunt Ilish by what was left of the barn, pointing and screaming for her Burt. The only thing left of him was a pile of charred bones atop the springs of the barn bed. He smoked and stank long after Sheriff McKay and his deputies got there.

"Good God Almighty!" McKay repeated over and over, shaking his head in disbelief. "Wonder how Milt's old dog happened to be in the barn."

"Eb told us when he went to get you that must be Old Mame burning there," I said.

He looked at my aunt, who was still rooted to the same spot, and pointed to a deputy. "Get her inside, see if you can get head or tail of how this thing started. And you go tell Bode Jenkins to tell Miss Maudie—no, wait," he told another deputy. "They've been gone all day to town, Miss Maudie went to put in for her devorce from Burt Troat today. I saw 'em there."

He bent over the bones. "Good God Almighty, that ain't a dog

I smell cooking, it can't be. It's Burt Troat? He wasn't worth a hill of beans, but nobody ought to die this way," he said, turning aside to cough.

Though the smoke had been heavy and black and the air thick with the burning meat smell, I hadn't really realized in my numbness that it was a human I smelled, a person I knew, laying there in the hot ashes.

And then I got so sick I thought I'd die.

Sometime in the night, Aunt Ilish, who was sitting in the rocker without rocking, sent me to fetch Jessie Red McKay. He stood before her, ashes on his face and hands, smelling of the meaty smoke. "I hate to say, Ilish, it was a killing. I found some empty shells."

"Shots. I heard the shots," she said.

"You see anything, Ilish?"

"A man with a shotgun and a axe run from the barn."

"You on your way down to visit Burt?"

She folded her arms. "I was feeding the chickens when I first heard Burt holler. I started to run down here. Partway, my telephoney—it's homemade from tin cans and bob wire—it give the trouble ring. I felt it was powerful bad. All the way down, I called to Burt to hold on, I'd be there. About to the cornfield, I heard shots."

"How many?" She shook her head. "What about the fire?"

"The barn was nigh gone, save for a corner this side, by time I got here."

"That the corner the man run round?" She nodded. "Guess you didn't see the man plain, Ilish, huh?"

"I guess I did. Plain's I see you."

"Do you know him?"

"No." She put her hands over her eyes and took a long breath. "No, he was somebody I'd never seen afore."

"Well, we're all done here for tonight, Ilish. We're taking Burt's, uh, bones to town for you." He sounded like he was talking to a sad little kid. "And Miss Maudie'll be told, if that helps you any. I'm sure sorry. Can I do something else for you in Rard?"

She nodded. "You can tell the undertaker I can't pay him for a spell. He sure hollered at me acause I didn't hold any insurance on

Henry Troat, a long ways back. Recollecting that, I took out a policy on Burt's life after Milt died. I didn't have to worry on Milt, Eb took care of his funeral." She lowered her head. "You can help me go about getting the insurance money if you get time."

"You want me to have him a grave dug in the Lynch corner and line up services for him, Ilish?"

"Miss Maudie likely won't help, so it's my place to," she said sadly. "Thanky for doing what I can't get to from here."

Before she left for the cabin, I asked her if she wanted me to write Burt's death in the Lynch family Bible. "I just want to help," I said.

"Best way to do that's to mind your own business," I was told, "and leave mine be."

# 19

Burt Troat's funeral was held in Rard—New Hill had yet to find another preacher—and drew a crowd that outdid even Milt Holt's. Opal being unable to go, and Eb refusing to, I drove my aunt in the buggy. She sat silent, unchewing. Not one tear had she shed for Burt in front of me. If she cried at home alone, it never once showed in her eyes. The one time I saw her show any feelings whatsoever, and that was surprise, was when Bode Jenkins entered the church and sat directly across the aisle from us. I halfway expected her to stand up and screech at him for Miss Maudie not being there, but she didn't move.

The service was short, starting with "Rock of Ages" by the church singers. It ended with the preacher saying good things about Burt, which showed he hadn't known him in life.

Aunt Ilish didn't say one word on the ride to the graveyard. We walked in behind Bode, who seemed to be there alone. Just as we got to the waiting grave in the Lynch family corner, the singers went into "How Beautiful Heaven Must Be," and a baby behind us cried. The preacher said a fast prayer over the closed coffin. When he was done, Aunt Ilish bent her head and coughed twice. That was her goodbye to her only son.

Back in town, I waited in the buggy while Aunt Ilish went to promise the undertaker payment from Burt's insurance policy money when it came. I also waited outside the courthouse while she signed Burt off relief. I was so tired from being up the two nights and three days since my cousin's terrible death, I leaned my head against the buggy seat and right away fell asleep.

"Gold Lark Farker." The whisper of Sheriff McKay was close to my ear. "You like your Aunt Ilish much?"

"I don't like her any," I said, coming awake.

"You notice her not crying for her boy?" His head was so close I could smell the oil in his curly red hair.

"She acted like it wasn't Burt in the coffin," I said.

Without looking directly at me, he said, "For the time being, I'll forget you said that, if you'll forget you said it." He watched Aunt Ilish come down the courthouse steps and added, without turning his head, "I'll be down at Onion Creek come tomorrow noon. Got something just me and you can do."

Tipping his hat to me, he hurried to help Aunt Ilish cross the street.

# 20

For most of the day Jessie Red McKay and his deputies searched the farm. "No sign of that man anywhere," he told us when they quit around two. "Just told Ilish up at the cabin I'm no smarter now'n I was this morning," he said.

"What you trying to find?" Opal asked from the front room bed, where she stayed all the time now.

McKay shook his head. "Won't rightly know what I'm looking for till I find it," he said.

I figured from that he didn't want her to know what he'd said he wanted to tell me.

Eb, who'd had either me or Opal cut his hair all winter long, mentioned his need to see the town barber. "Getting wild and woolly, full of fleas. Can I bum a ride to town with you, McKay?"

"My deputies going," he said. "Get your own way back."

"Think it's safe to leave the girls here alone?"

McKay turned to me. "You know how to shoot?"

"Nate Brice had a gun I learnt on," I said.

Jessie Red took Milt's rifle down and blew in the barrel. Handing me the gun after he'd put in the two shells I'd got him from a dresser drawer, he said, "The gut's a good place to aim at."

I commenced shivering the minute the men left and was still shaking a few minutes later as I took the water bucket down to the creek. At first, I couldn't see the sheriff anywhere and was wondering if he'd forgotten me when I heard a "Pssst!" across the bridge. Jessie Red McKay stood in the buckbrush motioning me closer.

"Can you do something for me and keep your mouth shut about it?" he asked when I joined him behind a big elm tree.

"Acourse I can," I said.

"What I want you to do for me's go all over the house and under the hewn log first good chance you get. Need to find the missing shotgun I know Brother Dossie always kept at the cabin. His woodpile's shy its axe, too. You get your hands on either, drop anything you're at and get it up to Vestman's quick. Urch, he'll call me on his telephoney. You wait for me there."

"You know who the man is?" I guessed.

"Got a dom good notion." He reached out a big hand to pat my shoulder. "He's far gone now, just atween you and me and the gatepost. No call to be scared."

"I ain't," I lied.

"You fill your bucket, go in and fasten the doors, if you'll feel safer. That mule you got'll snort loud if somebody comes. And you got the gun. Now, don't you worry. I'll find Eb Holt, start him back here long afore dark."

The darkness came, but not Eb Holt. Opal's pill let her sleep while I stood guard at the front door against a killer. I hoped that if he had to come back tonight after the rest of us, he'd go to the cabin and kill Aunt Ilish first. Then he would kill Opal, while the two bullets I left in his belly would slow him enough that I could run for Vestman's. I would marry Eb before Opal was cold in her grave.

When Eb at last returned, I lit the lamp at the dresser and let him in when he growled my name at the door. He pushed past me like I wasn't there.

At Opal's cry of surprised pain, I ran to the front room where Eb had pulled her up and was slapping her awake. Drunk as he could ever be and still stand, he looked from Opal to me.

"So you're both named Lark, ain't you?"

We nodded together.

"Well, come on, tell me. Which one's the little two-bit whore all the camp boys laid with?"

Neither of us answered.

"She had plaits and a blue relief dress and her name was Lark." His face was purple. "And sometime in the winter, she bobbed her hair. Ain't that something, she bobbed her hair." He was shaking so hard I thought he'd fall.

"I went to this place in Rard for a beer—one lousy bottle of beer, mind you—and here's this camp boy there, one of the bosses who don't move round so much. I tell him I used to be a camp boy in Oregon and you know what he tells me? He tells me about a little bitch named Lark he met at New Hill church last summer, who lets you stand in line three deep for two bits a lay. He pictured the barn to a T. He's not been there lately, though, not since about time I moved in. By Christ, I don't have to wonder why."

I was afraid to look at Opal.

"Goldilocks, I'll ask you first if it was you he talked of?"

"No." It was too late now to help Opal, even if I'd wanted to.

"You look me in the eye and swear you've never slept with a camp boy?"

"Yes, Eb, I sure can," and I did.

"Then it's you, Opal, ain't it? You didn't come to me a poor girl raped a few year back by some man you didn't know, like you told me at Christmas in the barn. You didn't come to me robbed of your cherry, you slut. You come as a sum bitching knocked-up whore!" He pulled her up by her hair, only to slap her down when her feet hit the floor. "No wonder you couldn't stand me touching you much. I never offered you a quarter, did I?"

Opal stayed where she fell, tears running down her cheeks.

"So the kid you're carrying could be anybody's but mine, and what a bastard sucker I am!" He slapped her again.

"Don't, Eb." I was afraid he'd kill her and go to jail for it and then he'd never be mine. "It can't be helped now."

He doubled his fist and knocked me against the devonette. "You think so, huh? Well, that's where you're pure wrong. Get all her things bundled up and get her out of my sight fast. I'll kill her, by hell, if you don't."

"Eb, she can't. She's wobbly from her pills. It's too dark out, she can't see."

"Shut up, Goldilocks. Crawl your ass to Ilish Troat, Opal. Tell her if she ever tries to tell folks your bastard's mine, I'll kill her, sure there's little green apples."

I stuffed Opal's few belongings in a floursack with her pills, tied it, put it in her hand and got her to the kitchen.

"Opal, go up to Urch's, get him to take you in," I said.

She gagged in answer.

I turned to Eb. "Can I take her up in the buggy?"

"The buggy's mine. So's the mule. They don't budge. You got one second to get her out of my sight." He doubled his fist.

He was in the rocker opening a bottle while I, soon to become his one and only now, helped my cousin out of his life.

# 21

Sprinkles of blood leading toward New Hill showed on the bridge when I went down for wash water at daylight. My heart thumping, I saddled Old Jack without first feeding him his breakfast biscuits. I followed Opal's trail as far as the school, where it stopped by the mailboxes. Expecting at every bend of the road to find my cousin dead in the ditch, I raced the mule to Doc Helton's.

Evelyn met me at the door. "Opal's here, Goldy Lark. Doc found her last night on his way back from Copeland's. She's weak from blood loss, but she'll pull through."

"She have her baby?"

"A dead boy. Ivy's got him on the kitchen table. Opal's in no shape to make funeral plans and we figured Ilish wouldn't help her. Eb neither." She moved to shut the door. "Coming in or not?"

"I don't know," I said.

She opened the door wider. "If I was you, I'd anyhow see Opal. Neither Ilish or Eb's apt to. Asides, you're letting in flies."

205

Opal looked so pale under the blue ruffly bed cover, I'd have thought her dead if she hadn't raised up when I closed the door in Evelyn Helton's face.

"Oh. Goldy Lark." She sounded like she'd been screaming all night, and from what Bree had once told me about how having a baby hurt, I guessed she'd carried on her share.

I went closer, trying not to look at the bruises Eb had put on her face and arms. "Opal, I don't know what to say."

"You could've helped me last night, but you want Eb for your own. I can see it by the way you look when I say his name. My little baby's dead acause you let him beat me up. Words ain't any good to me now," and she turned to the wall.

Evelyn Helton hurried in to shoo me out to the kitchen.

I found Ivy in the linoleum-flowered room, bending over a little table where Opal's blued baby laid. She was washing the black Indian hair with a cake of storebought soap and a mail order washrag, squeezing the rag out in a big granite pot, not seeing me. She couldn't, for the tears.

I said her name so's she'd know I was there.

She wiped her eyes with her sleeve and looked up. "Oh, Goldy Lark. I'm taking last care of Eb's baby. I want to."

My first thought was to slap her into next week for the soft, soft way she said Eb's name. But my second thought told me not to knock the dead baby from her arms; it would look bad for me. She'd be punished enough when she lost Eb Holt to me, and she'd have to hurt the same way I'd had to when Opal grabbed him right from under my nose.

So I watched as she finished washing the baby, dried and powdered him, and dressed him in white rompers with pink ducks on the bib. Last of all, she wrapped him in a storebought blanket, her tears falling faster. She kissed the ugly little wrinkled face and opened what I guessed was Doc's office door.

"H-He's ready, Daddy," she called to Doc and carried Opal's baby to the door.

I hated Ivy Helton as I watched her squeeze out the storebought washrag, dry the pretty pink soap on her apron and drop it in the apron's pocket. I hated her even more when she dumped several potatoes in the granite pot without first emptying the water.

"You can't have Eb Holt, Ivy, not ever," I said through a thick tongue. "The reason why's you and Opal both slept with the camp boys and took money for it. Eb, he won't piss on you when I tell him all I know."

"I got saved since then, Goldy Lark."

I looked at that white face that was Evelyn's from the yellow bobbed hair to the red bobs in her white ears and said, "I'll lie on you. I'll tell Eb I see you all the time with some camp boy in the bushes."

"I didn't know you wanted him that bad." Her tears were dripping down onto the waist of her striped storebought dress.

"You do now." While I was at it, I added, "And best you dump out them taters, Ivy. You'll cook 'em in the dead baby's warsh warter and Opal'll have to eat some."

And then I didn't hate Ivy Helton nearly so much.

# 22

Eb Holt didn't seem to hear me when I said the baby died. He didn't seem to hear me again when I said Urch Vestman said to say Opal had put in for a divorce. "He said she worked in the store a few days, then up and left. He don't know where she went to," I added, thinking it best not to say Opal had stolen twenty dollars and two pair of silkies from Urch the minute his back was turned.

Real late that night, I found out I'd been wrong. He did care, but he'd been too drunk to think or talk.

"Goldilocks, tell me it ain't so." He was in the rocker with his clothes on, moving back and forth in big pain. "Tell me she's not gone from me for good. Oh, God, I can't hurt this way no more! I love her so damn much I'd cut off my head if she asked. And she ain't nothing but a two-bit whore!"

I leaned over to take his hand. "I can't say it didn't happen, Eb. I can fix you some eats, that's all I can do."

"You get me another bottle, Goldilocks?" I thought he would shake himself apart.

"Urch said he was all out," I lied.

"Then you go away, let me be. If I don't want to die now, I never will," and he commenced to cry.

That was how Jessie Red McKay found him at daylight. With both hands he hauled him to his feet and shoved him down to the creek, where he pushed him in head first.

Eb came up spewing water from his mouth and nose. "Go on, drown me if you got a notion to. I don't care. I'll never cry over anyone ever again and I'll never care for a girl again,' he said, holding both hands to quiet his shakes.

"That go for Goldy Lark Farker, too?"

Eb looked at me like I'd been the cause of all his worries. "She's Ilish Troat's kin, can't you tell by looking?"

"She was good enough to take care of your daddy when you couldn't, I recollect."

"She's still a God damn mishling who looks like Ilish Troat," Eb said.

McKay pushed him back in the water. "For a penny," he said, "I'd jail you for hitting Opal and making her lose her baby."

"Man finds out his wife's whoring, he can hit her all he wants to." Finally able to stand, Eb started blubbering again.

"Guess you'd best clear out of here afore I run you off," McKay said. "Look at you, Milt Holt's son, bawling like a baby. Don't you have even a smidgen of his goodness?"

"I never claimed to be half the man Pop was," Eb sniffed.

"Get his things," McKay told me.

"Don't, Goldilocks." Eb swiped at his tears. "I won't go to jail, McKay. I'd smell Burt there."

"Get going, girl," McKay said again.

Eb made it to the bridge. Sitting down with his head in his hands, he asked, "How's come I can't swap Ilish Troat for the cabin, since Burt burnt my place down?"

"Reckon you could do that, if she don't mind," McKay said.

"Goldilocks," Eb told me, "go tell the old heifer I like her so much I'll give her a pick of who to live with, you or me."

The sheriff grabbed my arm to stop me. "You go," he told Eb. "A little walk upcreek might sober you up a while." Watching Eb staggering up through the buckbrush, he said, "You been looking all over the house, like I told you to?"

I said I'd been all over the whole house and found nothing that didn't belong there.

"Well, let's go over it again while there's a chance," he said.

He took the front room and the kitchen, giving me the back room. There was still no place there to hide anything. The rag box held just rags, the bed held mattresses and covers. Under Burt's cot were a few quilts we didn't need in summer, under Opal's was my dirty jeans and relief dress and my other pair of bloomers.

I heard McKay opening the dresser drawers, then pulling my devonette from against the wall and pushing it and a giant wad of dust back. He was standing on the creaking dresser trying to crack the loft opening loose when I got done, his face reddening more with each smack of his fist.

"Dom thing's never been off, reckon, since the house was built," he finally said, jumping down to wash his dusty hands. "Couldn't be what I want up there."

The one place left was under the hewn log, where I again found only spider webs with the dirt and dust.

"Guess that man Aunt Ilish seen run took the axe and Brother Dossie's shotgun with him," I said. "You think they'll ever find him?"

He rubbed at his nose. "Any day now, just any day."

In about ten minutes more, a pale Eb came down the path with puke on his shirt, Bode Jenkins and Aunt Ilish right behind. Bode had a floursack full of Aunt Ilish's things, a jar of goose grease, and her pillow. She carried her Harper's Homespun and her tap. McKay stayed long enough to warn us all about getting along before washing his hands again, this time in the creek.

All that week I was kept busy going back and forth from the house to the cabin, from the cabin to the house. I brought down Aunt Ilish's relief eats and toted Eb's up. I moved down the rest of her clothes and moved his mother's rocker up. I caught her nigh-grown brown leghorns and dumped them in Old Jack's empty shelter after I took the mule, saddle, bridle, curry comb, harness, and water tub up to Eb. Then I got cursed at by him for not being able to also get the buggy up through the rocks and buckbrush where it had never gone before.

I was within sight of being done when Aunt Ilish missed a poke of Virgie Jenkins' dried green apples. She didn't give Eb a chance to lie to me about them. Tearing up through the brush, she returned in minutes with what was left.

Thoughts of Milt Holt's "overgrown boy" feeding that "solid gold mule, who's rightly mine, what's rightly mine" so riled Aunt Ilish that she made me move the woodpiles.

Thanks be, both were very, very low.

The other big thing to happen that week was my aunt's agreeing to let Bode Jenkins pull her aching tooth with the pliers he brought from home. Bode got the tooth out, all right, but her mouth was nigh swollen shut for over three days. It was good to have the house quiet for a change.

# 23

"The city people's powerful slow paying me my Burt's insurance money," Aunt Ilish said every day the mailbox showed empty. "This keeps up, I'll be in the poorhouse afore I know it. Guess you know, Goldy Lark, with me being in charge of you, you'll go, too."

"I ain't got money to keep us out," I said.

She passed me a hateful look. "Tell me another'n afore that'n gets cold."

I watched her shove the end piece of a tobacco twist into her mouth and wallow it from side to side. "This is my last chaw. We're out of coal oil, too. Walk to Vestman's afore it gets too hot."

She spat in the mudhole. "Hie, now." Removing her chew, she laid it on a clean plate. "I'll make this last till you get back. That way, you can wait for the mail. It might run early today."

To my surprise, Ivy Helton was working the store. She laid two tobacco twists on the counter and went to the back for the coal oil, acting like she didn't like me. I didn't say anything else to her till, on my way out, she handed me a bottle for Eb Holt.

"Urch said give it to you if you come up, put it on Eb's bill," she said, trying to pitch her head like Lucy Lee Copeland Jenkins.

I took the bottle and asked, "Where's Urch?"

"Old man's sick." She fiddled with an ear bob. "Anything else?"

"Just Eb Holt, but you don't have him," I said, happy to see tears come to her big blue eyes.

I smiled all the way down to New Hill.

After a long, two-hour sweaty wait, I was still smiling to myself over the look on Ivy Helton's face when I smarted off. But I knew my aunt would find it anything but funny when the mail finally ran and she had no insurance money letter.

When Eb Holt didn't answer at the cabin, I left the bottle in the doorway. I hurried down home to find Aunt Ilish by the woodpile, so mad she was trying to cry. A big bloody hunk of her heel hung loose. Dried blood covered the axe blade, its handle, and part of the chop block.

"I could've cut my head off and you still wouldn't bring me a money letter, would you?" she snapped, seeing my hands empty.

"What'd you do?" I asked.

"What's it look like I done? I cut myself, that's what I done," she snapped.

"Your hand slip?"

"My head slipped." She gave me a look that would have fried a bedbug. "Bode Jenkins, I mean. Who'd you think, Santy Claus?" She was so boiling she shook. "He comes up here finally, wanting me right now, just like that, the old tom cat. He's even brought me a jar of milk, fancy that. I told him to his face he's not the best man I ever had want me. Now he's gone! And I could die afore daylight for all you and him and the insurance people care."

I held out my hand. "Come on, I'll help you up."

"I'll help myself, never you mind."

I brought her a dipper of water after she'd settled at the table, ducking just in time as she threw it in the mudhole. "I'd wanted warter, I'd asked for warter." Then, seconds later and in a kind voice, came, "You go down to Bode's. Tell Virgic to give you a poke of goose feathers. Though don't say they're for me. Tell her Eb Holt cut his hand on rusty bob wire and he don't want to take lockjaw."

"Anything else?" I asked, hoping to save myself another trip, when she changed her mind about Bode.

"Goldy Lark." Her voice softened. "Atop a gooseberry bush, biggest one of three on Bode's creek side, there's a cut of binder-twine, bow-tied. You undo it and tie it in a loose knot on your way back."

"I will, Aunt Ilish."

At dark she was asleep in the kitchen doorway. Her cut heel rested on a board lying across the washpan full of damp, scorched, and smoking goose feathers, which would draw out any chances of lockjaw. She was nigh helpless. She wouldn't try to keep me from doing what my heart told me must be done tonight.

And Eb Holt would be sleeping from the bottle I'd brought. He'd welcome me naked into his bed and from that second on, he'd forever be mine.

There was enough of a moon that I could see my way to Aunt Ilish's tap in the dresser drawer. All I took was the tap itself. I couldn't chance any extra noise for a glue gun I didn't know how to work, first place. I scooped up a handful of goose grease, to be used instead of what my aunt put in the glue gun. Opal had told me the glue should be laid on the black circle that ringed the tap. The goose grease should work there, the same as the glue.

At the creek I washed the tap and dried it on my dresstail. The black circle I filled with the goose grease, adding more for good measure. The tap hurt and wouldn't go in all the way, but I figured Eb could push it up to where it should be. Every nerve of mine was screaming Eb's name as I went to him up the path.

My hopes for the night dimmed at the sight of him, shirtless, by the cabin door, untangling fishlines by lanternlight. And, for a reason only he knew, sober. When drunk, Eb would have loved me the right way, I was sure. Sober, he'd be just growly old Eb.

Then, funny enough, he greeted me with a friendly grin.

"Goldilocks, how'd you know I been thinking of you all day long?"

My heart and the tap thumping like woodsaw motors, I dropped onto a nearby rock. "I bet."

"Honest. Aimed to go down see you time I got done here."

"Why?"

"Oh, just thinking, well, I aim to marry Ivy Helton when I'm rid of Opal and move up to Doc's till I can build my place back."

I jumped to my feet. "Not her, Eb! She's a camp girl, like Opal. She'll break your heart all over again."

He actually laughed while taking out his makings. "You're just a jealous little bitch, Goldilocks, ain't you? You still want me to finish what we started downcreek last spring, don't you?"

"Ask Jessie Red McKay if it ain't so." I was barely able to hear my words for the sizzle in my head. I hadn't had that sizzle since Opal had left.

Eb finished rolling his smoke, twisted the end, lit a match with his thumbnail, and puffed. "Goldilocks," he laughed, "you're a piss-poor liar, you know that?"

I could stand anything but him making fun of me, so I commenced to cry.

"Well, now, little Ilish Troat's boo-hooing acause I found out she's no cleaner'n Opal, ain't she?"

"E-Eb, I told you I never—"

"Acourse." He still laughed. "You're a Lynch, you got birthed knowing how to work off a man, like Ilish Troat and Bree and Opal done. Hell, Bree went after Pop when Mom died like a duck on a june bug. She was about fourteen at the time. Then Henry Troat died and Ilish Troat took Pop away from Bree. They both had Bode Jenkins and Nate Brice, then Bree went after Urch Vestman. She'd got him and the store, too, if old Villie hadn't took her away from Urch. Now Opal's going the same way." He puffed smoke at my face. "Now I'm nigh rid of your damn family, Goldilocks, you think I'm dumb enough to marry you, dammit?"

The sizzle in my head had now changed into such a big hurt I couldn't think of anything to say back.

"Save yourself time, Goldilocks. Just go find Opal, let her show you how to get rich." He pitched his smoke away and moved closer. "And don't go telling any lies on Ivy Helton, else you'll be crying sorry you ever met me."

As he spoke, the tap jumped out of me and rolled down into my bloomer leg, spinning wild when it hit the elastic casing at my knee. I naturally grabbed for it, causing Eb to slap his legs and howl with laughter.

"Mention money to you Lynches, watch you hurry to pull down your itchy drawers."

The hate out of him for a while, he was whistling when I left.

I took the tap from my bloomers at the creek, washed and dried it and, stepping over my sleeping aunt in the doorway, returned it to its box seconds before she awoke.

That was the night I started crying Eb Holt from my heart and my life.

# 24

From the bridge next morning, I watched Bode Jenkins turn his wagon and team to head up for New Hill. He'd tied his horses to a post oak and was starting to the house before seeing me and the water bucket blocking his way. He'd been whistling till he saw I didn't aim to move.

"Where was you last night when I was up here seeing to your sick aunt?" I knew this was going to be a nasty talk because of his nasty tone.

Since I was the one to be asking questions, and what had happened last night between me and Eb Holt was none of his business, I said. "You and Bree. Tell me the truth about that."

He looked up to the house like he was expecting Aunt Ilish to come down and take his side against me and said, "Ain't my place to tell you about your mom. Ask Ilish."

I raised my chin. "No. I'll go ask Virgie."

He took several giant steps toward me, his hand raised. "Don't you go no closer to my place'n you are right now."

I stood my ground. "Well, then, you send Green up here, I'll ask him what I want to know."

Now his face was a foot from mine, so close I could see the sweat pop out on his bald head, watch the black hairs curling inside his nosehole. The knuckles of his free hand white against his overalls bib told me he'd sooner loosen my teeth than look at me.

"I just want to know about you and Bree," I said, not daring to blink.

"Ain't nothing much I can tell, save she was born a whore." He dropped both arms, and took a step backward. "She had ever man she'd ever looked at by time Harley Farker come along. That what you want to hear?"

"If it's the truth," I said, hoping Aunt Ilish couldn't hear him from the house.

"Well, I'll start counting men for you." He wiped his sweaty bald head with a blue bandana and commenced to count. "Milt she had when she was younger'n you are now, bet. Then there was me she tempted. I took Virgie and Miss Maudie and Green back to her Greene County home so's to get free and marry Bree. Time I got back two days later, she was loving someone else."

"Another man?" Milt, Bode. Oh, Bree, who else?

"Nate Brice." His eyes wouldn't meet mine. "Bree, she took him smack out of Ilish's bed to hers. Twice, for spite. To pay Ilish back for taking Milt Holt, reckon."

"That makes you the second man she took from my aunt?" I was having a pretty hard time trying to keep everything he'd said straight.

"No. The first." Bode Jenkins found his feet easier to talk to than my face. "There was others after Milt and Nate and me."

This was another bad dream, bad as last night's talk with Eb.

"That's all I know of, save Urch Vestman, maybe old Villie, too." He suddenly put his fist tight against my cheek and commenced pushing me backward hard. "Now you move from my way, else I'll knock you aside."

Too numb over hearing old Villie Vestman named twice as maybe a lover of Bree's, I backed off the bridge to let him pass.

"I don't ever aim for you to claim Green's soul, like Bree done mine," Bode said, starting to the house. "You just forget you ever heard his name."

I started to laugh at his dumb talk, and with the laughing came the head sizzle, which stopped any words I might have had.

I tried to cry when Bode had got Aunt Ilish in the wagon on her way to Doc Helton's, but something other than crying would have to make me feel better. For I had no tears I could shed after crying all night over Eb Holt. What would I cry about, if I could cry? That my mom had been as much a whore here as she'd been back in Pelper County, maybe even born one, like Bode Jenkins had said? Was Opal a whore because Aunt Ilish was one? Could I ever hope to be somebody big, like I wanted to be?

Sure, I can, I told myself, mad now, I can still be somebody, but it won't be easy, knowing what I know now about Bree.

"You damn right I can," I told myself aloud, raising my chin. "You damn right I will."

I stayed a while by the mudhole thinking about Miss Emmer Cox, now wishing I'd answered her letters; if I had, maybe she would have come to see me this summer. I didn't hold any thought of Roy for long. He and I were as dead that way as Eb Holt and I, and it had all been because of the other women in my family being whores.

It was nigh ten when I finally brushed the turds made by my aunt's brown leghorns from the table and made myself some fried bread. The chickens swarmed around me, begging to eat, dropping their mess everywhere, even on one foot. I shooed them out and shut both doors, also Old Jack's so they couldn't come in that way, and decided to sweep their mess from all three rooms while I was at it.

That meant pulling out the old cardboard rag box and sweeping good where it always stood. Next, I swept under the bed, then under Burt's cot, a spot that last summer had been covered by many quilts. Some of those quilts had been burned when Milt Holt died, others had been burned in the barn fire; now only three or four were left.

What I found besides chicken turds answered a lot of questions. It was a sort of cellar, or maybe had been in Joshua Lynch's time, with a wooden lid that fit tight into the floorboards. Two men Burt Troat's size could have dropped through easily and nobody in the front room or the kitchen would ever have known the difference.

I knew Sheriff Jessie Red McKay should know this was how Burt Troat had gotten out and back into the house when he'd burned Eb Holt's place, and years before, when he'd killed Almy Copeland.

I raised the lid after a hard struggle, moved it aside, and looked down into the big black-shadowed hole. Enough light showed through the washed-away clay mud chinking that I could see a ragged quilt. Beneath it was a big relief poke. From it I lifted Brother Dossie's shotgun, broken in two, and an axe whose blade showed bloody wads of hair the color of Old Mame's. In a smaller poke underneath lay several cakes of Aunt Ilish's store-bought soap, all partway used. Sticking to a pretty pink soap scrap was a wadded piece of white crepe paper. I didn't know until I'd straightened the paper out that I'd find a little greenish-gold heart tied onto a bright red string.

# 25

I had to wait a few hours to tell Jessie Red McKay of my find because Bode Jenkins and Aunt Ilish returned just as I got the lid back on the cellar. I hid the pokes under Opal's bed, aiming to start for Vestman's the minute Aunt Ilish went to sleep in the kitchen doorway and Bode went home. It didn't work as planned, for Bode told me the medicine might make my aunt dizzy, and I shouldn't leave her alone. I used a whole hour cleaning up the chicken turds and cursing myself for not hightailing it for the law the minute I'd found the cellar and the pokes. Since I couldn't leave the house with Aunt Ilish awake, I had to make sure she slept.

Almost as if by magic, I remembered how my aunt had melted down extra pills of Milt's the time she and Burt made Opal lose her baby. So I put two of her pills in her coffee when she asked for a cup. I watched her drink several sips, smiling to myself for my smartness, and left the house when she snored extra loud.

"Goldy Lark!" I was even with the woodpile.

I turned to see her hateful wide-awake eyes fastened on mine. "Think you're smarter'n I am, don't you, putting pills in my coffee, Goldy Lark? Didn't you think I could tell by the way you're acting you wanted to leave sick me alone again?"

Damn, I thought, now I'll never get away today.

"Put them pokes down. Come hear who this man is Bode said you asked him about this morning," she ordered.

"Bode's already told me it's same's Urch Vestman."

She shook her head. "Bode couldn't tell you, Goldy Lark, acause Bode don't know."

"You got one minute afore I go for McKay," I said.

She pushed her cut heel closer to the smoking goose feathers and wiped her fevered face before biting off a chew.

"Bode, he told me you'd found out I wasn't the only Lynch woman not wearing angel wings. From Eb Holt, he guessed. I want you to know I'd sooner cut out my tongue'n tell you what you're making me say."

"Acourse, Aunt Ilish, acourse." I left the pokes by the woodpile, and with my foot pulled a stick of wood closer to me. "Acourse, Aunt Ilish," I said again, seating myself.

"You said Urch, Goldy Lark. How's come you said him?"

"Bode said he thought . . . " I stopped, not wanting myself to say what Bode had said about the Vestman men and Bree. "Well, last summer," I started again, "when I first got here, I asked him if it was true he wanted to marry Mom once, like she'd said. He told me it was so."

As expected, her eyes flashed fire at the mention of Bree Lynch. But after a few tries at working her jaws and a giant spit, she was able to talk.

"So how's come they didn't get married?"

"Urch said there was a fight."

"Fight!" she snorted. "War's more like it."

"You trying to tell me old Villie stopped the wedding acause he thought Bree wasn't good enough for Urch?"

"You hear me all wrong, Goldy Lark." She spat tobacco juice at a brown leghorn but missed it. "What I'm trying to say's the reason old Villie didn't want that little bitch mishling for his daughter-in-law's acause he wanted that little bitch mishling for his own bed."

It couldn't be so, Bree and that mean old man. Never! Life had to be kinder than that.

"My time's up," I said, starting to rise.

"Just you hear me out, Goldy Lark." Tobacco juice hit the poor chicken full in the face. "There's lots more to it. There's Brother Dossie's great church that could someday still rise up the creek yunder, due to pretty Vestman money. Help us forget some of the shame Brother Dossie heaped on our heads, when we see saved folks walking up them steps of solid gold."

A sudden head sizzle gripped me and then, just like that, I knew what she was trying to say. "You're aiming to get Vestman money from Urch for a promise you won't tattle what you think you know on old Villie Vestman and Bree. I got half a mind to tell McKay that myself."

She aimed her mouth at another unlucky chicken. "Best you keep all your mind and hear what I say." Phutt! She got the poor chicken smack in its rear.

"You got one more minute," I said, thinking maybe I owed her that much of my time.

She bristled. "I'm still in charge of you, Goldy Lark, so you do what I say." The unblinking snake eyes fastened on mine. "I ain't proud of a Lynch crawling in bed with old Villie Vestman, the Good Lord knows that. But I'm lesser set for the whole county and half of Arkansaw hearing how a rich Vestman, or both of 'em, for all I know, paid Harley Farker to take that certain Lynch bitch away from old Villie. That little bitch, she same's told me so once."

"You're crazier'n Aunt Cloma," I said.

"Crazy, am I?" she snorted. "Just you wait'll I start getting everything I want at Vestman's store free of charge, then you'll see, you'll see."

"Bye, Aunt Ilish."

"Goldy Lark Farker, damn your soul forever if you set a foot off this land!" I heard behind me, "Oh, if I could just stand up and get to you, I'd kill you dead!"

Turning fast to leave, I bumped into Sheriff McKay, scaring him like he scared me. He took the pokes I offered and said, "Good God Almighty!" after pulling out Brother Dossie's shotgun and his axe. He repeated the words after looking inside the soap poke.

I pulled out two of the house's big foundation rocks to show him the cellar's outside door. "There's another door under Burt's cot. The pokes was all hid in there."

"Well, Ilish, what can you say about all this?" the sheriff asked my aunt, who'd been watching us in tight-lipped silence.

Aunt Ilish's pointer finger was aimed my way. "That one there, she found them things where the man I told you about must've dropped 'em when he run from the barn when Burt died. She'll lie about 'em being mine, acourse, if you ask her to say the truth."

"I won't ask many questions here," McKay said. "I'm saving 'em for Burt."

"Don't you talk of my dead boy!" Aunt Ilish, trying to stand, landed hard back in the doorway. "Don't you have any shame saying a thing like that on the dead?"

"Your Burt, he'll still be alive and kicking when the law nabs him as he's getting his mail, Ilish." Sheriff McKay dropped onto the stick of wood I'd just left. "See, Ilish, you told all the wrong people your business. Bode, he's been my Onion Creek deputy, just watching your place, ever since I told him Milt's old cooner a'stead of Burt Troat died in the barn fire. Bode, he wants to get Burt good for all the bad things he done to Miss Maudie. And Urch, he just plain don't want folks taking money they ain't earned from his store."

Another hateful look was my aunt's answer.

McKay smiled and shook his head. "Bet Milt had a big belly laugh where he's gone at seeing his old cooner get a bigger funeral crowd'n he did, huh, Ilish?"

A used tobacco chew landed close to McKay's foot.

Sheriff McKay rubbed his wet shoe against the stick of wood and said, "Reckon your Burt just wanted to try a third time to buy himself a car with money not his, huh, Ilish?"

That brought a quick and nasty, "Just trying to get your life insurance money afore you're dead and the money never comes in anyway, well, that ain't against the law, I know that. So you got one second to get yourself off of Lynch land, Mr. Sheriff!"

"When I go, Ilish," McKay said, "you'll go with me."

"Well, what for now?" Aunt Ilish's bottomless black eyes showed fear for the first time. "It ain't my Burt's burning down the Holt place you want him for, is it? You got somebody who'll say they seen him do it?"

Sheriff McKay turned to face her. "Her name was little Almy Copeland, Ilish, and I've got the heart necklace her folks give her the last Christmas of her life. Your Burt, he kept trying to take it away from her up at school; her folks finally complained to the law. My daddy wrote in his report how him and Milt Holt got after Burt. He was told to leave the little girl alone at New Hill or anywhere else. That report says that necklace was gone when little

Almy was found dying. She herself named Burt as her killer afore she died. You need any more reasons, Ilish?"

McKay turned to me. "Go get your things, girl. You wouldn't be safe out here with Eb Holt so falling-down drunk it's all Urch can do to handle him. Asides, I got a place in town for you."

"You ain't putting that lying little bitch in with me!" screamed Aunt Ilish, knowing now the sheriff meant business.

"Won't be room for her," McKay said, "by the time you and Opal and Ivy Helton all get there."

My aunt bit her thumb and didn't answer.

"Can I go up to the cabin and see Urch?" I asked. I had to know all about the Vestman men and Bree before I left Onion Creek, never to return.

"I'll jangle her telephoney'n I want you back," McKay said.

"Goldy Lark, you stop!" I knew my aunt wasn't going to let go of me easy. "Don't it mean nothing to you'n you walk out by the woodpile to know your daddy's blood got shed here on Lynch land? Don't it mean boo Lynch blood got shed in that green bed in there to give you life? Don't you have no heart in you for all the things on this land that mean so much to me?"

When I didn't answer, she added, "Now you hie inside and get a gander at yourself in the looking-glass and you'll see Meadow Lark watching you, and she'll be crying acause you and Opal, you brought bad luck to this place by cutting off your ong, pretty Churkey hair!"

"That ain't what caused all this, Ilish, and you know it," McKay said. "You and Burt, you done it all by your lonesomes."

"I guess that means you'll be coming to see me in the graveyard, don't it, Goldy Lark?" And Aunt Ilish commenced blubbering something I couldn't understand.

"She wants her Bible," Sheriff McKay figured out for me. "Get your things while you're there."

I jumped from the hewn log into the front room for my floursack on the devonette. Not wanting to chance another cold, hard winter wherever I'd be, my government relief coat went in the sack first. My dirty clothes I got from under Opal's bed went in next, then my relief jeans and red shirt, none that were too smelly dirty. The clean relief dress and floursack bloomers I'd washed only the day before were put atop the sack before I tied its end.

The Lynch family Bible was in my hand and I was turning to leave when I remembered what else I'd been told to do. I looked into the cracked looking-glass but didn't see my Cherokee grandmother. What I did see was a pretty—oh, yes, I was, I'd become so since living close to Eb Holt and loving him—young black-eyed girl with a freckled nose and hair the color of midnight framing that pretty face. More Bree's face now than Aunt Ilish's, though without the happy smile. Laughing had never been easy for me. When my times got better, that meaning when I was somebody at last, I meant to laugh and cut up just like my Bree. Only I'd make my life happier than she had made hers and my laughing would be real.

What Bree should have and maybe could have done with her life but didn't, I aimed to do with mine.

I promised the girl in the looking-glass that, no matter what life sent at me in the years to come, I would never hang my head for very long, starting right now. Thinking so, I returned the Lynch Bible to its dresser drawer and went to let Aunt Ilish finally know she was no longer my boss.

"Your leg ain't broke," I told her at seeing her long pointy finger being aimed at me. "You want the Book, get it yourself."

And then, just because I couldn't leave here without getting a little even for all the hateful things she'd said and done to me, I went into Bree's happy little dance. I didn't know I could touch my nose with my tongue till I tried to and did, moving like a rooster with a hen he aims to climb on and ride. I made myself smile wide in hopes of looking some like Bree.

When I finally looked at Aunt Ilish, she was belly down in the mudhole, her fingers fixed to choke me to death.

# 26

Urch Vestman was at the leaning shelter Eb had built for Old Jack, eating a biscuit. He stopped chewing when he saw me, passed the remaining bite to the mule, wiped his mouth with his fingers, and swallowed.

"Looks like Jessie Red took your word on Opal and Ivy Helton being camp girls," he said.

"I thought you'd told him," I lied.

"Told you I don't do things like that to my neighbors, Goldy Lark."

"I ain't here for that," I said, dropping to the grass.

Pain showed on his face as he said, "Guess I've always knowed and dreaded the day'd come you'd have to know about Pop and Bree," and settled beside me.

I knew then Aunt Ilish hadn't been lying all the way. "You tell me the truth," I said.

"It ain't pretty," he warned, sitting near me.

Mean old Villie fighting with his son over a young half-breed, someone he hated deep down for being born different, anyhow. How could it be anything but ugly?

"To start off," Urch finally said, "I was always in love with pretty Bree. I asked Pop if I could marry her when she turned fifteen. You can likely guess he hit the ceiling with his mishling, mishling goings-on, cussing me out in German. I got the blood cut from my back with the horsewhip. And me a grown man. He thinks old world, Pop does, where a man don't know his head from a hole in the ground till he's been married four year and got three kids, or been in a war. He threatened to run me out of the store without a dime to my name if I didn't forget her.

"I never got a chance. When I told her I'd be poor all my life she quit me fast. For my pop. In varely no time, she was laughing and dancing, sticking out her tongue to touch her nose. For him. You sure you want to hear the rest?"

"All of it," I said, trying not to notice my hurting heart.

He took a deep breath and said, "It was smart thinking on her part. With him, she could have the store and him along with it. Worst part there, he wasn't sure he could marry her, for fear what folks'd say after all his mishling talk. He'd give her some chew gum or a pretty to keep her coming back, all the while promising her the whole store'n they got married. She was already starting to look for somebody new the day Harley Farker followed her and Milt and Ilish from Rard."

I stayed still, hurting so inside.

"Well, that day Harley, he was so took with Bree on the courthouse steps, he wasn't far back on her way home. So when they stopped at the store for Ilish to pick out a wedding dress for her and Milt's marrying that night, Bree set in the buggy, Harley, he reined up and they talked till Ilish and Milt come back out. I saw all this from the house, so I know.

"That night, Harley shows up for the wedding at New Hill. Asked me if I knowed where he could find work. Pop saw him eyeing Bree and figured to shove her off on Harley when he got good and tired of her, if he ever was to. He put Harley to work 'round the place for two dollar a month till spring. He let him stay in a empty storeroom and put Old Nance in our barn. Me and him played fox and geese to pass the long winter nights. I got to know him pretty good. All he talked of was he'd hitch with Bree when he got some money, not knowing he was tearing my heart in two. I always thought Pop must've heard him, acause next thing I know, Pop truly wants to marry Bree. That give me the best notion ever, to keep my place in the store and not have to spend the rest of my life in the same house with him married to my Bree."

"You give Harley Farker money to marry her," I guessed.

"A whole hundred dollar, Goldy Lark." He almost whispered it. "I took it from its hiding place in the store one night Pop was sick with grippe. When Harley got back from seeing Bree that night, I give him the money, said it was extry I'd kept back to pay him when he got ready to leave. I told him not to let anyone know, specially Ilish, or he wouldn't have it long. He lit right back down to tell Bree. Afore daylight, they was ready to marry. They hitched the next Sunday noon.

"I made myself go to see her get married to someone asides Pop, and be safe from him. It wasn't very easy to do, that part. When I told Milt what I'd done, him being Onion Creek's deputy, I asked him to have it called a robbing. I asked him not to tell the first Jessie Red McKay about it acause he'd blame Harley Farker long afore he'd blame me. Milt, him still loving Bree like I was and wanting her to marry a decent man, took care of it for me. He had me tell Pop about it in German and I wrote the report for Milt, him not able to read and write, in the same tongue. See, nobody round here except Pop and me could understand German, and I always wrote Milt's reports anyway as a favor since he couldn't write. Milt, he burnt it after Pop seen it. When Pop would see old Sheriff Jessie Red McKay, he'd jump him about his lost money and get so riled about it, pretty soon old Jessie Red, he told me to shut Pop up, he couldn't figure out what Pop took on so about. Guess Pop still thinks Harley Farker took the money."

"My father ever find out what you'd done?" I asked.

"Not from me. But if he'd been accused, I'd told the truth, leastways my part in it, but not Milt's." He took another deep breath and whispered, "Tell me I done the right thing, Goldy Lark, will you?"

"It don't matter now," I said.

He stood to help me to my feet. "Look, I know I'm a liar and a thief but McKay don't. I'm hoping he never knows."

"He won't hear it from me," I promised, rising to leave.

"Goldy Lark, wait. Eb likely wants to see you. Come daylight, he's taking Old Jack and go live with Jane Bell's people. He's hurting something awful."

So am I, I thought, so am I.

"Look, McKay says he's taking you to town to stay. You don't have to go, you know. I'll tell him you got a home with me." He leaned closer and, maybe thinking the trees and grass had ears, whispered, "Goldy Lark, I love you."

I started downcreek, my feet moving faster with each step, and Urch followed. "Make out a bill for what my family owes you, Urch. I get on my feet, I'll pay you back to the penny," I said.

"You didn't hear me right, Goldy Lark." He was behind me on the path, breathing hard. "When Pop dies, I'll marry you, give you half of the store. You can work for me till then."

Work for him taking care of old Villie, he meant. Feed him like a baby, clean his stinking hind end, wipe up his puke like I'd done for Milt Holt. He must think I was dumb as a rabbit, to ask that of me.

"This ain't Bree you're talking to," I told him, starting to run just as the sheriff's telephone jangle told me it was time to go.

# 27

Aunt Ilish was muzzled with a floursack, or she would've screeched, prayed and cursed all the way to jail. She rode between Urch Vestman and Bode Jenkins, clawing them with her fingernails until the sheriff stopped to add handcuffs. Still not bested, she kneed Bode when he leaned close to help McKay. She twisted and fought like a cornered rat all the way to Rard. It took the three men, the two town deputies that had come to Onion Creek and a man passing by to get her through the courthouse doorway, little as she was and hog-tied, too.

On the sheriff's orders, I waited in the car. Even from there, I could hear through an open window the cat fight between Opal and her mom when they laid eyes on each other for the first time in weeks. I could still hear it as a deputy left with Urch Vestman and Bode Jenkins, probably to take them back home. Even after the sheriff took me several houses past the courthouse, it was nigh loud as ever.

"Glad you ain't up with 'em?" McKay asked, and I nodded.

He stopped before a big house painted white and carried my floursack up the front steps. I stayed on the porch while he went to turn on the same kind of lights that were at Vestman's store and Doc Helton's office.

"You can stay in Pearl's company room, girl. It's straight back, the bath next to it. You go in and clean up. I'll have Pearl scare us up some grub'n she gets back from prayer meet."

"She know I'm here?"

"I told her I hoped you'd likely come back with me," he said.

"I'd be fine on the porch." I looked at the neat front room with its big armchairs, flowerdy devonette, rugs on the floor, and real wallpaper on the walls; I felt too dirty to sleep in such a fine house. "I don't want to be in your woman's way, Sheriff."

He threw back his head with a big belly laugh. "Pearl's not my woman, she's my sister. I live next door with our Mom."

"Well, I just thought you and her was married."

He laughed again and shook his head. "Ain't got me a woman

yet. The one I tried to get, she didn't want me. The one who wanted me, I wouldn't have. My lucky number three, she's finally come, but she don't know I'm after her yet." He touched my arm. "Late. Best you clean up a bit, huh?"

I washed everywhere, even on my feet, with the pretty pink soap and storebought washrag in the lilac-smelling bathroom, and put on my other bloomers and relief dress. I combed my thick black hair with my fingers and might have smiled at myself in an unbroken looking-glass if I hadn't suddenly realized there was nothing to laugh about. Maybe a quick rest in the company room would ease the tiredness, take away the tears I felt would surely come.

The room was big size, with a feather bed just like Miss Emmer Cox's bedroom back in Pelper County, with storebought pillows and a fancy pink cover. There was a plaited rug on the clean, wooden floor, and another looking-glass over a big dresser. The blowing window curtain was white, bringing to mind the one in Doc Helton's office I'd daydreamed of wearing as a veil for my marriage to Eb Holt. It danced above a pretty chair in one corner.

The second my back touched the chair's cushion, thoughts came that I was gone from Onion Creek for good, but homeless for the second time in less than a year, and then the tears overtook me.

I guess I cried hard at everything bad that had ever happened to me, starting with Harley Farker's death. My world would have been much different, I knew it would, if he'd lived to take me and Bree away from Onion Creek. Nate Brice wouldn't have been there to mistreat us, and I could have gone a lifetime without ever knowing Aunt Ilish, my Troat cousins, or Brother Dossie and Aunt Cloma Lynch. That way I'd have been spared the extra shame I'd have to face at the trial. And since I'd never have known either Eb Holt or Roy Cox, I wouldn't have picked someone who couldn't truly love me back. I cried because all my dreams to be somebody might end with the trial's finish.

I must have been noisier than I'd thought. Next thing I knew, strong hands clamped me against a thumping chest, and Jessie Red McKay said, "Go ahead, girl, cry. You got a lot to cry about," and I really cut loose.

"I-I'll n-never be somebody n-now acause folks'll n-never forget the bad t-things my f-family's done," I could finally say.

"Now, that's just not so, Goldy Lark Farker. Why, my Grampa McKay, he stole anything that wasn't nailed down, and his daddy afore him sold chickens back to the same folks he'd swiped 'em from. Nobody brought that up when old Jessie Red, then me two years back, run for sheriff. They voted for us, not our family."

"Y-you didn't h-have nobody in your f-family like B-Bree. She w-was . . ." The words I had sworn never to say to another human were almost closing my throat. "P-poor little B-Bree, she died from whoring. W-what'll folks think'n I have to say that?"

A big hand wiped at my tears. "I had a letter from the Pelper County law telling me all about your mommy, Goldy Lark Farker. I burnt it. Now nobody save me and you knows. And the lawyer men coming in, they won't ask you nothing asides what you found in the Lynch cellar. Won't take you hardly no time to tell that."

"Then I guess you'll send me to Vestman's to take care of old Villie and marry Urch'n the old man dies?" I guessed.

I was surprised at McKays laugh. "You wouldn't want a man old enough to be your daddy, Goldy Lark Farker." Both big arms tightened their hold. "You need somebody my age to marry." He bent to kiss my cheek. "You need me."

"You've funned me enough. Let go," I said, twisting partway free.

"No, I can't do that. Why, the day you come to Rard, I saw from the quick way you answered me you didn't tell lies easy. I noticed you being down and out didn't keep you from holding up your head. You being a pretty little thing and kind, to boot, that didn't show all the way till I saw how you took care of poor sick Milt." He pulled me closer. "Don't you know by now you're my lucky number three?"

My answer was to shut my eyes and hope he truly wasn't making fun of me. It would be nearly as good as life itself to marry a man who smelled of chewing gum and today's sweat that would be washed away by bedtime. Sleeping in a clean bed in a clean house had always been part of my dream. I'd never held a thought as to Jessie Red McKay being my lucky number three, but things, of course, can change.

"I jig-danced home from work the first time I saw you to tell

Pearl I'd just met my lucky number three. If you don't believe me, ask her if it's not so."

Then, just like it had been planned that way, a woman who favored him in the face stuck her head in the door. "You can let your girl loose now, Jessie Red. From the way she's smiling, I doubt if she aims to run far," she said.

If I'd tried, I knew either my head or my feet would have stopped me cold.